Shawn's Prisoner

Louise Furley

Shawn's Prisoner

Louise Furley
Copyright 2021
All Rights Reserved

ISBN: 978-1-7378341-6-8 (Paperback)
ISBN: 978-1-7378341-5-1 (eBook)

Cover art by *Pixel Mischief Design*
Image courtesy of *Shutterstock*

ALSO BY LOUISE FURLEY

A Mafia Romance series

Distilled Duplicity
His Winnings
Adara
Jozadak

Satan's Brood series

Devil's Prince
Devil's Seed

Dutch Military Special Forces series

Jungle Treasure
Jancarlo

Other titles

Jezábel and the Assassin

Solitar

Vijay

Halo Valley

Isle of Orainn

Shawn's Prisoner

List of characters:

5 male prisoners, 4 male deputies, 2 female deputies, 1 female prisoner

Male Prisoners:

Shawn Darkonn
Beau Dyce
Daf Jamieson
Zachary Stockton
Caleb Taylor

Female Prisoner;

Cherriana Delighya

Male Deputies

Chief Deputy Vance Malone
Ritchie Marx
Tomas Trent
Jim Vega

Female Deputies

Leena Shipley
Bella Calla

Chapter One

The five male prisoners were already secured and sitting one to a seat on the prison transport bus. Three officers in their olive green uniforms were scattered around safeguarding them.

Behind the wheel the driver worked the day's crossword puzzle, and the chief deputy stood in the open doorway. Another officer waited just outside the bus door.

All eyes focused on the last prisoner being led up the walk. The female prisoner's hands were cuffed behind her back and two female officers on either side of her held her arms.

One of the males on the bus whistled a long low note, muttered under his breath, "Boy, am I gonna dream about that tonight with my fist in my pants."

Prisoner Beau Dyce leaned his red head forward to whisper in the ear of the prisoner in front of him, Shawn Darkonn. "There weren't supposed to be any females on this bus, looks like we got three coming."

Shawn nodded, his eyes narrowed on the approaching women.

Beau shook his head and said, "That is not good, Shawn, but check that girl's hair. Hell, like all the colors of a sunflower, bro. Can't be real, tis like a big wavy cloud around her shoulders and curls spiraling down her back."

Shawn turned slightly in his seat to Dyce, a sarcastic brow rose. "Are you through? You gonna write a damned sonnet about the lass, Beau? Put your *bluidy* eyes back in your head."

Smirking at his friend and fellow prisoner, Beau Dyce leaned back and replied, "She's a bonny *bure*, lad. Aye, maybe I will write a song at that."

The men watched the officers bringing the girl to the bus. Walking awkwardly with her hands bound behind her, she wore a red dress that fit snugly over her slender yet softly curvaceous figure. The short skirt flipped just below her thighs as the shapely legs propelled her slowly towards the bus.

Dwarfed by the larger females, her blue eyes radiated such vivid panic her terror could be seen a mile away. If she hadn't been supported, she likely would have swooned from sheer fright.

The prisoner in front of Shawn, Daf Jamieson, dreads tied back in a ponytail, rested an arm the color of shiny mahogany on the back of the seat. The huge bicep bulging under the orange jumpsuit would make Hercules jealous.

Military tattoos on his upper arm stretched when his muscles flexed. His gaze also on the girl, he twisted his head slightly to say to Shawn behind him, "Looks like jailbait."

One of the corrections officers, Tomas Trent, informed him, "Can't be, she's being extradited to a woman's prison in Montana, has to be at least 18."

When the women reached the bus, the female officers hesitated, apparently trying to figure out how to get the prisoner with her hands shackled behind her back facing several very high steps, up and into the bus.

The last male deputy, the oldest at 50, Ritchie Marx, was still outside the bus combing his curly salt and pepper hair. He tucked the comb in his back pocket, wrapped his chunky hands around the girl's waist, lifted the petite young woman up all the steps in one move and handed her to the chief deputy, Vance Malone.

Appearing quite pleased to have custody of the girl, a leering grin split the forty-something Malone's thick face. He rolled a hefty arm around her waist, high up, just under her breasts and held her taut against him.

Her hands bound behind her, she struggled, twisting, trying to pull away. He laughed at her efforts like he was plucking the wings off a helpless pinned fly.

Malone maneuvered her into the front seat and sat down next to her. He unlocked her manacles, brought her hands around in front of her and then cuffed both wrists high up to a bar next to the window.

The door swung closed after the last three boarded.

The two female officers, Leena Shipley and Bella Calla, stood halfway down the aisle chatting while everyone got settled. Leena had a gun holstered on her hip, as a corrections officer, Bella did not.

Sitting back casually, Shawn Darkonn observed the occupants of the bus through lowered lids. He watched the girl prisoner trapped next to Malone struggling to get away from him. The husky deputy chuckled and whispered in her ear.

Judging by the way her pale face flushed with color, he wasn't talking about going to church on Sunday. She turned her head and the rest of her cornered body to the window, writhing away from him.

From his seat, Shawn could see shame, abject fear, and the glint of tears in her big eyes.

The girl was the only one cuffed the way she was, as if the deputy had deliberately put her on display, and to keep her suspended so she couldn't fight him off. She was utterly vulnerable to the letch sitting beside her.

The male prisoners had only one wrist comfortably shackled low to a horizontal metal bar along the armrest.

His voice like the low sound of an animal's rumbled warning, Shawn growled, "*Miss*."

Leena Shipley, in her late thirties, a tall, slightly overweight brunette turned hazel eyes back at him. He jerked his head once, motioning towards the front of the bus.

Leena followed his line of indication and saw Vance Malone with his arm around the female prisoner, pressing his barrel-chested body against her. Rolling her eyes, Leena huffed, "*Shit*." Her long legs striding swiftly up the aisle, she poked the chief deputy in the shoulder. "Malone."

The girl had her legs tightly crossed. Her cuffed hands were above her shoulders locked against the metal pole by the window, tears streamed down her face.

Malone's big meaty paw was high up her thigh, trying to shove between her legs. Glaring annoyed at Leena, he snapped, "What?"

Leena set her hand on the back of his seat, the other on her broad hip in the tight, olive green polyester pants. "Come on, Vance, you know the procedure. One of us has to be next to the female."

"Get lost," Malone sneered and turned back to the girl. "It's going to be a long trip and I have something here to keep me entertained, right honey?"

Grinning at the defenseless girl, he chucked her chin then slid his heavy hand around the back of her neck forcing her to face him. He leaned in like he was about to latch his fleshy lips on her small mouth.

Her voice slightly irked like she was talking to a child she was about to paddle, Leena snapped harshly, "Vance, you get up right now or I'll have the other officers help me get you up."

4

Exhaling a grating sigh, the irritated deputy released the girl and slid to the end of the seat. He shuffled to his feet with a beleaguered grunt.

Before leaving, he leaned down with his hand on the back of the seat. Combing brown hair straight back off his forehead with fat fingers, he drew one of those thick fingers down the girl's round cheek and said with a sly promise, "Remember, babydoll, we still have a party planned."

She tried to turn her head away from him. Cupping her chin, he roughly pulled her face up close to his and whispered in a guttural leer, "A party with just me," his hot breath steaming her skin, he smirked, "and you."

Although clearly terrified, the trapped girl labored to glare coldly at him, but the trembling plush lips and streaming tears negated the defiant glare.

Sitting behind them, his voice gruff with strength matching his powerful body, the skin of his dark face darkening further, Daf Jamieson said to the deputy, "Leave off the girl then, man."

None of the officers commented, but redheaded Beau joined in, "Yeah, bugger off, you asshole."

Not taking his eyes or hands off the girl, Malone sneered at the felons, "Fuck off, you Scotty dicks."

Still meanly pinching her jaw with his big hand, he said with a cringe worthy smile to the female prisoner, "It's okay, babydoll, I find those tears pouring out of those angry, frightened eyes a bitch of a turn on. Not that you need any other enhancements."

His lusty gaze showered so heatedly down her body she recoiled like he had physically groped her.

She jerked her chin out of his hand with anger, to his amusement; he liked a little fire in his conquests. It was more fun when they fought him. The lust turned into a snarky smirk, he gave her an insolent wink, a promise of things later to come.

Patting the side of her face with a thick hand, he left her and flopped down on another seat, propping his feet up on a first aid kit on the floor in front of him.

Leena slid in and took his place next to the girl.

The bus finally started up and headed to the highway. His back against the corner of the window, Shawn slid down in his seat stretching his long legs under the seat in front of him. Crossing the arm not cuffed over his stomach he went to sleep.

Scratching his short-cropped beard as red as his curly hair, Beau Dyce asked the deputy in the seat across the aisle, "Jim, how long do you expect it to take for us to get from North Dakota to the prison in Montana?"

In a faint Hispanic accent Jim Vega replied, "We are going way up north, northwest, supposed to take 15 to 20 hours, maybe more. We will be passing the Kootenai National Forest, skirting the Cabinet Mountains Wilderness.

"The road we will be traveling on winds up and around some other mountains. Other than the high road up the mountain, there are no other roads or buildings in that part of the wilderness, so, I pray we do not break down or it will be a long damned walk out."

Crossing his bony legs, at 5'9 Jim Vega was the shortest of the officers. The only other person, other than two of the women that was shorter than him was prisoner Caleb Taylor.

At forty, Caleb was small and wiry and losing his hair which was also wiry. A quiet, nervous man constantly straightening his glasses like an uncontrollable tic, Caleb had been an accountant and had gotten caught embezzling from a huge corporation. He had five years to serve.

Beau said to Officer Vega, "Doesn't your wife miss you on these long trips?"

Vega chuckled with a swagger in the way he smoothed his short dark hair back with his palms. "Naw, but my girlfriends do. The wife is busy carpooling our daughters."

Beau nodded with an unreadable expression then laid his head against the window and did as Shawn had, closed his eyes and nodded off.

Altogether, there were 14 people on the bus; the driver, 5 male corrections officers counting Chief Deputy Malone, 5 male prisoners, 1 female prisoner, and 2 female officers.

The driver drove for four hours before stopping for their first break at a rest area.

Deputy Malone stood up first, stretching and yawning like a donkey after chomping a dry dinner of musty hay. He dragged a hand across his damp mouth then wiped the hand on his uniform and said to the driver, "You getting off, Stan?"

Shaking his head in the negative, settling back in the worn cushioned seat, the grey haired driver crossed his arms and closed his eyes planning a quick catnap while the rest took breaks.

Shifting down lower in his seat, he replied, "Nope. We got an unlucky number on this bus, 13. I ain't going nowhere until we get to the prison."

Chuckling, Malone shook his head. "That makes no sense, Stan. There are 14 of us altogether."

His eyes closed, the driver muttered, "I don't count me, I'm an extra, you all are the passengers."

Leena Shipley and Bella Calla unchained the female prisoner and took her off the bus first.

Deputy Malone's hungry eyes followed the red dress swinging up the walk to the building's restrooms. For

7

security, the men were taken to the restrooms one at a time after the women returned.

Shawn was last off. The big strapping black-haired man was handcuffed to the shorter, thinner Jim Vega.

Standing outside the bus with the female prisoner, drawing on a cigarette, Leena squinted at Shawn through a stream of smoke as he was returning with Vega.

Next to her, Bella chuckled. "You're liking what you see, girl?"

Leena's eyes traced the tall prisoner coming down the walk. "Oh yeah, hon." Her gaze straight at Shawn's broad shoulders. "I'm loving Shawn Darkonn's husky Scottish accent, his wavy black hair, and those midnight eyes."

Drawing in a long drag, squinting, she blew it out with her words, "Those black eyes look like they hold treacherous secrets deep inside, very hot."

"Huh." Bella turned ready to help the female prisoner up the steps. "What about those scars, Leena? Find them hot too?"

Her lips sucking on the end of her cigarette, Leena mused, "They hardly mar that handsome face, only give him a dangerous, violent edge. I bet he's rough and aggressive as hell in bed."

Her hazel eyes darted to Bella and back to Shawn who was nearing. "We've had a few talks. Even that deep quiet voice makes my panties wet." The female prisoner winced and blushed.

"Geez Leena, TMI," Bella moaned. "But I have to agree, we lucked out on this trip male hunk wise. Shawn and that dreamy Black prisoner, Daf Jamieson, and the gigantic prisoner Zachary Stockton are the tallest in the group. All have wide muscled shoulders like boxers." She confided with a grin, "I like 'em big too. All over."

Nodding in agreement, Leena tossed her cigarette to the ground and pulled her pack out for another one. "Oh yeah, hon, love those hard, sculpted arms and chests that are nicely outlined in the short-sleeved orange jump suits. The only one I have concerns about is that humongous prisoner, the quiet one."

Bella was nudging the female prisoner to the door of the bus. "Yeah, Zachary, brute's on the scary side. Guy is like a blond goliath. He's even damned taller and stockier than the other two leaner men, Shawn and Daf. He's built like a freakin' fortress."

Leena lit her second cigarette. "I'd do them all at once, no prob. Got three holes, yeah? But Shawn is my fav."

The female prisoner's face turned beet red. She ducked her head trying to turn away from hearing any more of the pudgy officer's salacious declarations.

Bella laughed. "Okay, on that note, I'm getting the girl set on the bus before Vance can get his filthy hands on her again." She gave the prisoner a little push up the steps, and followed her inside.

As Shawn and Vega approached, Shawn's eyes went to Leena's cigarette. Her smile flirtatious, she said, "Want one, tall, dark, and sexy?"

A corner of Shawn's mouth pulled in denting a dimple in his cheek that instantly drew Leena's attention. "*Sea,* pardon me," he corrected, "yes, that would be great."

Leena gave him a cigarette. She held the lighter close to her chest so he would have to lean over to her to get it lit.

He cupped his hands around the cigarette and lighter, his eyes didn't dip down the front of her shirt like she'd hoped. Still, she all but shook her breasts in his face.

Jim Vega took out his smokes and the three stood quietly for a moment puffing.

9

Shawn asked Leena, "What's up with the lass? I thought this was a male only transport."

The tall brunette tucked her shirt in deeper, deliberately causing the polyester green uniform to tighten across her drooping breasts and plump belly. All of the officers only wore the bare minimum of weapons belts.

Their radios would be useless in the mountains, and the additional batons, Tasers, etc. would be uncomfortable sitting through the lengthy travel, so they were stored in a lockbox in the rear.

"Well, hotness," Leena sidled up close to Shawn, "it wasn't planned. Her extradition paperwork just came through. I think Malone had something to do with it."

Jim Vega finished his smoke, un-cuffed himself from Shawn and got back on the bus.

"Hmm." Through the window, Shawn could see Malone trying to talk Bella Calla, a solidly built, athletic Latina, into letting him sit next to the girl.

Bella was shaking her head, her dark brown hair in a tight knot barely moved.

"So," Shawn asked Leena, "what's up with the dress? Why isn't she in a prison uniform?"

Blowing out a funnel of smoke, Leena shrugged. Her brazen gaze checked out the prisoner from his strong shoulders down to the orange pants. Zeroing in on the zipper as if trying to see behind it, her gaze darted up to the scars on his impassive face, finally settling on the inscrutable black eyes.

"We only had sizes 2X to 4X. There're some big girls in the jail. The jumpsuits were so big they just slid right off her. The dress isn't even hers. When she was first brought into holding, some of the other girls wanted at her. They shredded her clothes before the deputies could get in and get the women off her."

Shawn's black brows rose to his hairline, then drew down sharply. "You're kidding."

Shaking her head, Leena sucked on her cigarette. "Nope. Like a pack of junkyard felines tearing at a kitten. Some of 'um don't care male or female. She's a beauty and young, the deputies should have known better than to put her in there with those hardcore heifer-bitches."

Exhaling audibly, she flicked the butt of the cigarette knocking the ashes off. Her eyes still on the prisoner's face she didn't notice the ashes float down and land on her shoe.

A flicker of anger crossing his stoic features, Shawn muttered in a low voice, "You need *tae* get that dress off her."

Leena snickered. "Yeah, you sound like everyone else."

He frowned in annoyance. "*Na*, no, not what I meant. I meant you need *tae* get pants, a belt and a looser shirt *tae* hide those curves on her. She's too accessible like that. Gonna cause nothing but trouble amongst the males."

"True that. The chief has been trying to bang her since he laid eyes on her." Clamping the cigarette between her teeth, one eye squinting with the effort, Leena pushed escaped strands of brown hair back up in her bun.

Loose flab on her upper arms wobbled in the short sleeves with her efforts. She clipped two fingers around the butt again taking it out of her mouth and crossed her arms.

Shawn glanced down at Leena, his forehead furrowed in question. She was tall but he had a lot of inches on her. She was at least ten years older than him, he was still a few years shy of thirty, but there were ages of hardness in his shuttered eyes.

11

Taking a puff, he held his cigarette between the pads of his fingertip and thumb and curled it back in his palm, exhaling the smoke like a slow drawl.

"Yeah." Leena told him, "She's only been in our custody for three days. She was being held in the county jail pending her trial. She was briefly in the prison so she could be transported per the extradition. Malone couldn't get near her in the women's side of cells, but he finally managed to get to her in the laundry room this morning.

"Like you said, the dress made it too easy. He had her on the floor and was pushing between her legs tearing off her panties, when a practice fire alarm happened to go off and another deputy found 'em and wrestled him off her. The slob keeps trying to feel her up every time he gets near her."

"Why the hell wasn't he reported?" The dark brows now slashed straight down, his nostrils flared fiercely. He looked so angry Leena was taken aback. Shawn inhaled deeply and held the smoke in before harshly blowing it out.

She lifted one shoulder in a slight shrug. "It's prison, honey, no one much cares. If he wasn't so blatant he could get away with more. Mark my words, that sly horndog will have that girl pregnant before we get her to the prison camp."

"What's she being extradited for?"

She smiled cagey and amused. "Murder," she replied.

His eyes shot up to the young woman cowering in the blue vinyl bus seat. "Her? You serious?"

Taking a last puff, Leena nodded. "Yeah. To be honest, I don't believe it myself. I read the report, sounds fishy, like some guy is trying to railroad her into being with him. You'd need to read it to understand." She tossed her cigarette. "Let's go."

They climbed back on board and the bus took off.

Chapter Two

They were nearing 15 hours of driving. It was closing in on dawn yet still twilight dark, most of the passengers were asleep.

The only light on the narrow, winding road came from the silver moon, and the bus's headlights bouncing over weathered blacktop and along rows of trees like black gothic spires flashing by.

It was hard to sleep with the bus bumping, rocking, and squeaking. Navigating the hairpin turns coiling up the mountain was tiring the driver. He'd only had brief naps here and there when they stopped for breaks.

Holding onto the seatbacks to keep his balance, Deputy Malone came up to the driver, leaned down to him and murmured in a low voice so as not to wake the other occupants, "Want me to give you a break, Stan?"

The driver yawned. "Ah, Vance, it's against policy, but what the hell." He yawned huger. "It's also dangerous for me to keep straining to see in the dark after fifteen some odd hours. All right, just for a short nap."

The two men traded places while the bus was in motion.

Snores and grunts, creaks from the rocking vehicle, and the tires rumbling over the rough pot-holed road were discordant sounds reverberating in the dark bus.

An hour before dawn, everyone dozing, no one noticed the bus speeding up, careening wildly, surging downward suddenly out of control.

The bus started pitching, then it barreled into a skid before it hit the shoulder of the road and leaped air-born-rolling side-over-side, crashing down the bank of the mountain.

Awakening in disoriented terror, the women screamed, the men shouted as they were jolted, seat-belted bodies thrashing back and forth, and banging against the sides of the hurtling rolling vehicle.

The bus kept rotating until it finally slammed into a tree, coming to a shattering, steaming halt on its side. Smoke poured out of the cracked engine, steam whistled, squeaks and pops sounded all around as the crushed bus settled.

The battered passengers sat stunned, gasping, trying to see in the dark and grasp what had happened.

"Malone," Shawn called out over the babbling panicked people. "It might catch fire, you need *tae* get everyone off, *now*."

Deputy Malone, seat-belted into the driver's seat, sat in shock, his hands still clutching the wheel.

"Malone!" Shawn yelled.

The deputy struggled out of his seat pulling out his gun and aiming it at the prisoners. His voice shaky he ordered, "Jim, Tomas, you unlock the prisoners. Leena, Bella, take the girl off after the men are all out. Ritchie, go outside first and keep your weapons trained on the prisoners as they come off."

14

He turned to the driver to give orders, then stopped abruptly and cursed, "*Oh fuck.*"

He stepped over to Stan who hadn't been belted in. The man was on the floor of the bus, his smashed head covered in blood. Malone checked his pulse, shook his head, he was dead.

No one moved as Malone dashed around the bus checking on everyone.

Besides the driver, another corrections officer also not seat-belted was deceased. The prisoners had been cuffed and belted, they were all uninjured except for minor bruises.

Officers Jim Vega, Tomas Trent, Ritchie Marx, like the prisoners, only had minor injuries.

Malone dragged an arm across his face, his long loose cheeks red from his exertions. Huffing and puffing, nerves fraught from the terrifying accident choking his voice, he croaked hoarsely to his crew, "All right, get them moving."

Ritchie Marx crawled out the damaged door to take a shaking stand as Vega and Trent hurried to unlock the male prisoners and usher them off the smoking bus.

After the men were taken off, Leena and Bella unlocked the girl, in their panicked haste they roughly pushed her off the top step.

A short cry squeaked out of the young woman before she flung her hands out into nothingness to break her fall-

Shawn sprung to the door and caught her in midair. A *whoosh* blew out of her lungs when she landed roughly in Shawn's hard arms.

He held her briefly, looking down into the terrified blues before setting her carefully on her feet.

The girl was obviously in shock. Her cheeks suddenly reddened in the ashen face, shallow fast breaths jerked from her, her hand fluttered at her chest. Shawn kept one big hand wrapped around her slim upper arm holding her steady until she calmed.

Embarrassed, brushing her hair out of her face with trembling hands, she tugged out of Shawn's grasp and moved away from him.

When everyone was out of the bus, shaken with fearful uncertainty emerging in the middle of the night into the dark unknown wilderness, they gathered into a frightened clutch.

Confidence and authority ringing in his voice, Shawn directed the deputy, "Malone, get everyone away from the bus in case it blows."

Shawn gathered the women and led them across bristly grass to the shelter of some trees. Prisoners Beau and Daf went with them. The others followed in a crooked line leaving Deputy Malone standing alone in a stupor.

Malone marched his thick legs over to Jim and said, "I want Darkonn cuffed, his hands behind his back."

Vega went immediately over to the prisoner. An apology on his olive-toned face, he pulled Shawn's hands behind him and clapped the cuffs on.

Stalking after the rest of the group, Malone stopped and stood in front of Shawn and barked an infuriated demand, "Who the hell died and made you boss?"

His hands manacled behind his back, a lock of black hair flopping over a dark eye, Shawn shrugged one huge shoulder. He said mildly, "Everyone on the bus did. You are ineffective as a leader."

"Really?" Malone sneered sarcastically, then without warning slammed his fist into Shawn's jaw, snapping his head to the side. The big man staggered backwards. As he gained his balance, Malone punched him again, and again.

The girl in the red dress ran over and threw herself between them yelling, "Stop Deputy! Stop it, he's defenseless-"

Whack! Malone backhanded her so hard she stumbled several feet before landing stunned on the ground. Malone's bright red mark covered almost the entire side of her face.

The deputy turned back to Shawn with his meaty fist raised, but with a roar of fury, Shawn leaped in the air, twirled around and snagged his legs around Malone's neck like scissors and took him down hard on the rocky ground.

Landing on his side, his wrists still bound, Shawn tightened his legs. Malone's flaccid face turned beet red, gagging and choking he tried to reach for his gun.

His voice edged steel, Shawn snarled, "Go for it, Malone. I will break your fat neck like a twig before you get it out of your holster."

When Malone stopped struggling, Shawn released him and climbed to his knees. Panting, Shawn sat back on his heels. Looking through black hair hanging over his eyes, he coldly regarded the husky man clutching his throat coughing and gagging.

Gesturing with his head to the stunned girl on the ground where she sat with a dainty trembling hand pressed to her injured face, Shawn growled at the wheezing deputy, "Next time, you piece of shit, keep picking on someone your own size."

Jumping to his feet, Shawn trod over to Leena, and ordered, "Un-cuff me."

She hesitated before moving. Then watching Malone on his hands and knees hacking, huffing and puffing, trying to catch his breath, Leena unlocked the chains. Shawn took them from her and hung them on the back of his belt.

17

Then he said to Leena, "We need a-" *blam-* Malone had gotten to his feet and pulled out his baton and whacked it across Shawn's back. Then he clubbed him in the head before Beau and Daf and the officers grabbed him and pulled him away.

Shawn collapsed to the ground, falling on his back.

The girl jumped to her feet and raced to the crumpled bus. She came right back out with the first aid kit Malone had earlier had his feet propped on. Hurrying over to Shawn, she knelt down beside him setting the kit on the ground.

The entire group watched her with rapt interest as she put two fingers on Shawn's throat.

Like lightning, his hand snaked out and grabbed her wrist. He pushed her over and rolled on top of her. Holding her wrist, he put his other hand against her neck.

The side of his palm angling into her throat, he threw his leg over hers immobilizing her. His deep voice a guttural threat, he growled, "What are you doing, woman?"

Through her pressed larynx, she rasped, "I- I- I have medical training. You were unconscious, I was checking your pulse."

"Hmmm, is that so?" His gaze took in the bright hair pooling on the ground around her head, a lock partially covered a wide, crystal blue eye.

Lying on her back helplessly anchored by his powerful body, he was so close his breath tickled wisps of fine hair around her face. She looked up fearfully at the hard face that glared so fiercely.

His inscrutable eyes seemed to pierce right through her. Weighing double what she did, he was crushing her. His hand covering her throat made it difficult to speak, she whispered desperately, "Please…please get off of me."

Lowering his head, Shawn's impassive gaze scanned her body under him. When it reached back up to the striking blue eyes glimmering with frightened tears, a corner of his mouth pulled in.

Releasing her throat, he braced his weight on his forearms. His face still bare inches from hers, he looked at her through locks of raven hair pitched over his brows.

Shawn could feel her breasts shuddering against his rocky chest, her legs shaking under his. If he stayed like that another minute she would have something else to fear from him.

In a heartbeat he rolled off her and jumped up. Then bending back over, he grabbed her shoulders and lifted her gently to her feet.

He brushed her tears away with his thumb. "Lass, never get between two brawny brawling men. A slight wee lass like you will only get hurt." He held her arms to steady her until her legs stopped shaking, then he let her go.

Backing away, lips trembling, she looked up at him through a fringe of lashes tipped with tears and crossed her arms protectively over her chest.

Malone moved towards Shawn again with the club raised.

His face a deadly mask of hard eyes and tight mouth, Shawn warned him, "Come near me with that thing again, Malone, and I'll shove it so far up your ass you'll never shit again."

Redheaded Beau Dyce, as muscular as Shawn but a few inches shorter, along with Daf Jamieson, dreads hanging down his back, huge arms painted with tattoos and built like a tank, caught up Deputy Malone's arms, holding him back.

19

Officers Jim Vega and Tomas Trent grabbed Shawn to keep him from physically confronting the deputy. The two combatants glared at each other.

Holding onto Malone, Beau said, "That's enough, Chief. Shawn always means what he says, you're putting your life on the line. Bro's deadly even while restrained, eh?" He glanced over at Shawn, a smile tugged at his mouth behind his cropped red beard as they shared a look.

Shawn easily shook off the two deputies, and Beau and Daf released Malone.

Swiping the back of his hand across a bloody cut on his cheek from Malone's strikes, Shawn said to the deputy, "Now that I've let you try to prove yourself, and you failed miserably, what's next?"

Surprisingly, Malone said, "Come with me." Turning on his heel he traipsed away from the group. After a few heartbeats, Shawn went with him and Beau and Daf followed a few steps behind.

During the whole fracas, Caleb Taylor, the quiet embezzler, stood next to the equally silent Zachary Stockton.

Huge and rock solid, with cordons of muscles stretching across his back and burly arms, Zach had a spiky blond Mohawk, the sides of his head were shaved and dark brown. 'Eat shit and die' was tattooed across the back of the psychopath's neck.

Zach had no intentions in getting involved. As soon as his head stopped spinning from bashing into the bar over the seat in front of him during the crash, this was a great opportunity to escape, walk away. He was taking a hike as soon as he got his bearings.

The bus hadn't rolled all the way down the mountain. The group was standing on a wide terraced strip of grass amid clusters of trees, the black sky and crisp night air encircling them. Just the tips of the grass reflected the cool silver moonlight.

Off in a grove of spruce and oaks, Malone gave Beau and Daf a dirty look and said to Shawn, "This is for your ears only."

Crossing arms of thick sinew and muscle over his chest Shawn replied, "They are with me. You got something *tae* say, say it."

Malone glared with annoyance at Beau and Daf then shrugged. In a voice steeped in conspiracy, he said quietly, "I did this whole thing on purpose. Rolled the bus."

He smirked at Shawn's arched brows. Nodding arrogantly at the prisoner, the deputy grinned with compassionless conceit. "Yep."

"The hell you say?" Shawn growled.

Malone nodded again. "Yeah. There's an old legend about a prospector's mule breaking its leg and the prospector was forced to bury 200 pounds of gold nuggets along the banks of the Clark Fork River, either on or near the Fort Missoula Military Post."

"So?" Shawn set his hands on his hips.

"So, I studied and researched, and came to the conclusion that the stories are off, that the prospector really buried the gold out here past the Cabinet Mountains Wilderness.

"In some old maps and paper legends I found in the library it tells of a pass, Grand Crest Pass. Which is apparently almost invisible somewhere in the Landmere Mountains. The papers indicate the treasure is hidden in the pass."

"So? What the hell are you telling me this for?"

Malone scowled at the man. "You're an impatient son of a bitch you know."

21

Mirroring the prisoner with his hands on his stocky hips, a bit of flab drooped over his belt, Malone said, "Of everything I could get my hands on, there was nothing to state where the goddamned pass is. It's not noted on any map. I asked around for quite some time, there seems to be that no one has any idea where it is."

Squinting one brown eye at Shawn, he said, "Until I found out about you."

Stuffing his hands in his pockets, Shawn stood mute, as did the two men bracketing him.

A corner of his mouth pulled in, Malone said, "The word is that when you first came over from Scotland you lived out here for a couple of years before you and your two Scotty buddies there got arrested for arson. The word is that you likely know where the pass is."

Beside Shawn, like unmatched bookends, redheaded Beau and dark skinned Daf both had trace smiles visible in the yawning pale light starting to peek over the mountains like an opening yellow eye.

When Shawn still said nothing, Malone's sigh was as heavy as a mating moose. "Lord, man, get a clue, you thick headed moron. What I'm trying to say is, I need you to take me to the pass."

Shawn crossed his arms back over his chest. "And why would I want *tae* do that?" Beside him Beau and Daf snickered like schoolboys.

Malone took a deep breath. "Because you can buy your freedom if you take me there." He exhaled slowly. His small, brown eyes darted to the other two men then back to Shawn. "I can report that you died in the crash and when they can't find your body it'll be assumed wild animals took you."

"Uh huh," Shawn snorted. "And what about all the witnesses?" He nodded towards the group standing amid the trees.

"No problem. After you lead me to my treasure I'll say you tried to escape and I had to shoot you. Again, the wild animals will have demolished your body and scattered the parts."

Taking his time to consider what Malone had just said, Shawn glanced at his two friends. He could see Daf's broad white smile in the still dim twilight.

Back to Malone, he said, "Their freedom too, or tis no deal. Plus 50% of the gold."

His frown pulling his entire flaccid face down, Malone contemplated the barter for several minutes.

Shrugging broad round shoulders, he agreed. "All right. All of the others have to come too, at least for a while. It has to look like we're just finding a way out of here. There're no cell towers out here. No roads, zero buildings, no one will be able to get out anyway without you showing the way.

"Not that I care about them but I don't want any chance of one of them squawking my business to anyone we might come across until I'm away from all of you. Once I locate my treasure we'll ditch the witnesses. They can find their own way out."

He glanced up the mountain the bus lay crumpled on. "We can't possibly get back up the steep mountain to the road we were on, you need to lead us out another way."

"Aye," Shawn concurred. His dark eyes settling on the shorter, heftier man built like a small bull with wavy brown hair combed messily back off his forehead. He glared at the little round brown eyes. "You murdered two good men, Malone."

23

The deputy's brows jumped, his eyes slid sideways to see if any of the others across the way heard Shawn. Then he turned back to the Scotsman and shrugged carelessly again. "Sometimes people have to give up what they have so others can have a better life, right?"

"Another condition, Malone."

"Yeah?" The deputy eyed him ready to argue about it.

Shawn said, "My two friends and I won't be chained, but I want the other prisoners, the two men, Caleb Taylor and Zachary Stockton, restrained at all times. When we're outside I want each cuffed *tae* an officer. I don't want *tae* be responsible for unleashing them on an unsuspecting public."

Malone's nod negligent, he didn't care one way or another about the convicts. The male ones anyway. Be all that much better for him if they disappear. "Fine, whatever. We have a deal. Keep your traps shut to the others about the gold, we don't need more fucking fingers in my pot."

He glared at Daf and Beau who grinned back at him. Irritation twisting his voice, he snarled, "Let's get going, the sooner we start, the sooner we get my gold and get the fuck out of this hellhole." He turned and headed back to the waiting group.

"Oh, one other thing," Shawn said as Malone started to walk away.

The deputy ground out an aggravated sigh turning back to him. His brows rose in question.

Shawn informed him coolly, "I will have responsibility for the girl."

Malone gaped at the prisoner. His face reddening in agitation and wrath, cheeks shaking, he started sputtering. "No fucking way. The bitch is mine-"

Cutting him off, and ensuring there was no mistaking him, Shawn stood resolute with his arms crossed over his powerful chest. His expression was cold, hard, biceps straining in the orange jumpsuit, legs braced. He told him, "The female prisoner will be under my charge. Discussion is over."

The man's enigmatic expression alone would give Malone nightmares. He turned without agreeing and marched back to the group. Shawn, Beau and Daf stood talking quietly for a minute before following him

The three men rejoined the rest of the congregates, then Shawn veered off and started walking towards the bus.

Malone running after him, called out, "Where the hell do you think you're going?"

Shawn came to such an abrupt stop in front of the deputy, Malone staggered back a step.

Shawn said, "Malone, you can't shackle me or shoot me, you need me. There're things on the bus I can use. There's a home for wayward teens that was closed down suddenly a few months back, and is in this area a couple of miles out. Due *tae* some severe illness, they removed all the occupants including staff in a hurry, there might be supplies we can use. We'll head there first."

He strode to the bus and crawled inside which was difficult as it was lying on its side. It had been easier for the small woman in the red dress to get in and out. Beau and Daf like two grizzly bears clambered in right behind him.

When they came out, they were buckling holsters around their hips that they had found in the back security box.

All three had shotguns strapped over their backs. Malone blanched when he saw his prisoners armed.

Zachary Stockton's eyes lit up, he started towards the bus. Shawn said to him, "There are no more weapons, Stockton."

Zach came up short, scowling at Shawn. Both extraordinarily muscular men, Zach was bulkier and had a few inches on the exceptionally tall, leaner Shawn. They glared at each other, daring the other to take a swing or back off.

Eventually Zach backed down. Storming away, he muttered, "Fucker."

Shawn gestured with his head to Malone, reminding him to shackle the other male prisoners.

Annoyed at being told what to do, the deputy nonetheless spoke with Tomas Trent and Ritchie Marx. The two officers went straight to Zachary and Caleb.

Tomas, a shade below average height, strong but more wiry than buff, cuffed himself to the small accountant Caleb. Marx, a beefier man chained himself to the giant Zach.

Shawn strode over to Malone and before the deputy could react, Shawn grabbed his gun whipping it out of the holster and stuffed in the back of his belt.

"Hey-" Malone's hand went to his hip too late. The lines in his face deepened and sharpened, he took a step towards Shawn with his hand out. "Give me back my weapon, you fucking thug, that wasn't part of our deal."

Shawn stood with his arms crossed, legs apart. "Tis part of my deal, Malone. You want your gun, come and get it."

The deputy stood still, his hand dropped to his side. He knew from the brief fight they'd had, he didn't stand a chance against the stronger man. It appeared that the prisoner had allowed Malone to strike him just to see what he was made of. Darkonn had moves Malone had never seen before.

"That's what I thought," Shawn derided, then walked away leaving the deputy staring with impotent rage at his back.

Chapter Three

Carrying one of the dead officer's jacket in his hand, Shawn trod over to the girl in the red dress. Before she could stop him, he swung the jacket around her.

His voice a low gruff order, he told her, "Keep this on until we can get you better clothes."

Startled, she started to pull the jacket off but he grabbed her wrists to stop her.

Leaning his head close to hers so she could read in his unequivocal eyes he would brook no argument to any of his commands, he ground out, "You will do exactly as I say until we are out of here. You will not try *tae* escape, you are going back *tae* prison."

She tried to twist away from him saying, "You can't tell me what to-"

He whipped her back to face him, squeezing her delicate wrists so hard she winced.

Seeing the shot of pain cross her heart shaped face, Shawn loosening his grip slightly. His expression harsh, he said coldly, "I can, and you will obey everything I say."

Towering over her, still holding her wrists, he pulled her in close forcing her to look up at him. Her forearms were pressed against his chest.

His voice quietly deep, he threatened, "If you do not, if you try *tae* run or go for any of our guns, I will first break both of these tiny wrists of yours then I will put my hands around your beautiful white neck and crush your windpipe until you cease to breathe."

His black eyes glittered his threat menacingly at her, the scars jagged white against his tanned skin, he looked like a vicious heathenish outlaw.

Already frightened and exhausted from not sleeping due to having to watch her back every second, the petite young woman's eyes widened like terrified blue saucers before they rolled back in her head, her legs gave out and she crumpled.

"*Shit-*" Shawn cursed under his breath catching her up in his arms. He had wanted to scare her into submission, not frighten her to death.

He called to his friend with the red hair and red beard, "Beau, get me the other dead guy's jacket." Beau jogged to do his bidding. He came out of the bus with the jacket.

"Lay it on the ground," Shawn told him. Beau obliged, kneeling down he spread the jacket out on the grass.

Leena came over. "What's going on? Why are you carrying her?"

Laying the girl on the jacket, Shawn said wryly, "The murderess while foolishly brave in some respects, is quite fearful and squeamish in others." Out of the corner of his eye he saw Malone looking over with lewd interest.

Under his breath Shawn muttered, "*Scumbag.*" Kneeling next to the unconscious girl, he tugged her dress down to cover her legs that curled to the side, and pulled the jacket he'd given her closed.

Leena laughed harshly. "Malone's not the only one, I told you the tough girls tried to get at her too. I've tried to keep an eye on her, she seems somehow- seriously naïve or green or something."

Shawn set one hand lightly on the unconscious girl's shoulder and gazed down at the pale young woman who had so idiotically yet valiantly tried to make Malone stop beating him. He asked, "How's that?"

"Well," Leena said with a bawdy chuckle. "The women told me that when they were telling her what they wanted to do to her pussy, she didn't understand what they were talking about."

Laughter gurgled out of her. "She had said couldn't understand why they would do the things they were saying to a cat, and besides, she didn't even own a cat. When they explained, she turned so red she started choking. It was hilarious."

Standing up, his head slightly cocked, with a sidelong glance through a tangled lock of black hair at Leena, Shawn said, "I don't see the humor in it." He turned away from her affronted face and said to everyone in general, "Let's gather up what supplies we can from the bus and head out. Tis almost light."

Seeing the female prisoner stirring, coming around, he turned back to Leena and told her, "Stay with her until she gets her bearings." He walked away not seeing, or caring about the officer's pique at being made a nursemaid.

Before they started to leave, Shawn went over to the bus lying on its side and forced the hood open further, which wasn't easy as it was crunched and half cracked open. At least the smoke had stopped pouring out.

Beau joined him and asked, "What are you doing, mate?"

His head under the hood, Shawn's voice was muffled. "I want *tae* make sure tis not operational, I'd rather drive than walk."

"Tis on its side, Shawn."

"I know, bro, but there's possibly enough of us *tae* right it if it runs."

It only took a few minutes of tinkering before he came to the conclusion the bus was dead. Leaving it, he said to the assembled people standing around watching him, "All right, let's go."

They trooped down the rest of the mountainside. The girl, back up on steady feet, Shawn in the lead grasped her arm and pulled her to walk beside him then he let go of her.

He had placed Daf in the middle of the group making Malone walk in front of him, and had Beau at the end. He wanted to know where everyone was at all times.

On Shawn's right, the girl had to move quickly to keep up with his long strides. Between her possibly trying to run for it, or even worse, being assaulted from within the group, he decided the best place for her was in his sight at all times.

Hearing her panting beside him, he realized she would never make it if she had to work so hard to keep up and he slowed his pace.

The sun rose lazily over the sleeping land making it gleam like the crown jewels of England. Lush wavering grass sparkled with dew drops like rainbow sequins sprinkled on the blades. Leaves every shade of green flickered around royal, sky reaching trees.

The valley floor gave way to emerald rolling hills mottled in the sunlight. Surrounded by mountains lighting up majestically slowly, like a blanket lifting off the dark peaks turning them platinum.

After several miles of hiking, Shawn found the abandoned detention home. He broke a window, climbed through, went around and opened the door to let everyone in.

They discovered a treasure trove of things inside. Clothes, toiletries, packaged and canned food, canteens, bleach tablets to purify water, rope, backpacks, blankets, tools, blessed biodegradable toilet paper, packs of cigarettes and on and on.

They all managed to find clothes to fit, even the biggest men. The officers also changed out of their polyester uniforms into jeans, shirts and hiking boots.

Shawn told Leena to take the girl and get her something appropriate to put on.

An hour or so they all met up in the main room collecting supplies and backpacks to load them in.

Shawn turned when the women came out.

The girl was wearing a snug set of jeans, buttoned down blouse and hiking boots. The clothes were not as loose as he would have liked, they did nothing to hide her lush figure. At least she had a belt to keep those jeans more secured.

They all found jackets. Shawn had them keep the deceased officers' jackets too, along with rolled up blankets, although it was late spring, it would get cold in the mountains at night.

Walking over to the girl, Shawn dropped a straw cowboy hat on her head. "You wear this whenever we're in the sunlight, that fair skin will burn like paper under a magnifying glass."

Stuffing backpacks, they rolled blankets over the packs, hauled them on their backs and filed out of the structure. Shawn boarded up the window he broke and pulled the locked door closed behind him.

While everyone gathered outside, he wandered around the side of the building until he found an old animal trail in the tall grass.

He strode over to the girl and brusquely informed her, "You stay beside me, at all times."

Ignoring her resentful frown, he announced to the group, "Let's go," and waved for the rest of the people to follow him.

"How come we aren't following the dirt road the people that lived here drove in on?" Jim Vega asked as they maneuvered into a loose line.

Shawn couldn't tell them he was leading Malone to a treasure so he said, "The road winds almost straight up the side of the mountain. Tis steep and slick, it will be too hard *tae* climb up it. And we'd be climbing, Jim, the road is nowhere near level at any point."

"How come you know that shit?" Ritchie Marx asked.

"Lived here some time back," Shawn responded. "Question hour is over, let's head out."

The group started hiking along the trail.

After a minute, Beau strode up beside him to talk. This left no room for the girl on the narrow path so she dropped back.

Caleb the embezzling accountant, not cuffed at the moment as Shawn had directed, straightened his glasses to peer at the beauty now beside him.

"My- my name is Caleb, Caleb Taylor," he stuttered, holding out a scrawny hand. Reluctantly, she politely shook his hand. He said, "Uh, so what's your name, pretty girl?"

She smiled weakly at the thin man in his forties and not a great deal taller than her.

His eyes were blurry behind the round glasses, the thin spindly hair noticeably thinner on the top of his head.

Wrinkles deepened in his pasty face as his interest in her showed. His teeth slightly crooked in his anxious smile.

Nervously, she pondered telling him anything. He was a criminal, her own status was very shaky. The less any of them knew about her the better. She sighed, all of the officers knew who she was and why she was in prison. She would just as soon keep her personal life private.

Resigned to everyone knowing her sordid business, she said in a quiet voice, "Um, my name is Cherriana, Cherriana Delighya."

"Wow, that's a mouthful. Is that like Samson and Delilah?" Caleb adjusted his glasses higher on his narrow stubby nose to peer more closely at her.

Apparently used to the question, the corner of her lip pulled in. "Yes, sort of. My parents were actors with creative ideas."

"Uh huh. It's very nice. Do people call you something shorter like, Cheri?"

Staring at the ground so she wouldn't trip over anything in the unfamiliar hiking boots, she nodded. "Yes, they called me that at the convent where-" she broke off suddenly, biting her lip. So much for not giving out any personal information.

"Oh? Really? Were you a nun?" He hesitated, a half a step behind her, admiring her bum in the tight jeans. Even in boots tromping over uneven ground her hips had an enticing feminine sway. "They didn't make nuns like you when I was in school."

Mad at herself for revealing too much, she said curtly, "I was not a nun. I grew up there, I was-" she shook her head, closed her mouth. "Never mind," she walked faster.

He picked up his feet, feet too big for his skinny frame and moved beside her. "So, honey, Cheri, what are you off to prison for?"

This she *really* did not want to talk about, keeping her lips closed she moved more quickly staring straight ahead.

"Honey, Cheri, wait up!" Caleb peddled to catch up to her. In the meantime, Vance Malone saw his chance and jogged up to walk next to the girl.

Elbowing Caleb out of the way, he said cheerfully, "Hey babydoll, miss me?" He tried to catch her swinging hand. Snatching her hand out of his grasp Cheri crossed her arms over her chest, which caused her pace to slow.

This was fine with Malone. He dropped an arm around her shoulders and held on tight when she tried to shrug him off. Behind them, Caleb scowled a black hole through Malone's bulky back.

"Leave off the lass, Malone," a timbered gruff voice from behind ordered the deputy to let go of her.

Knowing it wasn't the frail accountant, Malone glanced back over his shoulder. Seeing the big dark man glowering at him, Malone snapped, "Bug off, Daf Jamieson, mind your own business. Enjoy your freedom from bars. Go find your own girl, there are two others more than available."

Turning his attention to Cheri, Malone pulled her close and kissed the side of her head laughing when she struggled to get loose and fight off his lascivious roaming hands.

Daf grabbed Malone's collar, yanked him back then shoved him so hard he spun in the air and landed splat on his butt. Furious, the deputy went to push back up to his feet and go after the prisoner.

Daf stood with his beefy hands on his solid hips like an angry Mack Truck and stared him down.

The commotion caught Shawn's attention up front. The Scotsman strode down the line to see what was up.

"Daf? What's going on?"

Daf reached back and scratched his shoulder, ropes of heavy muscles jumped with his movements. He nodded at Malone. "Pig was all over her. She didn't seem to like it."

Shawn clapped Daf's shoulder. "All right, let's keep going." He said to Malone, "Stay away from her, Deputy, you can rape her on your own time. After the..." he glanced around, "mission is completed. You're on my time now." He grasped Cheri's arm and practically dragged her back up to the front of the line.

When they got there, he said to her in an angry low voice, "I told you *tae* stay by me. Stop with the slut behavior, I don't need the aggravation. Don't make me have *tae* come after you again."

Gasping, shocked at his treatment of her, she turned hurt and confused blue eyes up at the man.

Black stubble was already covering his strong jaw making him look even more dangerous than before. He glanced down at her. "What? You got something *tae* say, lass?"

She dropped her eyes and lowered her head and kept walking.

Beside her, Shawn commanded not politely, "Tell me your name lass, I can't keep calling you girl."

Remaining close mouthed, she stumbled over a few rocks and kept walking, then stumbled again.

His hand stretched out to catch her from tripping but she caught her balance. Irritation making his deep voice gravel rough, Shawn said irately, "Fair *leamin*, I don't like *tae* have *tae* ask things twice. Tell me your name. I'm going *tae* get really pissed off if I have *tae* ask you again."

Swinging her head at him, hair rippling across her back, with her own anger boiling, she responded, "I don't see how

35

you, a prisoner as well as me, think you are in charge of us, any of us. What right do you have to tell me what to do?"

"Aye, lass." He set a big hand around the back of her slim neck, under her hat which was not on her head but hanging by its string draped on her upper back. His grip not hard, but purposeful as his ire grew.

"I am the only one that can get us out of here, that makes me in charge. You are technically in custody, and since I am leading this group I am responsible *tae* ensure you don't cause any trouble, or run. I don't plan on taking the hit if you escape and go kill someone else."

Squirming against his hand on her neck, she complained, "What about the other prisoners, those two men, Caleb and the big scary looking hoodlum? I don't see you manhandling them." Twisting her head to get out of his clutch to no avail, she demanded, "Remove your hand from my neck."

Keeping his hand where it was, his thumb rubbed against her pulse. He allowed himself a tight laugh and a quick glance down at her. "You are a blustery wee one for someone so *nesh*, aren't you?"

"And you are just a big bully trying to push me around." Prying futilely at his hand on her nape, she asked scowling, "What is a *nesh*? Why did you call me that, are you insulting me?"

A dimple rippled on one side of his rugged face, he ducked his head slightly. "It means soft. You try *tae* act strong but you are soft."

Irritated at his words, Cheri sputtered, "That's just stupid." She grasped his hand harder trying to pull his fingers off her neck. Insisting, "Let go of me, you are not in charge of me," she twisted away, but he held firm.

"Stop fighting me," his voice hardened. He still held onto her firmly yet gently as she was so delicate. Which he decided not to mention seeing how angry she got over him calling her soft.

His intent was not to harm her, just hold her still to listen to him. His thumb continued lightly brushing over the pulse beating in her neck.

Still holding her, he moved her off the path and said to the next in line, Jim Vega, "Keep heading towards that rocky pillar. And hook those two prisoners back up. The weasily guy and that *rochle*, the rough Mohawk." He gestured to a stone column that jutted off the side of the mountain.

Vega nodded, and told Tomas and Ritchie to cuff the prisoners then kept walking, the others followed him.

Shawn led Cheri to an open stretch of grass then stopped with his hand still on her neck. Facing her, he looked down watching her expression change.

The girl's anger was fleeing, being quickly replaced by fear of the irate man that loomed over her. A sensation of danger like a coiled wild animal ready to kill clung to him.

His black eyes like a horse's, shiny, dark fathomless circles surrounded by long spiky lashes that curled just at the ends glared enigmatically at her.

Shawn let go of her then stood with his hands on his hips. His voice harsh as coarse sand, he said, "Listen wee spitfire. You are courageous and stubborn at the wrong moments. I am responsible *tae* get everyone out of here safely and that means everyone has *tae* do what I say, when I say, and how I say.

"To balk or argue about my instructions can mean the difference between life and injury, maybe even death. If I allow you *tae* ignore my orders then the others will too and that will put everyone in peril. You ken?"

She stared mutely at him, her hands at her side. She didn't know what he wanted her to say so she said nothing.

He continued, "*Tae* answer your question, the two other prisoners are the correction officers' problems. If I let them watch over you too I'm afraid you will, as a typical bonny woman, use your feminine wiles and allure *tae* trick them and before we know it you'll be gone.

"Unfortunately, I think you could also easily outsmart the two women. I don't want *tae* get more time in prison for aiding and abetting your escape."

Feeling the anger building back up in her, her brows, darker than her hair drew down between her eyes. "That is all ridiculous. I have no- no feminine whatever you said."

She looked from the strong frightening man to the mountains, the roses in her cheeks paled, the sparkling eyes dimmed. She swung her gaze clouded with profound fear back to him.

He watched her, his expression unreadable.

"I would rather die free out here in the woods than go back to- a- cage where unconscionable vile beasts can do what they-" her voice cracked. She took a short breath.

"Anyway, it is the women's job, Leena and Bella's to guard me. Not yours. I would ask you to let them do their jobs and- and like I said, stop manhandling me. I am not a doll for you to drag around."

The tips of his ears turned red, a pulse at his temple beat like a drum.

The sun was at its zenith, the strongest of the day, it streaked down on the top of their heads, lighting her hair like it was creamed butter. He took a step towards her with his hand out, she shrunk away from him.

"Dammit lass," he reached around her, plucked up her hat and dropped it on her head. Most of the group had found some type of hat to wear as protection from the sun, and from getting clobbered by a low tree limb when traipsing through the dense forests.

Her fear and dread, and the proud anger imbued in the dainty, highly feminine woman gave Shawn disturbing and confusing feelings. Expressing his confusion in ire, he dug his fingers into his lean hips so they wouldn't wrap around her obstinate neck. He took another step closer to her.

His voice so low like it dragged across hard dirt, he was barely audible as he ground out, "I don't care what you want or think. We're doing things my way. You do as I say and I won't have *tae- manhandle* you."

His face darkened, hands balled into fists. He said through grit teeth, "Lass, I'm warning you, if you don't do exact-"

"Cherriana."

"Huh?"

"My name."

He scrubbed his fingertips down the front of his face. Scratching the black whiskers on his jaw, he took a deep vexed breath and let it out. "Say it again." His eyes dropped to watch her small but full lips.

"Cherriana."

"'Tis different," he muttered, calming down.

She pushed the hat back off her forehead to look up at him. "Cher is from my French grandmother, Riana is from my Irish father's mother."

His black brows rose in interest. "Really? You're half Irish? So am I." He was surprised when he saw the pretty face grimace.

"Yes. The drunken abusive part. The state took me away when I was a toddler because he-" her mouth shut. Her soft features hardened then turned bleak. She crossed her arms, wrapping them around her body and stared down at the ground.

Seeing her anguish and not knowing how to respond, Shawn went to take her arm. "Come on, Cherriana, let's go."

But she took off towards the trail before he could catch her arm. A touch of a grin tugged up his lip, *so feisty that one.* He followed her and rejoined the rest of the group.

They came across an empty cabin Shawn decided would make a great place to spend the night instead of out in the elements.

Chapter Four

Finding the door unlocked, Malone marched right inside.

Behind him, Bella, her hair out of its tight knot and into a ponytail swiveled around taking in the space. "Except for being completely empty of furniture, it's not too bad," she declared. "Smells like woody lumber and smoky from the fireplace."

Her boots clomping across the wood planked floor she disappeared down a hall.

By the time she came back everyone was inside dropping their backpacks with tired groans. Bella slid her own backpack off surprisingly broad shoulders, big muscles for a woman pumped as she set it down.

She announced, "There is one bedroom with a small bed in it and a bathroom. There's cutlery and some canned food and a whole bunch of those survival packaged foods in the cupboards but there's no electric. But we have running water and the toilet works, and there's a ton of those biodegradable toilet paper tubes," Bella added gratefully.

"Must be a well with an osmosis pump of sorts," Shawn said, last in, stepping through the doorway with Cheri in front of him.

"We need *tae* get some wood for the fireplace so we can heat up the food. Daf," he said to the buff guy with the dreadlocks, "see if you can scare up something more satisfying for dinner."

"*Och ay*, sure bro," Daf replied, sliding the shotgun he'd taken from the bus off his back and into his hands. He disappeared back outside.

Officer Tomas Trent took the disgraced accountant Caleb over to a wall and had him sit down while he removed the handcuffs linking them together, then Tomas and Jim Vega went outside to search for wood.

Deputy Ritchie Marx chained to Zach brought him over and took the manacle off his own wrist and hooked Zach to Caleb, then he trod over to a corner and flopped down exhausted, bracing his back uncomfortably against the hardwood wall.

Leena dropped down wearily beside him.

"That a cross of David?" she asked the older man with the curly dark hair slivered with grey.

His chocolate colored eyes weary, he smiled blearily at her. "Yup. It is."

Leena said, "I've never seen it on you before." She stretched her back and worked the kinks out of her neck.

Ritchie's dark eyes slid sideways watching as she unbuttoned several top buttons on her thin flannel shirt and flapped her lapels complaining, "It's warm in here."

At fifty, Ritchie, a husky man, once fairly well built had allowed his muscles to turn to fat. He wasn't overweight, just not very toned, he stuck his legs out straight and crossed his ankles. "It won't be warm in an hour or so after the sun sets."

His head dropped back, his eyes closed. Leena squirmed closer to him until their arms were touching. One eye opened, he peered at her.

She said in a quiet, flirtatious voice, "I bet you got dark curly hair on your chest too, don't ya?" Flapping her lashes at the officer she snuggled against him. Leaning over slightly to give him a clear view down her shirt like she'd done with Shawn. Ritchie wasn't one to ignore an offer like that, so he looked.

Vance Malone went to find the bathroom.

Bella and Cheri were putting cans on the kitchen counter and opening some. With that done, Cheri refilled everyone's canteens that had quickly emptied on the long warm hike, and dropped chlorine tablets in them.

Done with her own self-imposed tasks, Bella wandered over and nestled down next to the hulking Zach. She chattered away quietly at the sullen prisoner while he sat with his blond head back and his eyes closed. He didn't even move when she traced the white supremacist tats on his arm with her fingertips.

The door opened, Jim and Tomas came in. Jim cradled an armload of thick branches. Tomas had a bunch of twigs tucked under his arm but he was clutching the doorframe and wincing in pain.

Shawn came over and took the twigs from Tomas. "What's the matter, mate?" he asked the twenty-something officer.

None of the men had shaved, a few sparse whiskers stuck out around Tomas' pallid face. Built like a wiry light pole, narrow with wide shoulders, Tomas had muscles but nothing like some of the other men.

Pain in his voice, he said weakly, "I cut my leg, it's bleeding like crazy." He showed Shawn his leg. His jeans were torn exposing a deep gash at least seven or eight inches long on his thigh that was bleeding.

Carrying the twigs to the fireplace, Shawn called out, "Cherriana, come here."

Hearing Shawn's commanding yet intensive voice indicating something was wrong, the young woman hurried out of the kitchen.

Dropping the twigs in the hearth, Shawn turned towards her and said, "Tomas is injured, can you help him?"

Looking up at him while he pushed his black hair off his brow waiting for her response, Cheri hesitated then moved to the officer and knelt down to look at his leg.

"Can you go sit on those crates?" she asked Tomas. There was no furniture in the large room except for some crates and empty boxes.

Tomas started towards the crates when Bella said, "There's a bunk in the bedroom, that'd probably be better for him." The cabin was bereft of furniture except for the bunk likely placed there for weary hunters to utilize.

Tomas changed direction and hobbled down the hall to the bedroom. Cheri quickly went to find the first aid kit in Shawn's backpack and some towels.

As they did that, Shawn and Beau tee-peed the twigs then started laying the branches down eventually setting a few bigger logs over them. Patting his pockets, Shawn found matches and worked to get a fire going.

Cheri trod down the hall and into the small bedroom carrying the medic box and towels.

Inside, Tomas was sitting on the bed with his back against the wall, legs stuck out in front of him. She hurried over and set the first aid kit on the bed then bent to pull the torn jeans away from the wound.

Not strong enough to tear the jeans further, she took out a pair of scissors from the kit and cut the material away from his wound. Picking up the towels, "Here," she said, placing

44

the towels over the gash, "hold these on it tight." He pressed the towels to his leg while she rummaged in the kit.

"My own Florence Nightingale," Tomas purred watching her.

Beau's big body took up the expanse of the doorway. His freckled face cheerful, he asked, "Can I help?"

Cheri regarded him suspiciously, she had a feeling Shawn had sent him to keep an eye on her.

His grin crinkled the freckles on his cheeks, over them the blues eyes blinked innocently at her.

She gave him a brief polite smile then turned her attention back on Tomas. Her lips pulled in tightly, she twined her fingers together displaying agitation. She looked so anxious Beau moved into the room and asked, "What's wrong, lass?"

Quietly so as not to panic Tomas, she said, "I'm going to have to stitch him up and there's no anesthesia…"

Beau arched a brow at her then smiled with confidence. "I got it handled. I'll be right back." Pivoting on his heel he left the bedroom.

Cheri turned to Tomas. His brown toned skin had turned pallid and clammy. He stammered, "You mean, you mean you're gonna *sew* me, my skin…"

Pushing her long curly hair back off her shoulder, Cheri set a hand on his arm and said kindly, "Yes, I'm afraid I must, it's the only way to stop the bleeding."

Beau returned with a bottle of whiskey clutched in a huge freckled hand. Cheri blinked at the bottle. "Where on earth did you get that?"

He grinned at her. "We're Scottish, love." He winked, red eyelashes smacked his cheek. "Tis called magic."

She rolled her eyes. "Uh huh, whatever. Start pouring it down his throat, as much as he can take."

Beau moved to them and handed the bottle to Tomas. "Drink up, me boyo, it'll be the only thing between you and the needle." He shoved the bottle into the man's hands watching Tomas' brown skin turn paler.

Reaching into the medical kit, Cheri took out the things she needed and laid them in a row on a towel on the bed.

After readying the tools, she put pressure on the towels on the wound while he drank.

It didn't take long for Tomas to start giggling. Soon his face bloomed ruddy and shining, his head lolled and bobbed with his slurred words.

"You've had enough laddie, I think." Beau took the bottle from him.

"Can you pour some over the wound too, to clean it?" Cheri asked the big redhead.

"Sure." Beau started to pour it over the gash and Tomas let out a shriek. Beau gave him the bottle back and said, "I'm thinkin' you need a wee bit more, mate."

After Tomas took a few more slugs, Beau took the bottle, slugged down a big swig himself, poured a bit over the needle Cheri held out and screwed the lid back on.

Cheri cleaned the wound and started threading the needle. When she went to stick the needle in Tomas' leg, Beau turned green and stammered, "Uh, I'll be back in a- a minute." He scurried out of the room.

Laughing at the large manly man with his weak stomach, Cheri started stitching. After sewing Tomas up, she dabbed antibiotic ointment over the gouge then wrapped adhesive bandages over it. He was drunk enough for the pain to be dulled but he still moaned and groaned.

Finished, Cheri cleaned up the equipment and returned it to the bag. She took the bloody towels and filled the bathroom sink for them to soak then went back in and sat on the edge of the bed to see how her patient was doing.

Checking his thigh to make sure the wound wasn't bleeding, she put her palm on his forehead to check for fever.

Tomas opened one bloodshot eye to peer at her. His face relaxed in a broad drunk grin. "Hey, Florence Nightenangel…"

She laughed at him. "That's Nightingale."

He muttered, "Whatever, baby," then he grabbed her hand off his forehead and pulled it down over the bulge in his groin and pressed it down hard. "Look what you've done to me, angel!"

"Tomas!" She jerked her hand out from under his. Before she could move away he lunged at her. Throwing his arms around Cheri, Tomas said, "Come angel, give your patient some sugar, c'mere." He tried to kiss her.

"Tomas! Stop it!" Cheri turned her face away and tried to wrench out of his arms.

He shifted to the side and pushed her down on the bed. Throwing his good leg over her to prevent her from getting away, he grabbed her wrists staking her hands over her head on the bed and lowered his mouth to hers.

"Who knew I would have my own little angel for the night. C'mon, baby, let me show you my gratitude." Grinding his erection against her, he crammed his mouth over hers smothering her screams. Clenching her wrists with one strong hand, he reached between them to the zipper on his jeans.

Suddenly Tomas was jerked up and off and hurled to the floor.

Gasping, Cheri struggled to sit up. She put the back of her hand to her mouth, then looked at it, there was blood on her hand. Tomas had cut her lip with his aggressive attempts to kiss her.

Beau dropped down, grabbed Tomas' shirt collar, yanked his head up and hauled his fist back-

Cheri shouted, "No! Don't hit him, Beau! He's drunk and injured, he doesn't know what he's doing!" She scrambled across the bed on her knees and grasped Beau's arm to stop him.

"Leggo my arm, lass, he has no business assaulting his kind nurse. He needs to have a lesson." Beau tried to shake her off, but she clung to him with both hands, begging, "No, please don't hurt him, he didn't know what he was-"

"Beau," the deep calm voice from the doorway stopped the redhead from pummeling Tomas. Shawn casually entered the room, his hands in his pockets. "Be a good lad and put Tomas back in the bed."

He said to Cheri, "You can let go of my tough guy now."

Her cheeks blossoming dark pink, Cheri let go of Beau who winked at her with a grin.

Shawn said, "Come here, lass." His eyes narrowed when she hesitated. Then she did as he bid her. Still on her knees, she slid off the bed to her feet and moved to stand near him but out of reach.

Clutching Tomas' shirt and belt with both hands, Beau easily lifted the now almost unconscious man off the floor and onto the bed. He stuffed a pillow under Tomas' head then ambled over to Shawn.

"Sorry, bro, I left for just a minute. I mean she was literally sewing his *bluidy* skin togeth-" he started to turn green again. Gulping hard, he said, "Anyway, I come back in and he's got her pinned down and was climbing all over her undoing his pants."

Shawn settled his condescending gaze on Cheri. "You see, lass, this is the kind of thing I am trying *tae* avoid."

He took a hand out of his pocket and brushed the blood off her cut lip with a fingertip. "I don't need you going back to the authorities and crying rape and they come after me for allowing it to happen."

Cheri gasped at his audacity, like she had asked the patient to attack her! She stood stunned for a second with her mouth hanging open. Then, rigid with fury snapped it shut and strode imperiously out of the room.

Beau grinned at Shawn. "Feisty little piece, isn't she?"

His lips pressed into a firm line, Shawn nodded. "Aye, that she is."

"You were right, Shawn, I think she's going to be trouble," Beau commented. "You're going to be spending all your time fighting the other men here, keeping them off her. Talk about catnip, it oozes unconsciously from her. Your best shot would be to take her to the nearest ranger or game warden station and dump her on them."

"Hmm." Shawn glanced at Tomas who was now snoring like a runaway train. "Let's go eat. Daf got a couple of rabbits. Don't say anything *tae* the women, you know how they get about killing bunnies. We'll tell them we found them in a cold root cellar below the shack or something."

After they ate, people hung out in small clusters chatting.

Leena and Ritchie were unabashedly making out in a corner.

Bella was trying to get to know Zach, she had taken his cuff off so he was not restrained to Caleb. The supremacist con was a man of few words. Bella kept yammering at him, until he finally stood up, grabbed her hand, pulled her to her feet and dragged her outside.

Cheri and Caleb washed the dishes and put them back in the cupboard where they found them. Cheri said nervously to the small man, "Do you think she'll be all right? Bella I mean. Maybe someone should go check on her…"

Caleb dropped his dish-drying towel on the counter and walked away from her without a word. When he reached a wall he slouched down against it.

The only light they had now was from the glowing fire in the hearth. They had laid blankets and pillows on the floor for their bedding. There was very little furniture but a lot of domestic items had remained in the cabin's closets and cupboards.

Cheri walked tentatively over to Shawn who was standing by the fire speaking with Beau and Daf. Shawn turned to her as she approached.

"Um, Mister…" she didn't remember his last name.

He supplied it, "Darkonn."

Twisting a length of hair around her fingers, she swallowed a few times. "Mr. um Darkonn, I'm a bit worried, you know, for Bella. She- she- went outside with that man, you know, the…"

His arms crossed over his chest, Shawn impassively contemplated the disconcerted girl. "So?" He wasn't concerned the prisoner would run off, it was pitch black outside with bears and mountain lions roaming. Zach might be psychotic but he wasn't stupid.

"Uh, well, she might be in- in trouble. He's a very big, mean looking, um, man. He might harm her."

Beau Dyce spoke for Shawn, "*Hinnie*, first of all, Bella went willingly with him after she'd been rubbing up against him all evening like a cat in heat. Second, that lass can well take care of herself. That hard athletic body, you've seen her shoulders, for a woman, she's quite strong. She's not like-" his eyes dropped down Cheri's soft and slender curvy body.

Embarrassed, Cheri's face burned red, a shimmer of sudden tears threatened to fall. Feeling dumbly helpless, she turned from the men and strode to the door, flung it open and ran out.

"Way *tae* go, bro," Shawn muttered.

Beau's lips pulled in, in chagrin. "I dinna mean to hurt her feelings, Shawn. She's bonny, a soft little lass, some men might like Bella's hard toned body, myself," he shrugged. "I'll take the soft, silky, the *nesh soie*, wee ones like," he nodded towards the door.

"*Nae dout*. Keep it in your pants, bro," Shawn said, heading for the door with Beau's snickers of, "Back at ya, bro," ringing in his ears.

Outside, it was as black as a deep hole, and had cooled down. A chill clung to the trees, dampening the grass.

Off to one side he could hear loud moans that he determined to be Bella and Zach getting to know one another. He stood for a second and listened to find where Cheri had gone.

On the other side of the building he could hear quiet weeping. "*Great*," he swore under his breath.

Strolling slowly so as not to frighten her, with his hands in his pockets, Shawn wandered around the cabin. He saw her huddled against the building. When he got close, he said softly, "Cherriana."

She gulped back a sob. He could see her dashing at her eyes. She didn't turn around or answer him so he moved closer.

Setting his hands on her shoulders, he gently turned her around. Her head was bowed, she wiped with embarrassment at the tears that still slid out.

Gruffly, Shawn said quietly, "*Nesh leamin*, what's wrong? Don't tell me you're upset because you're not a muscle bound jock like Bella. What's really upsetting you?"

The tears flowed harder, she wiped at them faster, her chest heaved with sobs trying to get out.

He cajoled, "Come, lass, don't go on like that." Shawn leaned his back against the building, drew her to him and wrapped his arms around her. He pressed her head gently to his chest and held her, stroking her back.

Fumbling in his pocket, he pulled out a handkerchief he had gotten from the juvenile home and handed it to her. "Dry your eyes, lass, tell me what is upsetting you so much."

The tears subsided, she wiped at them. Shawn's large fingers carefully cupped her chin and lifted her head. His dark eyes gleamed down at the distraught young woman. "Well?"

A body-shaking sigh escaped her, her lips parted then closed.

Shawn murmured, "Tell me, lass." An arm still around her, he let go of her chin and plucked some loose tendrils that stuck to her wet cheek smoothing them back off her face.

She sucked in a deep trembling breath then exhaled. Leaning back, taking another deep shuddering breath, she told him, "I'm going to prison, Mr. Darkonn, don't you see? I'm going to prison and I didn't do anything, I never," her throat closed, the tears streamed.

Shawn pulled her to his chest again, stroking her back until she calmed again. Gently he commanded, "Tell me about it."

Through gasping, quivering breaths, she said, "I was raised in a…a convent."

He nodded. "I know, Caleb blabbed your business *tae* anyone who would listen."

Lifting her head slightly, she sighed. "I never meant to tell him, it slipped out. Anyway, I was going to take my vows, I was going to become a nun and stay there. Then, Sister Marie had a talk with me. She convinced me that I had seen nothing of the world outside the convent.

"I did all of my schooling there, it's where I got my medical training. Anyway, she pushed me to start college for nursing, or maybe even to become a doctor." She stopped to take a breath, peered up at him to see if he was bored yet.

His eyes were trained intensely on her, he nodded as she spoke.

"So, my very first class, my first professor, he…was always around me, following me everywhere. He was freaky obsessed, stalked me. One day he got me alone in a classroom."

"Did he-" Shawn's arms tightened around her.

Her hands pressed against his shirt, tensely she clutched some of the material in her fists. Shaking her head, she replied, "No," and drew in a shuddering breath.

She whispered, "He said he planned to- to rape me, but he knew that I'd go to the police and there would be…evidence on…me. He knew he couldn't prove it was consensual because he'd either have to drug me, or force me, thereby leaving…damage. He…said he would kill me before he'd let me tell on him, so he had another plan."

When she paused, he prodded, "What was his other plan?"

Her bleak smile mirthless, she told him, "It was wild, outrageous, unbelievable. He said he would to marry me, then I could never...refuse him. Of course I said no. I know this is impossible to believe, as crazy as it sounds... But when I refused him, he deliberately framed me for a- a murder. He actually did kill...someone...and planted things of mine at the scene.

"He said when I come to my senses and agree to marry him he will destroy the evidence so there would be nothing to prosecute me with. Well," she drew another deep painful breath.

Shawn rubbed light circles with his palm on her back as she talked. "So, I was so scared. I knew I would be found guilty. I didn't dare, you know, marry the professor after he- he- killed someone. He would certainly have no hesitation in harming me, or- or killing me too ...so I ran while on surety bond.

"Obviously I was caught and am being extradited to Montana. It's all so...sordid and bizarre. I've lived a life of chastity with limited outside contact and knowledge of the world, now all I hear are threats of rape, and cursing.

"And words I've never even heard before much less comprehend what they mean, and people pawing me like I'm a caged animal at the zoo. I just don't understand it, not any of it." Her agonized sigh expressed her fears.

Shawn was silent, still rubbing her back. His eyes drifted down watching her hands splayed flat against his chest then agitatedly clutching his shirt, then she tried to smooth out the material.

Shawn pulled her closer, forcing her forearms to press on his chest.

She looked up at him. "Even you, you call me names I don't understand. *Leamin*, is that like cursing, are you cursing me?"

His lips quivered then pulled in. *"Na,* it means something like 'bright glow'."

Cheri contemplated this, unsure of what to make of it. It didn't sound disparaging, but it was hard to tell with this man. Her confused thoughts churned over her creamy face.

"You said *nesh* means soft, so when you call me *nesh leamin* you're calling me like a soft glow?"

One broad shoulder hitched faintly. "Something like that."

Not knowing what to make of any of it, she lowered her head and was silent for a moment. Raising her head weakly, her voice twisting with despair, she asked him, "Anyway, do...do you believe me?" At his grim countenance, she lowered her head again.

Quietly pondering her words, he stared at the top of her brilliant hair. Chucking his fingers under her chin he tilted her head up and looked down at the sadly earnest blue eyes tasseled with dark lashes like the fringe surrounding the blossom of a sunflower.

He watched her clamp those small plump lips together trying to still their trembles.

Stuffing his protective feelings, Shawn said evenly, "I don't know, Cherriana." He brushed a thumb delicately over the cut on her lip. "My experiences with women have been that most are conniving and deceitful."

She lowered her head but not before he saw the tears misting again. He repeated to the top of her head, "I don't know lass." Not enjoying the guilt he felt at causing her to weep again, he ran his hands down her arms then let her go.

Away from his body heat she started shivering. The temperature had dropped at least 15 degrees, the air hovered heavy and dank. A chill wind ruffled around the building blowing iciness at their clothes and hair.

"We need *tae* go in," he said.

His hand automatically cupped her elbow to help her tread the uneven ground in the dark haze. Clouds hid the moon and stars, the only light in the pitch-black night came from the fire inside the cabin glowing golden evanesce through the filmy windows.

At the door he stopped. "By the way, Cherriana," his tone turned cold and emotionless as it had been before, all the gentle kindness gone. "You will not leave this building again, or any other place we are, inside or out, without my permission or me with you. If you run, I will come after you, and you won't like it when I catch you."

He gripped her jaw forcing her to look at him. The blue eyes swelled with the suffering of being a prisoner with no free will. "Are we clear?"

She stiffened, her face set. He was being so nice and comforting, and now he was dictatorial and brutish, ordering her around again. Yanking from his grip, she went to sweep past him into the house but he grabbed her arm and held her still.

Dark eyes like black ice glittering at her, he said with a harsh brusqueness, "Let me make things more clear, Cherriana. If I canna trust you, *tae* even answer me when I ask you a question, then I canna trust you at all. I won't take the chance of you running. I will be forced *tae* tie you *tae* me for the *entire* time we are out here. You understand me? You would have no *preevacy,* I mean no privacy, no freedom at all."

His fingers tightened on her arm, he shook it when she didn't respond. He waited.

Finally she whispered, "I hear you." She jerked her arm out of his grasp and dashed into the cabin.

Chapter Five

Beau and Daf added logs to the fire to last through the night. Everyone else was settling down, choosing a place to lie down on blankets they'd taken from the first abandoned facility.

Shawn joined his friends for a brief conference. Beau would be sleeping by the hall leading to the bathroom and bedroom that Tomas still slept in. Daf would take his place by the kitchen, and Shawn the front door. Shawn trusted the deputies even less than he did the prisoners.

A giggly Bella and irascible scowling Zach stumbled back inside, shivering with their clothes and hair askew.

Shawn traipsed over and had a few words with Malone. Then Malone had a few words with Bella, whose face turned furiously red before she flounced off to the bathroom to fix the buttons on her shirt that were unevenly buttoned, and comb the leaves out of her hair.

Malone spoke next with Jim Vega and Ritchie Marx. Afterwards, Vega handcuffed himself to Caleb, and Ritchie waited for Zach to settle someplace then hunkered down beside him and secured himself to the huge convict.

Everyone wanted a shower, so half of them showered at night and the other half would shower in the morning to save time. The showers were fleeting, the water was like ice.

Leena was sitting next to Cheri, her back against a wall talking quietly with her.

Shawn came over and stood in front of them.

Leena grinned invitingly. "You come for me big and handsome?" Next to her, Cheri's head slightly inclined towards the officer, her expression appalled at the way Leena flirted with the domineering felon.

It didn't get past Shawn. He said, "*Na,* I've come for her. Come with me, Cherriana." He held a hand down to Cheri, daring her with mastery in his hard eyes to disobey him.

Her gaze flit from his face harsh with dangerous angles, to the extended hand, to the floor. Without looking at him, she reached up for his hand. He bent over so she could reach it and pulled her to her feet.

"Nighty night, hon," Leena drawled jealously after them.

Shawn led her near the door he was going to guard. Pointing to a blanket on the floor, he ordered, "Lie down there." Another blanket was laid out next to it along with two others as covers, their packs would be their pillows.

Clearly, she was to sleep next to him. He would be on one side of her, the other side was the wall. She wrapped her arms around her body, took an imperceptible step back shaking her head, the bright wavy hair billowed around her.

His boots planted shoulder width apart, arms crossed, he said quietly, "You have a choice, lass. You can get your pretty bum down right now on that blanket by yourself, or you can be embarrassed in front of everyone here while I put you down. You have one second."

When she didn't move, just stood gawking at him, Shawn uncrossed his arms and took a step towards her.

With a tiny shuddering sigh, Cheri lowered herself down on shaking knees, but went no further. Hearing his rasping impatient exhale, she cringed.

He crouched down inches from her, so close his long legs bracketed her, and with both large hands he pushed aside her hair that covered her like a buttery veil. Eyes blazing, he said in a savage whisper to her frightened face, "You try my patience, lass, *lay down.*"

Slowly, she unfolded and squirmed down to position on her side with her back against the wall and pulled her legs up to her chest. Her body twitched, pinpricks of fear ran up her arms when she heard his masculine grunt as he dropped down beside her.

Sitting up and facing her, he had a length of rope. She watched him take her trembling hands and tie her wrists together, ignoring her gasp when he tied the end of the rope to his belt.

Without another word, he drew a blanket over her then moved to lie on his side with his back to her and listened to her stifled sobs catching in her throat.

When Cheri woke the next day Shawn was not beside her. Her hands were free from the restraints. She groggily sat up rubbing her eyes, praying he had left the cabin. Her hope died as she saw him still there in the room.

He was in a corner with his two friends, their three heads together. Probably planning on how they were going to murder all of them and then go rob a bank.

A tiny grin at her fantasy pulled at her lips. At that second he glanced over at her. Straightening her mouth she turned her head away from him.

Shawn moved to the center of the group waiting for them to quiet down before he spoke. His black hair still wet from his morning shower, he'd rolled the long sleeves of his shirt up past forearms of a lumberjack laced with black hair. He set hands used to hard work on his tapered hips sheathed in mildly worn, snug jeans.

Except for his two friends, the rest of the crowd sat on the floor scattered around the room.

When the group settled down and looked at him, he said, "Okay. Tis going *tae* be a lot tougher going from here on out. We will begin hiking across a few acres of grass but then we'll hit a bit of forest before we begin ascending the mountain.

"Keep yourselves hydrated, and the most important thing is that everyone sticks close together. We are in a treacherous area, there can be sudden bottomless ravines, trickling streams that can flash flood into raging rivers, and of course wild, hungry animals that can see us but we can't see them. We have safety in numbers."

"Yeah," Malone chuckled sadistically, "like a herd of gazelles. All I need to worry about is that I'm faster than at least one of you."

Not responding to Malone's callous joking, Shawn narrowed a direct gaze at each person to make sure everyone was listening to his warnings and instructions.

Bella had her head near Zach's shoulder. A virtual giant, his flannel shirt was opened to the waist showing mounds of bulky muscles. Bella palmed his massive, hairless, tattooed chest. The psychopath was staring straight out with glazed eyes, he wasn't hearing anything Shawn was saying.

Malone now stood leaning a shoulder against the wall, his arms crossed, watching Shawn. His brow furrowed like he was still debating how trustworthy the Scotsman was.

Shawn perused the rest of the group. Everyone else was listening intently to him, eyes lit with adventurous or anxious anticipation, except for Cheri who looked wan and sad.

Beside her, Caleb picked at his fingers and obsessively pushed at his glasses, he looked about to lose his breakfast. Clearly he was neither the adventurous nor the outdoors type.

Shawn settled his attention briefly back on the girl, Cheri, the only other person than Zach who was not looking at him. She had her knees up and her arms around them. Her chin propped on her knees, she stared at the floor.

Before he gave the go ahead signal, Shawn went over to Malone and said, "Give me your watch."

Holding his hand away from the taller man, Malone scowled, snorted, no way this jerk was getting any more of his stuff. "What for?"

Shawn held his hand out explaining, "I can use it as a compass."

Total disbelief raised Malone's bushy eyebrows and he stuck his hand in his pocket. "No way you can do that."

Rolling his eyes, Shawn said coolly, "If you hold an analog watch flat with the hour hand pointing *tae* the sun, south is halfway between the hour hand and 12. 2. Hand it over."

Malone stared warily at him keeping his hand deep in his pocket. "You can look at the sun and know what direction it is. What else can you use instead of my fucking watch?"

Shawn planted his hands on his hips in exasperation with his boots akimbo, lowering his eyes but not his head, he looked down on Malone.

As if teaching kindergarteners, he said derisively, "I can of course use shadows. Stand a 3-foot stick vertically in the ground and mark the tip of its shadow with a rock. Wait 15 minutes, then mark the shadow again. The line connecting the two roughly coincides with the east-west line."

He went on, "At night, I can use the stars. Locate the Big Dipper and follow an imaginary line through the two stars at the end of the cup and extending into the sky *tae* a medium-bright star, which is Polaris, the North Star.

"Or, I can use the moon. If there is a crescent moon rising before sunset, its illuminated side will face west. If it rises after midnight, the brighter side faces east. Of course if tis cloudy or raining those things won't work.

"There are also ways of using plants, trees, water flow, etc. The fastest, easiest is the watch, especially if the sun is straight overhead unless tis dark. That answer your question?"

Actually surprised at all this information, Malone was speechless. He had no idea there were so many ways to tell direction. Still disliking the man, Malone's admiration for his skills in the wild went up.

Besides knowing the way to the crest, Malone had definitely chosen the right man for the job, but he still didn't want to give up his watch. The front part of his shirt was not tucked in, it hung messily over his belt. His sleeves were unevenly rolled up his flaccid arms. If he had a cigar hanging out of his mouth he'd look like a rumpled bookie.

His impatient irritation with the deputy darkening his face, Shawn grit his teeth to keep calm and said, "I can show you, let's go outside."

Knowing he was going to lose the battle, Malone just undid the watch and handed it over with pissed resignation.

Buckling it on his wrist, Shawn ran both hands through his damp hair, the wetness making it even blacker, shinier. He bent and picked up a shotgun slinging the strap over his shoulder so the gun rested at the side of his backpack.

He said, "All right, let's head out." He waited while everyone climbed to their feet and paraded out the door.

Before she could move, he strode over to Cheri, leaned over wound his long thick fingers around her arm and pulled her to her feet.

Yanking her arm out of his grasp, she cut her glance from him to the floor as if she couldn't stand to look at him, and snapped, "I can get up on my own, please stop jerking me about."

Shawn had shaved this morning but still a shadow covered his lower face that was a chiseled wall of no dispute.

He ground out, "If you would do as I ask the first time I ask then there would be no need for me *tae*...assist you. Speaking of that, let me reiterate the ground rules for the rest of the...uh excursion."

He watched her still staring at the floor, crossing her arms tightly over her chest in an attempt to keep him from seizing her again and dragging her out the door. If it hadn't been such a pitiful attempt at keeping him, twice her size, from doing to her whatever he chose to, he would have smiled at her bravado.

Now he frowned at her resistance as little as it was. "I would appreciate it, Cherriana, if you would look at me when I'm speaking to you."

He waited, expecting further resistance, but he needed to show a line of zero noncompliance with all of them if they were to succeed and make it out of the woodlands intact. He stuffed his surprise at seeing the blue eyes turn up at him, narrowed in defiance, but at least she complied.

"Thank you," he said stiffly. "Now, you will, as I said yesterday, stay with me at all times unless I say otherwise. Is that clear, Cherriana? Because if it isn't, like last night you will be tied to my side all day and night, and forfeit any *preevacy* for *anything*, I'm sure you get my drift. Well?"

Ice clinging to her rigid mouth and words, she said emotionlessly, "Yes, Mr. Darkonn."

His mouth quirked at the lass who was probably less than ten years younger than him calling him mister.

He turned to go when her hand reached out to touch his arm. He hesitated, looked down at her delicate fair hand on his rugged arm that was unexpectedly tanned for a prisoner. His dark eyes moved up to hers in surprisingly patient question.

"Mr. Darkonn," she didn't catch the twist of his mouth at her continued formality. She licked her dry lips before speaking. "Um, if you could just look the other way, or just not notice me slip away, I won't be any trouble to you. No one can blame you if I just…disappear?"

Shawn took in the creamy complexion, her beautiful features pinched in desperation. He'd been watching her interactions with the others. She was always helpful, pleasant, actually she was kind to everyone, even that pig Malone. Although she always stayed an arm's length from him.

Shawn was surprised as dainty as she was that she pitched in more than any of the others except for him and his friends, and that was only because she didn't have the strength, stamina or capabilities that they had.

She seemed oblivious to the carnal way the other men eyed her. Malone practically drooled when he was near her. With his head down, under impassive lowered lids, Zach's gaze relentlessly followed her movements.

The way the purity and innocence clung to her like a soft aura, Shawn thought that the story she'd told him has to be true.

When he didn't respond to her, her eyes dropped. Then, she licked her petal pink lips again and said, "So, um, then I will just go the other way when you all start down the trail…"

Shawn put his big hand on her shoulder and pushed her until her back was against the wall. Her blue eyes instantly lit with fear and dropped to the floor, her lips parted with a gasp. His shoulders blocked her view of the rest of the room.

He moved in close, leaned over and webbed her face with his hand. "Cherriana," he frowned when her eyes stayed downcast. "Dammit, you look at me when I'm talking *tae* you."

His angry breaths stirred the top of her hair. He could feel her trembling under his hand. With a heavy sigh he released her and stood back.

Her hand fluttered at her neck, she raised her eyes with a wince as if she expected him to strike her.

Shawn drew his sleeve across his brow. "I have explained *tae* you that you will be returned to prison."

Lifting her long curls, Cheri shuffled them back behind her shoulders and quickly wiped under her eyes. "You are a prisoner, and you are not going to go back. Why is it so important to you that I do? I am nothing, no one will even notice I'm missing. I can just slip down that small path by the back of the building."

The corner of his mouth pulled in. His gaze went from the bright silky curls to the big blue eyes over the plush little mouth, then down over her lush breasts. His eyes rolled down her shapely legs in the snug pants, he smirked. His tone sarcastic, he said drily, "Yeah, sure, no one will notice if you disappear."

Shawn reached out suddenly and gripped her chin again. The black eyes piercing hers with vehemence, he snarled, "I explained *tae* everyone the dangers of this wilderness. It gets *tae* freezing at night. Animals that are way bigger than you are out hunting constantly. We are surrounded by steep cliffs and deep ravines, you would not last the day, much less one night alone in these mountains. You would have no way *tae* find food or water, you would never find your way out alone."

She tried to pull from his grasp, he released her chin to hold her shoulder again. Cheri said to him, "Mr. Darkonn, please, I have a better chance to survive out here than I do in prison. You have to see that."

"It doesn't matter what I see, honey. You got yourself in your predicament, you-"

"I did nothing wrong!" she yelled, stamping her foot.

Shawn bit back a grin at her ferociousness.

"Just, please, please let me go. If I am caught I will tell them I just gave everyone the slip. If anyone gets in trouble it will be Deputy Malone. Please…"

In frustration, Shawn forked his fingers through his black hair making it stand up, he couldn't believe her stubbornness. He pictured her taking her first step on the side trail and a bear just grabbing her up and biting her in half-

He snapped at her roughly, "We are done arguing about this. Let's go." Before she could say another word, he moved his hand down to her lower back and ushered her out the door, closing it behind them. The rest of the group was milling out front waiting for them.

"We'd appreciate it, Darkonn, if you would fuck the bitch on your own time," Malone throwing Shawn's earlier words back at him drew snickers from some of the crowd and flaming cheeks from Cheri.

Shawn long-legged it over to the deputy, at the speed of light he hooked his fingertips into his chunky neck and squeezed until the deputy's eyes bulged out of his head.

His mouth next to Malone's ear, Shawn said in a dark growl, "Talk like that again, Malone, and next time I won't let go until you draw your last breath."

Releasing his fingers with a shove, he turned just as Cheri headed towards the trail she had asked him to let her disappear down. He stalked over to her and snatched up her arm, hauling her with him he started walking back to the animal trail they'd followed yesterday.

"Mr. Darkonn, please-"

"Shut up," he barked, forcing her to walk beside him, his steps faster in his pique. For cripe's sake, he'd just gotten through telling her how damned dangerous the land was and off she was going anyway.

His expression ferocious, Shawn strode hard with furious power.

Witnessing his rough treatment of the girl, everyone, except his mates, walked in silence for a while afraid of drawing his wrath.

A few miles of quiet hiking and Caleb whined in a whisper to Leena, "Geez, he has the hair-trigger temper of a lion that someone had suddenly snatched away his prey."

Leena's lips pulled in, she wasn't saying anything. Angry Shawn was scary Shawn.

The day broke clear and cool requiring jackets. They followed the trail for an hour until it brought them close to the foothills where it split. Part of the trail went up through a cleft in the hills, one went to the east and the other to the west. Shawn headed west.

As the terrain steadily inclined, Tomas lagged behind from the strain of his injury.

Shawn gave a short, sharp whistle.

In seconds Beau was behind him.

Shawn said to him, "I'm going *tae* scout ahead, stay with her," indicating Cheri. He disappeared almost instantly. It was growing warmer now under the high noon sun, people started peeling their jackets.

Beau moved up alongside Cheri and, gave her a big smile. He said cheerfully, "Hey there, lass, how's it going so far today?

The rueful faint scowl she aimed at the tall redhead with the trimmed red beard, twinkling blue eyes, and a peppering of freckles across his face, made him guffaw a burst of laughter. "Aye, lass, he can be a bit...overbearing, our Shawn."

Her head quirked at him, brows flat in genial agreement, "That would be an understatement, Beau."

This made him chuckle deep in his throat. "Aye, he can be bossy." His mouth curved at her wry nod.

"But you won't find a better man than him, lass. He'll have your back to the death if it comes to that, and has unwavering loyalty. He has an iron will, doesn't suffer fools lightly, actually not at all. He has the highest integrity, and will protect you from the worst life can throw at you."

His admiration for his friend practically radiated out of the twenty-something man.

"You sound like you know each other very well," Cheri said with friendly interest.

He nodded. "Aye, and Daf too, since we were tiny lads and all through the service-" he broke off, he'd said too much.

"Beau, I'm a bit confused, you said he has integrity but he, and you, and Daf are convicts in prison. I'm seeing a bit of a conflict there."

"Hmm." He caught her elbow helping her step over a large hole then said over his shoulder to the others, "Mind the hole, and pass it down."

Each person in line warned the one behind them of the hole.

Beau went quiet, she was asking questions he wasn't at liberty to answer. "All I can say, Cheri lass, is that you can trust him with your life, take my word." He moved to take a step behind her, they were hitting rocky, steep terrain and she was obviously not used to hiking up mountains.

No sooner did he do that and Cheri miss-stepped. Her foot twisted on a loose rock and with a scream she was airborne flying over the side of the steep ravine-

Like lassoing a calf, Beau jumped forward, threw his arm out and just barely snagged her shirt. He jerked her back from the mouth of the ravine so hard she fell into him and they both tumbled backwards to the ground with painful grunts.

Leena and Jim Vega the closest to them hurried over.

"Are you guys okay?" Leena asked with concern.

Cheri was literally sitting in Beau's lap. Breathing heavily, Beau had a goofy grin on his face. He was scared to pieces, it had been a damned close call. He held his arms tightly around Cheri, feeling her rushing panicked breath against his chest.

"What the hell is going on, Beau?" Shawn was suddenly in front of them, his face dark and edging to anger. He'd heard the scream and raced back.

At the moment, he could feel a flush running up the back of his neck seeing Beau holding the girl on his lap, and her blouse was wide open exposing the prettiest bra Shawn had ever seen. Black lace with a tiny pink satin bow on the front at the v. His eyes moved to her full soft breasts mounding over the- he blinked, looked away quickly at Beau.

Both Beau and Cheri looked scared, as did Leena and Jim.

Keeping his eyes on her face, Shawn stuck a hand down to Cheri and pulled her up, then did the same to Beau.

Beau wiped off the back of his jeans to steady his frantically beating heart. The ravine was wickedly steep, they should have been moving more carefully. He said as much to Shawn who was glaring at the girl.

"Shawn bro, take it down a notch. She tripped, and…" he inclined his head towards the ravine, watched Shawn glance over, then at the girl, his mouth pressed hard. "I had to grab her and jerk her back hard. It was, ah, close."

Beau's gaze moved to Cheri's anxious face then dropped to her chest still heaving in her panic. Red crept up his neck seeing Vega and Leena gawking at the curvaceous young woman.

"*Lass*," Beau croaked, grabbing the sides of her blouse he pulled them together.

Not knowing what he was doing, Cheri slapped at his hands and backed away from him.

Now the rest of the group was catching up, mouths dropped in question as to why the girl was standing partially undressed and everyone looked distressed.

Shawn quickly stepped in front of her and said quietly, "Cherriana, Beau tore your shirt catching you. He was trying *tae* cover you up." His eyes darted down her front then up so she would understand.

Cheri looked down and gasped. She clutched the ends of the shirt tugging them together. Many of the buttons had popped off. Her cheeks brightened like cherry red balloons.

Tying the ends of the blouse together under her midriff, she thought, *would her mortified life never end?*

Containing his composure, Shawn turned to Jim. "Vega, you and Leena take the lead, follow the trail."

He pulled Beau aside and he said under his breath, "I have *tae* go ahead again *tae* locate a turn off. I found big cat prints, I need *tae* see which way tis headed. Stay behind Vega with her, and," he smiled to lessen the chastisement, "I'd like *tae* see that she still has all of her clothes on when I return. Plus, you might want *tae* walk on the *outside*, mate."

He clapped a hand on Beau's shoulder briefly, and said proudly, "Good save, *brither*," before moving back up the trail without another word to Cheri, making her feel as if somehow he blamed her for deliberately causing another fuss.

Chapter Six

They journeyed without further incident but the group had to proceed more slowly as Tomas was still recovering from his wound.

Hiking the uneven ground, everyone watching out for hidden holes or jutting rocks with grasshoppers jumping back and forth in front of them like green leggy ping pong balls.

The crooked trail barely visible at times was partially shaded by ponderosas, their cones littering the ground around them.

Leaving groves of white pines, they moved to higher elevations where slender cedars and other firs and evergreens knitted like a multi-hued green shawl over them offering pleasant shade. Dried leaves crinkled and cracked under their boots.

"Oh!" Bella exclaimed from the middle of the line. "Look at the beautiful deer!" A deer with large ears was standing in an open clearing. As soon as Bella spoke it dashed off.

Big, blocking the sun in black jeans and black shirt, Daf told her, "He has a black-tipped tail, makes him a mule deer." His dark face smooth in a calm pleasant smile, he glanced at the strong athletic woman moving easily with long strides.

"What I wouldn't do for a gun right now," the man of few words, blond goliath Zach said mournfully, eyeing Daf's shotgun strapped across his backpack. "That's great eatin' there." He mournfully watched the deer prance into the woods.

Ritchie Marx was handcuffed to the giant hoodlum. The deputy's face clearly expressing he was tired of being attached to the psycho-monster.

Zach scoffed at Daf, sweeping the black man head to toe as if to determine what kind of detriment Daf could be to him. "You coulda' bagged it, man. What's the problem, you can't shoot, or you're a pussy or what?"

Scratching his chin, Daf pondered the enormous man. Like the Hulk on steroids, Zach was even bigger than Daf and that was saying something.

Daf didn't think he had an IQ because he never heard him say much, just growled and grunted and sometimes pawed his blond Mohawk with long thick fingers. Daf couldn't see Bella's interest in the *rochle,* rough thug.

Zachary Stockton had a long sheet of violent arrests. He was currently doing 10 to 20 for armed home invasion.

Daf was keeping a close eye on the muscled monster, he was a damned dangerous man to have on the loose and he wouldn't put it past the guy to murder them all while they slept, take their weapons and go search for the treasure himself. That's if he knew about it.

Shawn and Daf and Beau had discussed how much they thought the others knew about the secret mission. One thing they decided was that not just Malone and Zachary, but no one in the group was to be trusted.

Daf sneered to Zach, "Tis not season, *man.*"

Zach cold-stared him with a squinty-eyed withering, hostile look. Grunting, "Pussy," he stalked off with long loping strides dragging Ritchie behind him.

Daf noticed Ritchie had tucked that Star of David inside his shirt the minute he was tied to the supremacist crudhole.

Daf watched him moving away through narrowed eyes. He knew the freak was a white supremacist, the guy had 88's and thunderbolts, pitchforks, MOB, a mix of gang crap all over his bulked up body.

Shawn was right to keep the racist locked up, he was likely liable to hurt someone. Or someone, Daf maybe, might hurt him. He tightened the band around his dreads and powered forward.

The trail blessedly started descending, it was tricky still walking at a slope, but a lot easier.

"I see a clearing, *finally*," Leena groaned. They trekked down the trail until it leveled off for a while.

Kicking at stones, thin Caleb was not pleased to be there. Hiking and the outdoors, he hated all that fresh air and healthy shit. He yanked his hat down over his forehead to shield his pasty skin from the sun's relentless UV rays.

He heard some of the people, that hottie and the redheaded guy going on and on how beautiful was the rolling voluminous land with majestic trees, and swath of golden scrub like an ornamental chain stringing along the foothills blah blah.

Nature, Caleb thought, ick. The women got all excited when a dumb deer frolicked too close. He could see the hungry murderous look on Zach's face when he saw the deer. Same way he looked at the girl, Cheri, like delicious prey he couldn't wait to skin and eat.

Caleb shivered like someone walked on his grave. He was thankful that he wasn't her. Between Zachary the beast and Malone the creep she didn't have a chance of getting off this mountain unscathed. He sure didn't want that blond sicko looking anywhere in his direction.

Off to the distance Caleb could see a shimmer of blue. Water. Staring at the precious liquid and not at the ground, he could use a good dunk, or at least wash his hands and face-

"Agghhh-" he stepped into nothingness. Throwing out his hands as he fell he grabbed the side of the earth. Scrabbling with his frantic fingers and toes, trying to catch a hold of something to slow his descent, he caught a vine sticking out and grabbed it with both hands. Panting with exertion and shaking with fright, he looked down and almost passed out cold.

The others seeing him fall ran to the hole shouting in alarm.

The crevasse was deep, but not enough that he still might have survived the landing, but not the pit of rattlers he'd disturbed with the falling dirt and rock he'd brought down with him.

Long slinky bodies slithered and coiled and rattled beneath him. Holes pocked the dirt wall around them revealing their ways in and out.

Bella screamed, the rest started yelling. Beau dashed over and knelt beside the opening. Caleb was clinging to a root, his face a sweating white ball, his mouth flapped open and closed like a copy machine going bananas-

Daf dropped down beside Beau. "Hang on, dude," he shouted to the top of Caleb's terrified head.

Beau said, "Shawn has the rope, we need to get-" but Shawn was already there tying the rope to a tree and hurrying over to the edge.

"Caleb," he said calmly down the hole. The skinny accountant didn't answer him, he couldn't, his lungs had no air, his heart pounded out of his chest, panic constricted his windpipe.

"Caleb," his accent thickening with the dire situation, Shawn said softly, "*na dean*- don't look down. I'm dropping a rope *tae* you, grab a hold of it and we'll pull you up. You got it?"

Caleb didn't answer.

Shawn was lowering the rope as he was speaking, "Okay Caleb, tis right next *tae* your right hand, do you see it?" Caleb didn't move.

"Caleb, you have *tae* let go with your right hand *tae* catch the rope...Caleb," the little guy wasn't moving. He was frozen with fear.

Shawn stood up, murmured, "All right." Holding the rope, he took a knife out of his pocket and cut it in half.

"What are you doing?" Beau asked him.

Tying both ropes around the tree and one around his waist, Shawn moved back to the hole. "Caleb isn't going *tae* be able *tae* do this on his own. I can go down and get him, but you guys won't be able *tae* pull both of us up together. So I'll go, tie him, you pull him up then me."

He didn't wait for a response just trod to the hole and swung his leg over it looping the end of the other rope around his shoulder.

"Okay Caleb, I'm coming down *tae* get you, just hang on." Holding onto the rope with both hands, Shawn climbed down into the hole.

The last thing he saw was Cheri's worried eyes peering over the hand she had stuffed in her mouth aimed at him. He wondered if her concern was that he wouldn't make it back up, or that he would.

Easily repelling down the side of the hole, he reached Caleb. Jamming the toes of his boots into the dirt to brace himself, he said quietly, "All right, Caleb, I'm here. I'm tying the rope under your arms, you don't have *tae* do anything, the lads will pull you up."

Seeing Caleb's confused tilted head, Shawn cleared his throat to ease his accent so there would be no confusion with Caleb understanding his instructions.

Caleb stared at the dirt wall looking like he was going to explode with sheer terror, tears and sweat poured in a race down his face. Shawn threw the other rope around the wiry man, brought it under his arms and tied it.

"Okay!" Shawn called up.

All of the men and Bella, pulled on the rope. But Caleb wasn't letting go of the root.

Shawn yelled, "Hold up! Beau!" He saw Beau's red head peer over the hole with a big freckle-eating grin.

"Beau, he won't let go of the root. I'm going *tae* pry his fingers off. I'll give the go ahead, then pull him up."

Hearing Shawn's voice get deeper and his brogue thicken again by the second, Beau knew he was worried about getting Caleb up. He saluted Shawn in affirmation.

Steadying himself with the toes of his boots jabbing into the dirt wall, Shawn pried Caleb's numb fingers off the root and yelled, "Go!"

The group steadily pulled on the rope. Shawn watched as Caleb was tugged up in jerky bumps. When Caleb reached the top, hands reached over and hauled him out.

Shawn quickly climbed up his own rope with the speed and agility of a monkey in a tree.

The two men were safely sitting on the hard earth, breathing heavily. His glasses scratched but still intact, Caleb looked like he'd wet his pants.

Shawn dragged his shirttail over his own sweaty dirty face. Two small boots were suddenly in front of him. He looked up with his hand over his brow to block the setting sun. Cheri had two canteens, she handed one to each man.

Shawn took his, but Caleb was still paralyzed with terror.

Kneeling beside the small thin man, Cheri sat back on her heels, unscrewed the cap and held the canteen to Caleb's mouth and helped him drink some. "It'll make you feel better, Caleb, just drink and take big deep breaths. You are safe now," her gentle voice was a calming lilt.

Caleb sat rigid as a rod and shaking like leaf. Cheri helped maneuver him so he was leaning against a big rock. She moved next to him and pulled his head to her shoulder.

While stroking his hair and his face, she sang so quietly her soft voice was almost a hush, a relaxing lullaby. The other men stood around watching, wishing that at the moment they were the crooked accountant.

Listening to her trying to calm Caleb down with her quiet sweet voice, Shawn's own eyes drifted closed, he shook his head and blinked.

Climbing to his feet, concentrating on diminishing his accent, he said to Beau and Daf, "The little guy isn't going to be able to travel, we will stay here for the night. There's some boulders we can use for wind and animal barricades. Tell everyone *tae* put their blankets close together, tis going to be pretty cold out here. Here, help me with him."

Daf and Shawn helped Caleb climb to his legs of jelly. Beau took off Caleb's backpack, set it down then took out Caleb's blanket and spread it out in the middle of the clearing with everyone else around him so Caleb would feel protected.

They half carried the accountant to his blanket and helped him to lie down, his head on his backpack. Like a suddenly cut rubber band he curled into a fetus. He didn't move a muscle when Daf laid Caleb's other blanket over him.

Shawn said to Daf and Beau, "No fire, it'll alert anyone else out here that we're here."

They ate cold canned tuna and compressed survival packaged food. Some of the group wearily settled on their blankets on the cold, hard lumpy ground.

Malone sidled over to Shawn. He complained, "It would be helpful, *convict*, if you could find another empty cabin or something, you must know where there are others. It's damned cold and uncomfortable on this hard ass ground."

Shawn's mouth twitched at the deputy's disparaging convict jab. "Malone, I didn't ask *tae* be here, tis gonna be grueling *tae* get you *tae* Grand Crest, no one said it would be easy. You had *tae* have known we'd be sleeping outside and roughing it when you planned this little escapade."

Shrugging his thick shoulders, Malone wiped his nose running from the cold with the back of his hand. "I didn't really think about it. My thoughts were purely on how to get here." His eyes shifted to Cheri who along with Jim Vega was cleaning up after their meal.

He looked back at Shawn. "When we get there, to the crest, we hide from the rest of them and let them go on their own way. You lead me out, then when we're out of this godforsaken wilderness. You and your two buds move on and I'm keeping the girl with me."

Shawn's lids lowered to slits until his eyes were barely visible, just nicks of glowing black light. "Not gonna happen, Malone. She goes back *tae* prison. I don't want aiding and abetting a fugitive escape on my head."

"Yeah? What's the difference? You and your friends will be fugitives too until the authorities decide you croaked out here.

"You should worry about your own skin, and not hers…and she's got some damned fine silky skin don't you think? Makes me want to lick it all over, outside…and in…" He swiped at the drool from the corner of his mouth with his tongue.

Shawn looked at him in disgust, the deputy made his stomach turn, he was at least twice the young woman's age and sloppy heavy. "You're a bleedin' horny swine, Malone."

The deputy turned brown orbs of greedy lust to Shawn. "So what? I don't give a fuck what you think. When the time comes, you'll be hightailing it out of here to run and hide, you'll forget all about that hot little piece.

"Before you round the first corner I'll be all up inside her little snatch. Besides, at this point, I'm figuring you've got to be gay. There's no way you would not be hitting that out here where she can't stop you and there's no one for her to cry rape to."

Malone's face twisted nastily, his sneer grosser with his runny nose. "So which one of them is it then, the redhead with the beard or do you go for dark meat?" He turned abruptly and stalked off to his blankets.

Shawn watched the lawman throw himself on his blanket and cover up with another. The revulsion he felt for the deputy crawling up his throat, he strode over to Cheri and seized her arm harder than he meant to. The deputy provoked him so much he wanted to do bodily harm to the asshole. He didn't dare strike the guy even once, he wouldn't be able to stop.

He said to Officer Vega, "You can finish up, right Jim? Make sure Zach is cuffed. Caleb's okay, he's not going anywhere." Without waiting for him to answer, he swung around sharply and pulled Cheri to where he had laid out their blankets, and caustically with a small shove, said crossly, "Lie down."

Knowing he was acting like a brute, and she didn't deserve it, *that damned Malone,* he waited for her to get down on the blanket.

Seeing the fury radiating in his eyes, she didn't hesitate as usual, *thank God.* He lowered down next to her. Everyone was close together for body warmth, Beau was on Cheri's other side. Silently, she pulled her second blanket over her body.

Shawn lay on his back with his arm over his eyes, he was so bloody pissed he knew it would take a while for him to calm down.

Every time he closed his eyes he saw that fat hog shoving Cheri down on the ground, climbing on top of her, her helpless screams none but the trees and wild animals to hear. Malone grunting like a pig between her slender legs- *fuck*

Finally, a half an hour later his eyelids grew heavy, but a noise disturbed him. Cheri's teeth were chattering.

Rolling over to face her, he could see her eyes were closed, she was in her jacket under the blanket but she was shivering. Next to her Beau was snoring like a hibernating bear.

Shawn took off his jacket and said quietly, "Here, Cherriana, put this on." She hesitated then took it, wrapped it around herself under the blanket.

Moments went by and he could still hear her. She was gritting her teeth to keep them from clacking together, but he could see her body shaking.

Taking a deep breath, this was going to be harder on him than on her, he moved closer to her and lifted her blanket, said, "Come here, and lie against me."

Knowing she wouldn't obey, he reached out with both hands and pulled her to him, turning her so her back pressed against his front. Tucking his knees behind hers, he pulled their blankets over them both.

She tried to move away, he dropped an arm around her and held her firmly to his chest. Aware she couldn't get away from him, Cheri lay rigid as a marble statue.

In her ear, he said in a hushed voice, "This is only *tae* get you warm, lass. I am not going *tae* assault you, so just relax. If you stay all wound up like that neither of us will get any sleep."

It took a few minutes before she let herself slacken. She still shivered but less so. They'd both removed their boots.

Shawn murmured, "Tuck your wee feet between my legs, lass, they'll warm quickly."

He smiled against her hair when he felt her feet tentatively push between his legs.

As he drifted off, his last thought was that her hair tickling under his chin smelled oddly sweet like her name of cherries.

Chapter Seven

They started out the next day at the crack of dawn, grumbling and yawning, stretching cold limbs and complaining.

Shawn was waiting for everyone to get ready when Leena approached him, her large lips opened in a wide, mannish loud yawn.

When the yawn was almost done and her teeth and tongue were no longer visible, she put a hand over her mouth complaining through her fingers, "Lord, Shawn, shouldn't we have found a road or something by now?" She tugged her shirt down over her droopy breasts to cover part of her big hips.

Gazing down at the plain brunette, even plainer now with no makeup and harsh sleeping and eating conditions, he thought to himself *she looked like she might be down a pound or two, that's good, she should be grateful instead of complaining. Well, that's women for you, constantly bleatin'*.

His attention went from the tall, plump whining officer to Cheri who, still wearing his jacket that went down to her knees was quietly rolling up their shared blankets.

She was obstinate as hell, but never uttered a complaint or a harsh word to anyone, not even when fighting off the slobs that tried to fondle her whenever Shawn, Daf or Beau weren't near enough to protect her.

"Shawn?" A heavier whine infused Leena's deep voice.

"Aye?" He still stared at Cheri. "Yes? What was it you asked?"

A peeved redness burned across her chest. "Shawn, dear hunk, you could at least have the courtesy to look at a lady when she's speaking to you. Now," she set a hand on his arm, "stop staring at the skinny felonious slut and give me some attention."

He stiffened, his pupils flared, he pulled his arm from her clutch. "She is not a slut, don't start trouble, Leena. I thought you liked her." He turned his piqued face to her. "What is it that you want?"

She smiled smugly. "Now that I finally have your attention, I asked how come we haven't," she hesitated, her face softened into a vixen-ish blob. "On second thought, my question is, when we stop tonight I want you to bang me like you did her last night, hotness."

Jealous green tingeing her homely features, Leena nodded the top of her head at Cheri as she wound her claws around his arm.

Shawn's eyes rolled, what was it with these disgusting officers? He said hotly, "I did not bang her, I slept close *tae* her to keep her warm."

His measured gaze travelled intentionally down Leena's figure indicating she didn't need anything extra to keep her warm, she had plenty.

Jerking away from the lewd woman, he said bluntly, "Now bugger the hell off me." He stomped off to gather

Cheri and get on with the day's hike. When he approached the girl she handed him his jacket.

Cheri murmured shyly, "Thank you for your jacket...and...um other...kindness." The blush brightening her cheeks only made her look even younger and more desirable.

It made him relive when he'd had her wrapped up in his arms last night, her hot little body pressed against his. Pushing that thought way to the far recesses of his mind, Shawn took the jacket from her and helped her on with her backpack.

"Yeah," he grunted, and headed down the path he remembered from years ago.

They had been hiking for a couple of hours when Daf lumbered up alongside Shawn and Cheri.

Shawn already knew what he was going to say. "Aye, Daf, I see the clouds."

Ahead of them the sky was filling with heavy black clouds. Streaks of lighting ricocheted in and out and through them. A bit of a rumble growled in the distance. "I don't think there's anything nearby for us to get cover, not like a cabin or shed."

Seeing Shawn take a hold of Cheri's hand as he moved faster, Daf asked, "What about something to at least brace against the storm?" He walked more quickly as Shawn had picked up his pace.

"There're some caves to the north. Tell the others to move quickly," Shawn instructed.

Daf dropped back making his way rapidly down the line to tell everyone to move as fast as they could to beat the storm.

Shawn knew he was holding Cheri's hand pretty tightly, the ends of her fingers were white, but she didn't complain.

There was no way she could move as fast as him. His legs were twice the length of hers with a lot more muscle behind them.

He was considering picking her up and carrying her, it would be quicker, but he had already embarrassed her so much already he was loath to add to it.

Big blobs of rain plopped on them spurring the group to start running.

"Come on, honey." Shawn grabbed Cheri's arm hustling her to the partially hidden cave carved into the side of the mountain.

When they reached it, Shawn let her go to drag at the dense sharp scrub in front of the opening. If a person didn't know it was there, the cave was completely hidden from sight.

Giving Cheri a little push, he barked over the sudden crash of thunder and gusting rain, "Get behind me." He called out, "Beau! Daf!"

The two men appeared instantly.

Grabbing fistfuls of brush, Shawn yanked and jerked it out of the ground and to the side. "Help me clear this shit away. Tis overgrown since I was last here."

Beau and Daf hopped to it. The three men struggled to get the opening clear as the heavens opened and deluged the group like a waterfall roaring down upon them.

The second just barely enough brush was moved aside, the group rushed, funneling into the cave. Malone pushed inside first with Zach behind him, Bella was at his heels.

Shawn moved to hold back bigger branches when Marx holding Leena's hand jerking her with him shoved past.

Behind Shawn, Leena bashed into Cheri knocking her against the outside wall of the cave. She hit the rocky wall so hard she stumbled back several feet before falling to the ground.

The rushing dark clouds low and heavy with the torrential rain made visibility nil. The wild wind whistled and howled as it tore through the mountains.

When most everyone was inside, Beau and Daf ran in. As he moved into the cave, Shawn pulled some of the scrub back over to block the rain from the opening. At his back, Beau called out, "Bro, she's not here,"

Shawn swung around, his wet hair sending raindrops sailing. "What are you talking about? Who-" his eyes darted around the dim cave over the group huddled together in the damp dark. He thundered, "Where the hell is she?"

It was obvious Cheri wasn't inside. Shawn stormed to the cave opening, his friends at his heels. He said over his shoulder, "No, you two stay with them, I don't want any more missing," and he hurried back out into the squall.

As soon as he stepped outside, he shouted, "Cherriana!" The wind slapped his words and whipped his face, rain struck like bullets.

Shoving his blustering hair out of his eyes, he saw something move back by the side of the cavern wall. He rushed over pushing back scrub and branches as he went.

When he reached the source of the movement, he saw Cheri on her hands and knees buffeted by a wall of wind and rain as she struggled to get to her feet. Prickly branches from shrubs tore at her shirt holding her down.

"*Fuck, girl-*" Shawn stomped on the clump of brush and bent down. He dug his hands around her waist, lifted her up so her legs could wrap around his hips.

One arm around her back holding her tightly against his body and the other under her butt, he started back to the cave. Using his shoulder to push through the heavy scraping branches, he held her head against his chest covering her face with his hand to protect it from getting scratched.

As big and tough as he was, it still was a fight for Shawn to make his way through the raging tempest to the cave.

When he reached the opening, Daf and Beau were holding aside the worst of the thicket so Shawn could tromp straight inside.

They released the branches and moved away to give Shawn space. He was heaving and panting to catch his breath, but he still had Cheri wrapped around him.

He stood holding her for a moment, her arms clutched around his neck she seemed in no hurry to leave the warmth and strength of his solid body. His forearm a shelf under her bottom supporting her, he brushed back the sodden hair that streamed over her face.

His words barked out harsh and furious, "Cherriana, what in God's name were you-" he saw her face. She was scared to death. The knees of her jeans were torn and there was blood on her legs, and her palms were scratched.

Inhaling a deep breath, he said more quietly, "You weren't running were you?"

She morosely shook her head.

He brushed back more of her hair off her wet face, raindrops clung to her lashes. "Then what the hell- I told you *tae* stay by me. I thought you went inside with the others."

He saw her glance over at Leena who was leaning against the wall with Ritchie Marx, a guilty look spread with red across the deputy's chunky face. Leena's eyes slid shamefully away from them.

Shawn said softly, "She knock you down, honey?"

Cheri didn't say anything, her eyes dropped.

He gently set her on her feet. "I'm sorry, Cherriana, we unfortunately have some self-centered people with us. Are you all right?" He leaned over to check her scrapes and bruises.

"I'm fine, but you," Cheri stroked a hand over his arm.

Feeling his skin tingle from her touch, Shawn said, "I'm all right," he looked where she indicated. He had a deep gouge in his shoulder, his shirt was torn with it. "Must have been a branch. I'm all right." He brushed her off. But the wound was bleeding profusely.

"Bro," Beau handed him a towel from his pack. "Put this on it." He raised a brow at Cheri who nodded at him.

Shawn frowned at their shared look while pressing the towel on the wound. Beau brought the first aid kit to Cheri who set it down and immediately opened it.

"Sit down," she ordered the big Scotsman.

His black brows arched at her in wry irritation. "I am fine, woman, I don't need your help."

Beau was coming at him with the bottle of whiskey and Cheri was pulling out needle, thread, and antibiotic.

"Please sit down," she instructed, "you know it will be too hard for me to stich up your shoulder if you're standing." Holding the implements in her hands, she looked sternly at him like a teacher waiting for a student to comply.

Shawn looked from her stern gaze to Beau's mirthful one, then shrugged. Swiping the bottle from Beau's hands, he plopped cross-legged on the cold rocky ground. He twisted off the top and slugged down a good bit, wiped his sleeve across his mouth and said, "Well, get to it then, lass."

Trying to look severe, but with twitching lips, Cheri knelt to the side of him. She started unbuttoning his sodden shirt. He flinched from her, frowned, "What are you up *tae* lass?"

She said slowly like he was dull, "I need your shirt off. I can't do what I need to with it there."

When she reached for his buttons again, he didn't move, his gaze dropped to watch her hands undo the buttons.

It took some time, the buttons were wet and hard for her to push through. He could have done it himself more quickly and easily, but, his eyes on her fumbling yet graceful movements, feeling her knuckles brush his chest, he couldn't will himself to stop her and take over.

Shawn suppressed a shiver when she pushed the lapels aside and slipped her small hands under them to push the shirt off his big shoulders. His nipples puckered under the mat of dark hair as her warm hands skimmed across his skin.

Standing beside them, Beau watched every move she made. With a lusty grin he crowed to his friend, "Boy Shawn, you get all the luck."

Shawn tried to scowl up at him through wet locks of black hair, but Cheri's palms were stroking across his chest then back over his shoulders as she moved the shirt down his arms.

He knew he should lift his arms to help her remove his shirt, but he just couldn't move. His head was down, his eyes focused on the trails she was making over his body.

He forced down the tingling in his skin caused by her soft hands roaming over his flesh, his hard pecs bunched under her ministrations. Her smooth fingers slid under the material pushing the shirt down to his wrists. He held the bottle in one hand in his lap, the other was planted on the ground. His shirt pooled over his hand on the ground.

Beau knew what was going to happen next so he quickly made his exit. Shawn called after him, "Chicken."

Cheri took the bottle from him. His forehead creased like a child with his toy taken, until she poured some of the alcohol on his wound, then he bit back a gasp.

Hearing Beau snickering across the room, he clamped his lips shut and swallowed the pain.

Cheri knelt in front of him to look closely at the cut.

They were near the front of the cave where the light was the best although the storm raged all around the mountain. The rest of the group had tucked towards the back of the cave in a huddle, the warmth of the day had chilled with the rain.

Cheri leaned so close to Shawn her drying hair waved down his chest like a silky blanket. He felt heat start to burn in his loins as the silk tresses fluttered across, mingling in the dark hair on his chest and tickling his bare skin.

Then to get a better look, she leaned closer, bending a little over his shoulder, her breasts were almost touching his face.

Shawn's skin darkened, his Adam's apple bobbed with tight swallows. He closed his eyes as a hot flush roiled up his legs. "Uh," he couldn't believe his voice was shaking. He cleared his throat, "Lass, you, uh…"

Cheri put a hand on his right shoulder and patted it while peering at his injured left shoulder. "You will be fine, I promise, don't worry." She took his sudden agitation to be fear.

Then she leaned over too far and lost her balance. Falling forward, her chest landed against his face, her hands went to his shoulders to catch herself. Shawn quickly wrapped his hands around her tiny waist to stop her from falling further.

Holding his breath, Shawn opened his eyes. Her bosom was pressed hard on his face, if he opened his mouth one of her bouncy breasts would be in it.

He closed his eyes with a groan. Muttering, "Uh, here, lass," he propelled her back, steadying her to her knees.

She leaned back on her heels, her face crimson. "Oh, I am so sorry, did I hurt you?" Her bright eyes scanned his face to see if she had hurt him. "Did I make your pain worse?" Her attention went right to the wound on his shoulder, her brow creased with concern.

His face was scrunched up tight, he looked in terrible pain, she gently patted his uninjured shoulder. "I'm so sorry, I'm just a clumsy oaf."

The pain wasn't in his shoulder, but he sure wasn't going to tell her it ached much lower. His eyes rolled at her comforting pat on his shoulder. "I'm fine, Cherriana, here, you are so small tis hard for you *tae* reach me. Try this." He picked the bottle up out of his lap setting it to the side then moved his legs straight out.

Spreading his legs, he helped her to kneel with one knee on either side of his one thigh so she was straddling his leg.

He winced when he realized this wasn't any better. Now her breasts were wedged against his chest as she balanced herself, and *cripe-* she was straddling his leg with her private parts almost touching his thigh, *what the hell had he been thinking?*

Shawn kept his hands around her waist to steady her. Feeling the curve of her tiny waist under his large hands, his fingers almost met wrapped around it.

He fought the urge to squeeze her, to stroke his hands up her body to cover her plump breasts, clutch her rounded flesh with his strong fingers. Or roll his hands around her back to pull her closer- *damn, he needed more whiskey.* He moved her a few inches away from his body and sucked in a deep shaky breath.

Oblivious to his internal struggle to control his blazing libido, she sterilized the needle and her hands. Then she threaded the needle and finally stuck it in his skin. He flinched but didn't make a sound. He'd had a lot worse damage to his body, and endured a lot worse pain in his lifetime.

Shawn drew in another deep breath, but this was the first time a beautiful woman was stitching up a hole in his shoulder. With her fine breasts in his face, and her soft hair showering his chest while in a dark cave on the side of a mountain, in the desolate wilderness.

His gaze bounced around the cave at the other occupants wishing they would all disappear and leave him and Cheri alone.

He shook his head. What the hell was he thinking? The little witch has put some kind of spell on him. He opened his eyes a hair watching her face as she worked.

Concentrating, the tip of her tongue was just poking out of the side of her mouth.

Shawn felt himself drawn to capture that tongue between his teeth, then with his own tongue and lips he would- he growled impatiently, "Good God girl, are you done yet?" As cold and wet as they were Shawn was sweating like he was in the scorching Death Valley instead of a dank dark cave.

Still kneeling in front of him, her voice sweet and gentle she reassured him, "The wound isn't that extensive, I'm almost done, I'm so sorry to hurt you."

Shawn groaned. "It doesn't hurt, lass, I'm just tired of sitting here without moving."

Daf wandered over, picked up the bottle beside Shawn and drank thirstily ignoring Shawn's scowl.

"Bro, there are other bottles, over there," Shawn remonstrated him, jerking his head to the backpacks far across the cave and snatched the bottle back from him.

"Stop moving," Cheri scolded, still sewing. "You don't want a crooked scar do you?"

His slight grin lopsided, Shawn peered up at Daf who was smirking a blue streak down at him. "*Na*, doesn't matter lass, tis just one more added *tae* the rest on my ugly body."

"Oh no, your body is so beautiful, Mr. Darkonn," Cheri murmured innocently. "Big and strong with all those muscles." She leaned closer to tie the thread in a knot.

Now Shawn smirked up at Daf. "Don't you have something you can do, like go and see if there's any wood or kindling in here?" His brow arched in a look indicating for Daf to get lost.

Daf shot him a full wattage grin, looked at Cheri leaning over the half-naked Shawn in concentration then at Shawn's clear message to go away. "Okay, but I'll be right over there if you need me, just call, don't hesitate, don't-"

"Okay, Daf, got it," Shawn said shortly, frowning at his friend. Daf grinned at him and sauntered off.

"All right, I'm done." Cheri took the whiskey from him and poured some more on the stiches and the needle to sterilize it. Handing the bottle back to him, she swabbed antibiotic on top of the stitch and plastered gauze over it then taped the gauze down. She returned the supplies to the med kit.

"Here, lass," shrugging his shirt back up over his shoulders but not buttoning it, Shawn scrambled a few feet to lean against the wall of the cave, motioning for her to come with him.

With a sigh, Cheri got up and moved the few feet over then sunk gracefully to her knees and sat down next to him with her back against the wall.

He took a big swig of whiskey and handed the bottle to her. She eyed it warily then shook her head. "I don't think-"

"Go on then," he said, "tis storming out there and cold and damp in here, no better place or time *tae* chug down some strong liquor. Go on, it'll warm you." He pushed the bottle into her hands.

"Uh, okay." She took the bottle and awkwardly lifted it to her mouth.

"Here, wait, let me help you." Shawn wrapped a big hand around the bottle helping her bring it to her mouth and tilt it. "Just take a small sip, lass, I doubt you're used *tae* strong spirits."

She took a short drink then pulled back coughing and sputtering, her mouth dropped open. "Oh my gosh, that is- like- swallowing fire!" she hissed.

Beau and Dap looked over, and smiled. The petite beauty was sitting beside the big Scotsman and he was smiling and wiping the side of her mouth with his fingers and she was giggling at him.

Shawn took the bottle, swallowed a long nip then handed it back to Cheri. "Now, try some more." His voice had grown soft and light with the liquor warming him, his words slurred slightly, "This time, like I said before, *slowly*," he helped her tip the bottle.

She giggled again when whiskey dribbled down her chin.

"You need practice, *leamin*." His face loomed close to hers as he dabbed the whiskey off her chin with his fingertips. His dark eyes held her light blues, then he brushed the liquid off her lips, stuck his fingers in his mouth and licked them.

He watched her stare at him licking his fingers. Her luminescent eyes grew big, then misted, her lids fell limpid, her heated gaze trailed over his lips. He drew his knees up and dropped his hands over them holding the bottle loosely in one hand.

Murmuring, "You have some on your mouth too, here," Cheri's tentative fingertips lightly touched his mouth.

His skin darkened, his lips parted. He didn't move when she brushed them gently, shyly. When she went to pull her hand away he clasped it and brought it back to his mouth.

His heavy-lidded eyes on hers, his accent thick, voice deep, Shawn whispered, "You forgot *tae* lick them."

He put her fingertips just inside his mouth and lightly rolled his tongue around them then closed his mouth and pulled her fingers slowly through his lips. Seeing her pupils enlarge, his groin hitched in sharp twinges.

Thinking about putting his fingers in her mouth, her sucking them, *shit*, his jeans were growing tight, he shifted awkwardly tugging at them. He needed to stop looking at her, touching her.

He leaned back against the wall. She followed suit. His lids drifting down, Shawn said quietly, tell me, *leamin*, Cherriana, tell me about your childhood, at the, convent."

He felt her shrug beside him. She sighed with odd contentment. "Oh, there's nothing to tell, I mean, it was a convent, an orphanage in some ways, only for girls."

With effort, he studiously lightened his brogue. "Tell me anyway. Tell me about little Cherriana's exploits."

That brought a smile to her lips. "Okay." She thought for a minute.

"Well, we actually were quite busy. Besides of course our studies, we were in the rural countryside so we did a lot of horseback riding. We were quite lucky the convent had stables and rented them for income. We took care of the horses and were allowed to ride them..." she trailed off in a muse.

Enjoying her sweet soft voice, Shawn prompted, "Tell me more."

"Um, all right. When we were older we were part of the fire brigade. We rushed off whenever the alarm would ring in the village. We, uh, actually saved lives, it was wonderful."

Shawn turned his head to her. Her eyes were open but clouded with recalling her memories.

"We were near a huge lake with an old fishing marina. They brought us their nets to be repaired. We sewed up the tears so they allowed us to use their sailboats, and in the summer our team was part of the sailing races." Her cheeks glowed. She said with happy pride, "We won several times."

"Wow, you were pretty active for being in a convent orphanage. You must have made a lot of friends."

Her head tilted somberly, the happiness disappeared. "We weren't allowed to converse or directly interact with any outsiders as we called them. And throughout the years girls were adopted or aged-out so we didn't maintain long-term relationships.

"There was another children's home nearby. We were really so far out in the rural area that all the camps and homes for misfits, delinquents were out there. One of the children's home housed handicapped kids.

"We volunteered to teach them, to read, to ride the horses, to boat, swim, you know, try to help nourish them." A pleasant smile returned, filling her face.

Shawn was mesmerized by the look on her face, her voice, her stories, her. Their hands lay on the ground between them. Without thinking, he stroked her hand, lightly squeezing each of her fingers while she talked.

She told him of a few funny mishaps and adventures, falling out of a tree and breaking her arm. Then her voice slowed, grew hushed, until he realized she was asleep. Her hand curled inside his.

Seeing her head bob, he gently trussed it with his fingers, then he shifted her body to lay her head on his chest. He wound his arm around her to hold her from slipping.

As his eyes slid closed, he noticed pretty much everyone else was also taking the opportunity to rest, take a nap protected and drying while the storm raged around them.

Cheri's half-dried hair waved down Shawn's chest. He slid his fingers into the silky mass, combing and stroking it gently until he fell asleep too with the pattering rain as a backdrop.

Chapter Eight

The group rested for several hours until the rain let up then they started back out to continue hiking.

Late afternoon, Shawn brought them to another cabin he hoped was empty. Peeking in the windows he determined it was abandoned. He broke a window and let everyone in like they had done at the last cabin.

Tomas Trent sighed happily dropping his pack on the floor, he was walking better but was still sore. "This is great, thanks eagle-eye Shawn, no cold night again."

There was nothing inside, no furniture, dishes, nothing. Some of the men gathered firewood, Shawn and Daf made a roaring fire.

After they ate an early dinner, Bella came inside and said, "There's a well out back with an old pump thing attached to it. Maybe someone can fix it and we can shower again," she mentioned hopefully.

Finishing with the fire, Shawn, Beau and Jim went outside to see what they could do with the well. Daf left a few minutes later to find some more rabbits or something else for a meaty dinner. Everyone else just rested.

Cheri went to clean up the small kitchen like she always did because if she didn't no one else appeared likely to do it. There was a barrel just outside the kitchen door.

After rinsing them with canteen water, she took some empty cans out and put them in the barrel. Dumping them in, she turned around to go back inside when suddenly she was grabbed from behind.

A hand clamped over her mouth smothering her scream. An arm slammed hard around her waist and she was half carried, half dragged quick and rough across the grass to a dense thicket of trees.

Inside the crop of trees, he dropped her but kept a hard arm around her waist. Struggling, kicking and punching, she recognized the arm with the brown curly hair. Deputy Ritchie Marx had a hold of her. One hand tightly covering her mouth, he was tearing at her clothes with the other.

She managed to kick him in the shin, he yelped and struck her across the face then threw her violently to the ground and dropped on top of her.

Grabbing at her clothes, he tried to rip them off her, never uttering a word emitting only snarls and urgent grunts. Sweat on his forehead sprayed on her face. Thrashing under the beefy man, Cheri's arms flailing she felt a rock on the ground. Grabbing it up she slammed it into the side of his head.

Slightly stunned, he groaned and rolled to the side with his hand to his head.

She squirmed out from under him and ran for the cover of the woods. Hearing his footsteps pounding the earth behind her, Cheri ran blindly through the brush.

Running as fast as she could, she could hear him crashing over brush, the bushes crunching and rattling as he roared through and over them. In a frantic, heart racing panic she kept running, afraid to scream for help because then he would know exactly where she was.

Dashing desperately along a sparse trail, one side a precipice atop a hill, the other dense woods, Cheri realized she needed to get off the trail or he would soon catch her!

Just as she looked for some place to hide he leaped at her- she jumped sideways to avoid his hands-

Too close to the edge she toppled right down the hill. Her scream lost in the dirt, rolling and bouncing, jarred by rocks and stabbed by bushes she tumbled down and down and down-

Ritchie peered over the edge seeing her rolling down the hill. Cursing a blue streak, he muttered, *"Oh crap-"* and got up quickly.

He decided it was doubtful she would survive the fall. Good thing, then that black haired prick wouldn't come after him for tussling her. But damn he was frustrated he hadn't fucked her before she fell.

Wiping his sweaty hands on his shirt, he made it to the path and hurried back to the cabin.

It took a lot of elbow grease, but they finally got the pump to work in the well.

Shawn and Jim had a smoke, then satisfied with their efforts, the men complimented themselves and went back inside.

Washing up in fresh water for a change, Shawn glanced around the room. Twice. She wasn't there. Maybe she was in the bathroom. He turned towards it when Caleb came out and ambled over and plopped down on the floor.

Butterflies started churning in Shawn's stomach. Where the hell was she? She must be with Daf, he relaxed, *aye, she was with-* the door opened and Daf came in carrying a couple of hares. He took them to the kitchen.

Shawn rounded on him, "Where the hell is she?"

"Huh? Who?" Daf muttered, taking out a pocketknife they'd gotten from the first lodge to skin the rabbits.

Shawn grabbed a fistful of Daf's shirt to stop him. He demanded, "The lass, Cherriana, where is she? Isn't she with you?"

Daf looked down at Shawn's fist clutching his shirt. Shawn let him go. Daf said calmly, "I have no idea, mate. She's not with me. I was out in the woods." He turned back to his rabbits.

"*Bluidy* hell," Shawn cursed under his breath then ran and checked the bathroom to make sure it was empty. It was. There were no other rooms in the cabin. He rushed outside.

Scanning the perimeter, she was nowhere to be seen. Dragging a ragged hand across his forehead, Shawn blenched. There was only one conclusion, she'd run.

Remembering her words that she'd rather die out there than go back to prison gave him a chill. He needed to go find her, it would be dark soon. She would never survive the night.

He told himself he should tell Beau or Daf where he was going, but time was of the essence. Stalking around outside the house trying to catch a trace of which way she had gone, he saw outside the kitchen door a series of footprints.

Could be any of the group's. There were big ones and little ones heading towards the trees. He followed them to just inside the tree line, there he saw a small area where the grass was smashed down.

Then he spotted a button. He picked it up and recognized it as Cheri's. Stuffing it in his pocket, he followed two sets of footprints down a trail wondering if she'd fled with someone.

After a while he thought he'd lost the trail when he saw something like shiny filament hanging on a bush. Plucking it off, he held the hair up to the dwindling light. There was no other shade like it on the earth, sunflower, it was hers.

At least he was heading in the right direction. The sun was at the curve of the horizon. Thunder rumbled in the near distance, black clouds ominously lowered and blew closer, urging him to quicken his pace. Another damned storm was approaching.

A few dozen yards and he picked up the prints again. They led to the side of the hill. Kneeling down to look at them, it appeared there had been a scuffle, the prints were marred and covering over each other. The smaller pair stopped at the hill, the bigger prints retreated back towards the camp.

His heart thumping out of his chest, Shawn looked down the hill. A path of broken shrubs and mashed grass showed the way she'd gone.

Feeling sick, he kept looking for a sign of her. After several long unnerving moments- there- he saw her bright hair in the last of the sun's rays. She was moving in no particular direction, obviously she had no idea which way to go.

Then his heart clenched like a fist. He saw feral eyes gleaming in the dark bushes, then he caught site of a grey and white tail, several tails. Coyotes hung alone, wolves travelled in packs. Didn't matter, both kinds of canines would be deadly for her.

Fuck- he trampled down the hill, running as fast and as carefully as he could without losing his balance, trying to keep her in his sights. The light was fading fast and the storm was rapidly approaching.

As he descended, Shawn could see the wolves moving in on her, circling her. She seemed unaware of them by the way she kept traveling slowly.

When he reached the level ground, Shawn raced through the trees, crushing undergrowth, running as fast as he'd ever run before in his life!

Bursting through the thicket to the brief clearing, he tore across the tall grass- threw an arm around her, hauled her up in the air against his chest, raised his gun straight up and fired off two rounds.

Covering her ears she screamed, "Please don't shoot me!"

"Tis not for you," he said grimly. Tethering her to him with one arm, he held the other straight out with his weapon as he spun a slow circle to make sure they had gone. "It was for the wolves."

They didn't hear them leave, but then again Cheri hadn't heard them coming either.

Her voice a high pitched squeak, she choked out, "Wolves?"

He didn't have to actually hold her now, she wrapped her legs around him and threw her arms up frantically clinging to his neck.

"They're gone," he assured her, moving to set her down. But she clung like a koala to his neck, pressing her face against his shoulder too scared to look.

Stuffing the gun in his waistband, Shawn pried her hands off his neck. Putting his hands under her butt, he tossed her over his shoulder, then long-legged it swiftly through the deep grass.

The thunder rumbled, louder, closer, lightning flashed against the dark clouds blowing in fast. It was almost completely dark now.

"Put me down!" she shrieked, pounding on his back and kicking her legs.

"You keep hitting me, Cherriana," he warned severely, "and I will bind your hands behind your back and then see how uncomfortable you will be."

She stopped moving.

"That's better," he chided. The louder the thunder grew the faster he moved. Lightening crackled and streaked almost directly above them. Cheri set her palms on his back and pushed her head up.

"I warned you, lass *tae* stop fighting me, we need to find shelter quickly," he told her in a no nonsense tone. "I don't have time *tae* fight with you or chase you."

"I- I can't breathe," she gasped. "The blood has gone to my head," she flopped back down.

Holding her legs with one hand, and the other splayed against her back Shawn lowered her to her feet. He held her pressed against him for a moment both taking several long, deep breaths.

Thunder boomed and rocketed, lightening bolts slashed overhead, they saw it fork near the hill they had come down.

Pulling her back, he bent his head to look at her and said, "Cherriana," the sky flashed, illuminating her eyes, like petrified blue lightning.

Then the rain struck. Huge, golf ball sized drops, pelting them and making fast growing muddy puddles around their feet.

Shawn grabbed her hand and they ran. He headed to the rockiest part of the hill. A few boulders jutted out making a ledge at least five up the side. He picked her up and about threw her up onto it. Then he put his hands on the ledge and pushed up until he could get a knee hold and climbed inside.

Watching him push his entire body up the ledge, gasping for air from the hard run, Cheri croaked in awe, "You're like superman!"

His eyes narrowed harshly at her. "You need *tae* be quiet," he snapped angrily over the roar of the storm and scuttled back inside the shelter of the boulders as far as he could get, drawing her with him. He panted loud, short shallow huffs catching his breath.

"Why-"

He turned fiercely shooting black eyes like enraged bullets at her. His broad back hunched like a panther waiting to pounce. "You ran," he accused furiously.

His hands clamped in tight fists he turned away for a second to calm himself. Then when faced her again, he looked so enraged she wilted away from him against the rocky wall.

"I am so fucking mad, I could bite an iron bar in half. I should put you over my knee and paddle the hell out of your ass so you can't sit for a week!"

Slamming his back against the rocks, he reached out and gripped her chin with his fingers, rigidly holding her head up. A sheen of tears blurred the blue orbs.

He knew he was probably hurting her delicate bones and bruising the translucent skin with the strength of his fingers, still he thundered in her face, "You could have died out here, you dumb bitch. What the hell is the matter with you? What the fuck were you thinking?"

Her tears fell like the rain outside the ledge. He forced himself to calm down, working to control and lose the maddening rage, and the fear for her life that had struck his heart like a knife.

The incensed feelings dissipating, his gaze direct at hers, his voice now husky, he said with disappointment, "After the dangers I warned you about." His expelled breath huffed hard and gruff. "I didn't think you were that stupid." He let her go.

Her jeans soaked through, she pulled her knees up and wound her arms around them. In in a small voice, she replied, "I know I'm a prisoner, Mr. Darkonn, but don't I have the right to protect myself from- from the constant assaults, the endless attempts to force me to-"

She broke off in a gulping choke. Dropping her face in her hands, she set her forehead on her knees. The rain slightly darkened the wet tresses that fell, covering her face.

Watching her terrible despair, the anger stirred starting to return, but not at her. Feeling his muscles clenching, Shawn asked, "Are you saying you ran because someone tried *tae* assault you tonight?"

He cupped her chin again gently now, to peer at her. His brows bore down like black marker slashes. "Is that a black eye?"

Holding her jaw, he tilted her face, gently brushed the hair aside to get a better look at the slight purple bruise under her eye. "You didn't get that falling down the hill, did you?"

Her gaze dropped, she refused to look back at him.

He laid a palm gently against her face and said softly, "Tell me, Cherriana, what happened, who did this *tae* you?" His hand slid down around to cradle the back of her neck.

Hitching in a few shuddering breaths, she moved away and out of his grasp. His hand dropped to his lap.

Staring out at the sheets of rain that made a crashing liquid curtain in front of the ledge, she said miserably, "I only stepped outside the kitchen door to throw out the cans. He grabbed me from behind, dragged me to the woods.

When I kicked him in the shin he hit me then threw me on the ground and tried to rip my clothes off."

She looked down ruefully at another missing button and some more holes in her now soaking wet blouse.

Aghast at the attack, Shawn sputtered, "How did you..."

"Get away?" Knuckling her dripping eyes, she drew in a tight breath remembering the violent scene. "He was on top of me, I was fighting him. My hand landed on a rock in the grass. I- I hit him in the side of the head.

"It only stunned him but it was long enough for me to-to get away. He came after me, he was trying to catch- catch a hold of me when I fell down the hill."

Shawn dropped his head in his hands, rolled it back and forth, then he tipped it sideways to look at her. "Who?"

Her answer came out in a deep anguished sigh, "Officer Marx."

Shawn wanted to punch the wall of rock, but he would probably break his hand and he wanted to save his fists for Marx. He wanted to bellow his rage but that would only scare her more.

Unable to vent his fury, he rubbed his hands up and down his face then he dragged his fingers through his wet hair leaving furrows like rows in a black crop field.

Inclining his head at her with raised brows, he asked, "He saw you go over the hill?" She nodded. "He saw you fall and he didn't go after you, *tae* help you?" She shook her head.

"*Leamin*, tell me why did you kick him in the shins and not the balls, it would have incapacitated him longer?" Seeing the blush color her cheeks he realized it had never entered her mind. "You didn't scream for help?"

Embarrassed, she murmured, "He held his hand over my mouth."

Shawn raked his palm over his eyes, he struggled to cap his boiling rage. His voice rasped husky, he said quietly, "Cherriana, I would say next time, kick or knee him in the balls as hard as you can, but there won't be a next time. This was my fault for getting tied up fixing the water pump and leaving you vulnerable when I knew what dodgy scumbags we have with us."

His hands tightening into fists again, he said resolutely, "It won't happen again."

The roar of the rain decreased, the wet pellets shrunk as they lessened.

Silently he watched her tears fall, she turned her head away. But he could still see them sparkling in the moonlight that the clouds now passing let shine down. Reflecting off the wet rocks the light shone inside the ledge.

"Cherriana, come here, dry your eyes." He shuffled closer to her, pulled out his shirt and wiped her eyes with it.

She giggled while he dabbed at the trails on her cheeks. "It's not really helping, Mr. Darkonn, your shirt is as wet as my face."

Shawn maneuvered so he was sitting in front of and to the side of her, facing her. "Lass, my name is Shawn." He traced a fingertip down the side of her face, stroked it under her chin, then stopped, lifting her head up.

"Say it." He gently drew her closer with his fingers. In a hushed, tender voice he urged, "Say my name, Cherriana."

He watched her eyes drop to his mouth where they hesitated, then looked up into his dark spheres that pulled her to him like bewitching lures.

Their mouths were so close she could feel his warm breath, smell his manly scent, she whispered, "Shawn…"

A surge of fire coursed through him. He cradled her head and brought his lips down on hers, holding back, only faintly touching them. She didn't cry out or pull away, he pressed harder.

Her lips moved against his in an inexperienced but willing way that lit a fuse in him, excited him like he had known it would, inciting him to want more. Moving his fingertips to her mouth, he touched her lips and kissed them at the same time.

Her hands shyly slipped up his shoulders, up his neck and into his hair. Feeling her response escalate, Shawn brushed his fingers up the side of her face and with his mouth he slowly pushed her lips further apart so he could run his tongue along her top lip.

Her body sighing into him, he trickled his tongue across her bottom lip then inside to skim across her teeth, deeper, to find her tongue, teaching her how to taste, and be tasted, explore.

The kiss heated up, their mouths charged turning fiery and fused. Cheri followed his lead, did what he did. She moaned, melting boneless in his embrace.

Shawn held her in the crook of his arm, his fingers netted the side of her head, his thumb stroking her temple. Still melded together, his mouth scorching hers, pressing harder, devouring her.

He could feel her innocence, her plush lips nipping at his, shyly touching his tongue as he ravished her mouth turned him on like he'd never felt never before.

He whispered, "Cherriana," against the corner of her lips. Burning like a house on fire, he trailed passionate kisses and licks down her jaw, down further to suck gently then ardently on her neck. The back of his brain pounded just as hard telling him to stop as his body throbbed and burned not letting him.

The ledge was dark, cold, hard, damp, but it cocooned them, closing them off from the rest of the world. Hearing his own breathing loud and passion drenched, his moans making her shake with new found desire, Shawn finally forced himself to pull his mouth away from hers. He peered down at Cheri.

Her small head was cushioned against his brawny arm. Her dewy lips plumped and red. Her eyelids half closed, a slice of blue shone so sultry at him it made his knees weak.

But he had to resist, he should never have given into his desires. It wasn't fair to her, or him either for that matter, since he was going to have to deny himself her ardor.

Moving his arm, he pushed her gently to sit back against the wall. Her confusion matched his own pain, physically and mentally of having to push her away.

It took all of his control and then some not to sweep her back into his arms, or lay her down on the rocky ledge and- that was not something he could let himself think about again.

"Cherriana, I..." She looked at him, her beautiful face uncertain yet aglow with their lovemaking. Groaning, he rubbed his eyes to break their link.

"Lass, I shouldn't have done that. I- I'm so sorry, I..." This was so hard, she hadn't pushed him away, or screamed, it seemed she wanted him as much as he craved her.

But, he wiped his eyes then his mouth, he couldn't allow himself to think about the flaming desire he saw in her eyes. She was so very innocent, she didn't know what she was doing.

"I'm a...uh, you're a...we shouldn't, we can't..." *fuck*, how can he say it? Then he heard someone calling his name. The rain had stopped, they were obviously looking for them.

"Come on." He slid to the edge of the ledge, dirt and rock fragments shagged down in a dusty shower with his movements. His voice strained and weary, Shawn said, "I'll get down then help you."

He didn't look at her or wait for her reply, he jumped down then turned back for her. It was a few seconds before he saw her on her hands and knees look over the edge, her hair swirling down.

"Okay, lass, you're going *tae* drop into my arms." He almost chuckled at the doubtful look on her face. "I promise, I will catch you. Trust me, *nesh leamin*. Come now, sit on the edge then push off."

Her face a crisscross of wariness and nerves, Cheri scooted to the end, slipped her legs over, and stopped.

"I swear, I'll catch you. Just push off." He held his big strong arms up for her to see, his legs braced apart, rigid but with his knees slightly bent.

Closing her eyes tight, she slid off and dropped into his arms. He slung them around her, holding her tightly, breathlessly against his powerful chest.

Wishing they could stay like that forever, he gradually released his grip, letting her slide down his body, slowly, so slowly he felt her every soft contour and curve glide along his male hardness until she landed on her tiptoes.

His arms still around her, breathing in the scent of her, his mouth next to her ear moved towards her lips-

"Shawn! Shawn!" Beau was shouting his name.

His arms tightened briefly before he let her go. Tucking his hands in his pockets, he stepped back and looked down at her. Her expression was so confused and bereft.

"Cherriana," he said, his voice sounding ragged, the words scraping his throat. "I'm realizing you felt forced *tae*, uh, that...that you felt because you're under my control for the time being that you had *tae* let me kiss you. I, uh," he pulled a hand out and awkwardly scratched his chin. "Um, but you didn't, you don't, I was out of line, and I promise, it won't, I won't do that *tae* you again."

She stood motionless, clearly not understanding what he was saying. "But-"

Afraid that she would be even more scared of him now and take a chance and run again, cutting her off, he said through rasping breaths, "What I'm saying is, you don't have *tae* be afraid that I will, uh, force myself on you again."

He watched her through shamed, lust-glazed eyes. She just stared bewildered at him.

God, he'd never seen such a quiet woman express so much with just her face. Big luxuriant eyes fringed with sweeping tawny lashes, small straight nose with just a hint of upturn, and small lips too but plump. Right now they all blended smudging and crimping the creamy skin with confusion and shame.

He could hear the shouts getting closer. Then he noticed her ripped blouse, buttons gone, soaking wet. She might as well have been naked. It was quite obvious she was cold, her nipples poked right through the thin, wet material.

It's a good thing he hadn't noticed it until now. It made his knees so weak, and other parts so hard he didn't know how he was going to walk.

"Lass," he gathered the sides of her long hair draping them over her breasts to hide them. "I need *tae* find you some more clothes again," *and a thicker bra.* "Let's go."

Taking her hand, he led her to the voices calling his name.

113

Chapter Nine

They trudged to the foot of the hill.

Up at the top, Shawn could barely make out Daf and Beau scanning the valley. He waved both arms and whistled until they spotted him.

It took some time to get back up the hill. It grew much steeper as they reached the top.

Shawn put his hands around Cheri's waist, ignoring the shock of heat that shot through his hands to his loins, he held her steady so Beau and Daf could catch her arms and pull her back to the level land. Then he scrambled up behind her.

Beau held out an arm for Shawn to use to pull himself over the lip of the cliff.

Walking back to the cabin in the darkening evening, Daf in front, Cheri next, Shawn and Beau walked side-by-side.

The silence emanating from the missing couple was so tense you could touch it. Beau shot Shawn sidelong glances until Shawn finally frowned at him and shook his head, mouthed *later*.

When they reached the perimeter of the cabin, Shawn leaned over and said very quietly in Beau's ear, "You and Daf go take her inside. Stay with her, I mean *right with her* until I come back."

Curious, but Beau always did what Shawn said and sorted out the whys later. He flicked his brows at Daf then strolled over to Cheri and the two men walked with her inside the cabin.

Once inside, Cheri went right over to her blanket, lay down, curled into a ball and closed her eyes. Beau and Daf leaned nonchalantly against the wall closest to her.

Shawn entered in behind them and quickly searched out Ritchie Marx. His proof was in the way Ritchie turned white as a sheet when he saw Cheri return with him.

Shawn looked directly at the officer.

Ritchie's eyes widened turning to Shawn, but the rest of his body stayed turned.

Shawn jerked his head indicating for the officer to go outside.

Ritchie shook his head, moving deeper into the cabin. Shawn signaled him again but Ritchie started heading for the kitchen.

Shawn was quicker. He was beside Ritchie as he reached the kitchen.

All eyes watched the two curiously.

Shawn said in a low voice, his accent thickening in his wrath. "I'll drag you out, Marx if I have *tae*."

Seeing the bigger man's incensed fury clear and dark on his face, Ritchie shrank and took sideways steps around Shawn through the kitchen and out the door.

His biceps pumping in preparation, the enraged Scotsman followed him.

Once outside, Ritchie put his hands up defensively in front of his face. He cried in a babbling string of words, "I didn't do nothing to her, bro, I swear! She told you a bunch of lies, whatever she told you it wasn't true. I never laid a hand on her, and- and even if I did? So what? She's a convicted piece of tail, who cares? You've had your slice of her now it's the rest of us-"

Blam! Shawn punched him square in the nose. Blood spurted like a geyser, with a scream Ritchie's hands went to his nose.

Shawn hit him in the stomach, when Ritchie's hands dropped to his belly he slammed him in the jaw, then the eye, then Shawn just pounded relentlessly on the guy until he pooled into the ground.

Kneeling beside him, Shawn grabbed his collar in his fist and pulled his bleeding, bruised head up. Nose red and swollen, two black eyes, gashes, cuts, he was crying like a baby.

His tone pure ice, Shawn said evenly, "You are on your own now, Marx. You are not going with us. Go find your own way out. If I see you anywhere near us I will break your legs. You ken, you understand me?"

"What? No!" Ritchie cried, tears spilling mixing with the gooey blood. "No, you can't, I can't get out of here on my own-"

Still holding his collar lifting his head off the ground, Shawn slugged him again and said, "Don't come back inside."

His merciless voice dropped to a ruthless deadly threat, "Don't come near her, don't come near the group. If I see you, I fucking swear I will kill you."

He let Ritchie's head drop on the hard packed earth, then he reached and unbuckled Ritchie's holster and pulled it off the older man, slung it on around his own lean hips and buckled it, his knuckles dripping blood on the leather.

"Darkonn, you can't leave me without a weapon, how will I protect myself?"

Shawn said coolly, "The same way you expected that wee slip of a girl *tae* protect herself when you chased her over that hill trying *tae* rape her, and didn't go help her, or get help for her when she fell."

He stood up and without another look at the crying man strode across the grass and went back inside.

Inside, he joined his friends, still breathing heavy from the fight and his anger.

Daf said, "Uh, yeah?" Noticing Shawn's bloody, cut knuckles, blood spatter on his shirt, he said, "Tell us."

Shawn brought them into the kitchen, washed his hands and gave them a brief rundown, including his own behavior with Cheri.

Beau didn't hide his interest. "Whoa, no kidding, Shawn. Good deal."

Shawn scowled blackly at him. Staring down at his feet, he said grimly, "No, tis not a good deal. I blew it. I should never have damned touched her."

"Huh?" Beau said, surprised. "Why the hell not? There's nothing wrong with it. You said she was willing. The girl's a hot little lass, every guy here wants to get in her pants-" His embarrassed gaze dropped, then rose sheepishly to Shawn, "Uh, I mean other than us lads, right Daf?"

Shaking his head, his arms crossed over his buff chest, catching Shawn's dour expression, Daf said to Beau, "I think you should stop talking now, mate."

Agreeing, Beau shoved his hands in his pockets and closed his mouth.

Glaring at the pair of them, Shawn said ruefully, "There's plenty wrong with it, Beau. First, she's a prisoner, a convict, and I'm a..." he broke off. "Plus, she's so young, she doesn't know anything about men except they keep jumping on her like she's a pony and they want a ride. Now

117

I've done it *tae* her too. I think she only let me kiss her because she's scared of me, afraid to say no."

His head lowered, his ashamed eyes fell despondently to the floor. Shaking his head, Shawn ran a hand through his mussed hair. "I do nothing but bark at her and push her around. Of course she'd do whatever I say for fear of my wrath."

"You kissed her, Shawn, that's all. Don't make a bigger deal out of it than it is. She'll get over a kiss," Daf told him.

Pushing back a lock of wet black hair, Shawn slid a glance to where Cheri was lying down. Remembering the look on her face when he pushed her away, he said glumly, "That's not *bluidy* likely."

He wasn't going to get over it himself, it was the most electrifying kiss he'd ever experienced, and his brain kept yelling in his head begging him to go get more.

His lips pursed, Daf jerked his head tossing his dreads off his shoulder. "Okay, whatever. We have other more important things *tae* worry about. Let's hit the hay, boys."

Shawn went to Ritchie's backpack and took out a shirt then trod over to Cheri and knelt beside her. "Cherriana," he waited for her to open her eyes.

"You can't sleep in those wet clothes." He handed her Ritchie's extra t-shirt. "Go change into this in the bathroom. Tis big enough to cover you. Your clothes should be dry by morning. I'm sorry it has *tae* be *his* shirt but no one else has an extra one. Go on now."

He waited while she took the shirt mutely and went off to the bathroom.

The rest of the group was half asleep already when she came out. Shawn groaned silently.

She was wearing the t-shirt, and only the shirt. Her entire body was outlined by the light of the fire behind her, and she would be sleeping right next to him. He let out his held breath, there would be no sleep for him tonight.

Shawn had removed his own wet clothes while she was gone and not having extra clothes either, he was nude under his blanket. He turned away as she laid her clothes out to dry and then knelt to climb under the blanket.

He prayed she was warm enough even with her hair wet, it would be hell for him if he had to hold her mostly naked body against his to keep her warm again. His body shivered of its own volition with the strain to keep his hands to himself.

Doing math problems in his head helped him to eventually nod off.

The next day was a rigorous trek mostly uphill. It was hours before they headed down again back to a valley floor. They marched on all day mostly silent with weariness and trepidation.

People shot nervous glances off and on at Shawn. Aware he had banished Ritchie but not knowing why, they were afraid they could be next.

The wind rustling through the trees, crickets chirping, an occasional flap of wings as startled birds flew off, the trudging steps of boots hitting the dirt and kicked stones rolling were the only sounds in the wilderness.

Morale was low, everyone was tired, and those that didn't know about the search for the gold bars were starting to worry that they were irrevocably lost and would die out there.

Leena scrutinized the duskiness of Shawn's unshaven strong jaw then her gaze rose to those shadowed eyes filled with dark secrets. Sighing her lascivious itch with a full body wriggle, she whispered to Bella, "That hunk looks like a man masterful in sadistic brutality."

Her body wriggled lustfully again. "I bet he's sinfully rough, and capable of committing unspeakable and unrestrained wicked acts. *God* he makes me hot."

"Boy, that was a mouthful, you've been thinking about him pretty hard." Bella grinned, then said quietly, "I see goose bumps popping up all over your body. You're thinking about being alone with him, aren't you?"

Her pudgy shoulders rolled, Leena smirked annoyed. "Yeah, his attention is wasted on that puny inexperienced girl. He needs a real woman, he needs me to unbridle his wild predilections on. I won't break like that winsome child."

She glanced from Shawn to Cheri, they walked next to each other but hadn't uttered a word. Leena saw Shawn shoot sidelong glances at the girl, but Cheri not once looked at him.

Leena shrugged hopefully. "Maybe he's just being like a big brother to her, watching out for her like a brother would."

"Huh. Yeah, sure, not with that girl's body."

Leena cringed at Bella's sardonic snort.

"In that case, you're talking incest, hon." Bella snickered meanly. She added, "He tries to hide it but you can see the way he looks at her. It ain't with no chaste brotherly love, hon."

Still ogling Shawn, Leena scowled, twitching at the lust that prickled at her body inside and out. "Since he exiled Ritchie, I don't have anyone to excise my overwhelming carnal cravings. There's no one else that turns me on like that strapping Scotsman does."

Then, she elbowed Bella, whispered, "Check this." Moving up briskly, Leena penciled her way between Shawn and Cheri.

The pair still had not spoken a word to each other. Shawn darted periodic glances at Cheri like he was trying to read her mind, but she just stared straight ahead, her set face shaved away any emotions.

He started several conversations in his mind but dismissed them all, not really knowing what to say. Anything he thought of would only make things worse.

"Shawn, honey, you tall, dark and rough man," Leena cooed, moving imperceptibly closer and closer to Cheri subtly nudging her away and back.

"Leena," an irritated scowl apparent in his deep voice, Shawn said, "I've asked you not *tae* do that crap with the tall dark shit. Please just leave it at Shawn."

Shrugging one shoulder, Leena opened a few buttons on her shirt and tugged at the collar to expose her cleavage. "Sure, honey, whatever. It's getting hot, isn't it?" She fanned her blowsy face, sidling coy hazel eyes up at him.

The angles of his face were even more chiseled after days of lean eating and random shaving. It was all Leena could do not to salivate, desiring everything about him from his sexy lips to those broad shoulders.

It was growing warmer as the day progressed and they labored up the mountain.

Shawn was wearing only his white t-shirt. He'd rolled up the short sleeves in a young Elvis Presley-style and had tried to slick back his black hair that had needed a trim even before leaving the prison. But the front obstinately curled down over his forehead. The back curved over his collar.

Leena gazed at that lock of hair sweeping over his brow like she was dying to stroke it. Her eyes shifted down to his arms. Her nether parts throbbed every time his biceps bulged and flexed when he lifted something. He resembled the days of the greasers with their white shirts, black bomber jackets and motorcycles. There was even a cigarette tucked over an ear.

Leena had managed to subtly push Cheri behind them.

Cheri didn't care. She felt awkward and uncomfortable walking beside Shawn after what they'd done on that ledge.

She was so confused, and worried, scared and angry. And... now she had other feelings she'd never felt before, she didn't know what to make of them either. Her hands in her pockets, her head bent, the buttery hair partially covered her face like a wavy flowing cloud.

"Cherriana," Shawn's voice cut into her revelry. Slowing his pace, he reached back, took her arm and pulled her back up next to him forcing Leena to move over.

Still holding Cheri's arm, he said, "I told you *tae* stay next *tae* me. If you need a break, tell me and we'll stop." She made no response, he didn't let go of her arm.

"I could use a break, Mr. Hard and Hot," Leena burbled, sighing heavily like she was about to drop.

Shawn rolled his eyes but let it go. "All right, everyone, let's take a break."

Leena moved next to him on his other side and said, "How about a smoke?" She knew the girl didn't like the cigarettes and would move away from him when he was smoking.

Before he could answer, Cheri heard Leena and assumed he would smoke so she went to join Daf and Beau knowing that was acceptable to Shawn.

Leena watched Shawn watching Cheri trod over to his friends. "Come on baby, light my fire." A cigarette dangled out of her mouth, she raised her head so he could light it for her. They moved over by a boulder. Shawn leaned back with one foot up against it, blew out a spiral of grey smoke and watched it dissipate in the light breeze. Leena stood in front of him then moved until she was between his legs and put a hand on his shoulder.

"Leena, I don't-"

"Hush darling, men never know what they really want." She leaned in, placing pudgy hands with paint-chipped and broken nails on his chest, and slapped her lips on his before he could stop her.

Shawn put the hand without the cigarette on her hip pushing her away. Over her shoulder he saw Cheri staring at them. *Shit.*

Wiping his mouth with the back of his hand, he said, "What the hell was that, Leena?"

She wriggled back in against his chest. Flinging an arm around his neck she mashed her breasts all over his chest and tried to kiss him again.

"Goddammit Leena, what the fuck is the matter with you? Get off me." He stood up shoving her.

Across the grass, Cheri was sitting with Beau on one side and Daf on the other, she was laughing at something Daf had said.

Shawn's heart flip-flopped. He hadn't seen her really laugh truly without inhibition yet, or even smile big, just some giggles.

She was dazzling. Beau and Daf were vying for her attention, trying to tell her the funniest story.

"Oh come on you big lug, Leena purred. "That little girl is too petite for a powerful vigorous, *big* man like you. She wouldn't   be   able   to   take   you...   all   of you...all...the...way...in. I can. You want to with me,

Shawn." She set her hand on his man's package and squeezed. "*God* you're huge, just like I-"

He snatched her wrist pulling her hand away. Now he knew how Cheri felt with everyone trying to grope her all the time. The light hair caught his eye, Cheri was watching- her face was pinched as if in pain.

Stepping away from the wanton woman out of reach of her clutches, furious that it looked to Cheri like he had kissed her and thrown her away, rejected her, and then was all over this woman.

Shawn said fiercely, "Leena, what's the matter with you throwing yourself like that at a man? Have you no respect for yourself?"

Leena tried to move back into his embrace, hair that hadn't been brushed since this morning swished limply in thin brown waves over her shoulders. Tucking the frizzy strands behind her ears she said with a bawdy leer, "Honey, when I see something I like, I don't play games, I go after it. You don't like games, do you?"

Shawn threw his cigarette on the ground, stepped on it. Elbowing her away from him, he said, "I like *tae* do my own choosing." He stalked away, over to where Beau, Daf and Cheri were telling jokes and roaring with laughter.

When he reached the trio, grinning at him, Daf said, "Tis late, Shawn, what do you say we just camp here for the night? Everyone is exhausted and hungry." He nodded subtly at Cheri. The girl's eyes were drooping, she struggled to keep them open.

Shawn nodded. "Yeah. Okay. Let's start a fire and lay out the blankets."

The group ate and settled weary aching bones down and was soon drowsing.

The sky darkened as the sun lowered behind the mountains, in seconds it was pitch black. The night had cooled, everyone was asleep and tucked tightly under their wool blankets.

The three men, Shawn, Daf, and Beau, light sleepers, woke suddenly with uneasy feelings.

Standing next to Cheri who was still sound asleep, Shawn pulled his jeans and boots on, he didn't bother with his shirt and was already disappearing into the brush by the time Beau and Daf followed him.

In the thicket, Shawn whispered to them, "*Na*, you two stay here and protect the others. None of those corrections officers could fight their way out of a paper bag. *Daena* let Cherriana out of your sight." He took off.

"Now we're bleeding babysitters," Beau complained. Then he smirked at his friend. "He's got it bad, huh?" He saw the flash of Daf's smile as they went back to the others.

Slipping soundlessly through the brief knot of trees, Shawn worked to adjust his vision. There was nothing as dense and blind as a forest at night.

Fortunately there was a full moon offering a meager glow slightly illuminating the blackness. Its cool silver light coating shiny leaves and creating indiscernible shadows.

Shawn heard engines. At the edge of the woods, he stayed just inside the tree-line hidden in the murky crowd of broad trunks, and waited.

He didn't have long to wait.

Hearing the buzz of engines, lights broke through the dark switching up and down and across the rough terrain. An off-road vehicle came into view, another was right behind it.

Both vehicles had spotlights attached to the side, the lights were being maneuvered at clumps of trees.

When they reached the trees, they stopped. Several men hopped off carrying bags and vanished in the dark expanse of timber.

Stepping back into the forest, Shawn silently traipsed back to the camp. Everyone was awake.

Beau, Daf, Malone, Vega and Leena met up with him. In a quiet voice, almost a whisper Shawn said, "Tis illegal poachers jacklighting. They're hunting nocturnal animals using off-road rides with spotlights."

"Is that a problem?" Malone asked, grimacing when Shawn signaled him to keep his voice down.

"Could be," Daf answered him. "It's illegal to use an artificial light on a highway or in a field, woodland, wetland or forest while having in your possession a bow and arrow, crossbow, firearm or other device capable of shooting a projectile."

Malone said, "What are you, a walking law book for cripe's sake? So what? What's that got to do with us?"

"Yeah, what do we care what they're doing?" Jim Vega questioned, scratching his unshaven chin. He tightened his belt, rearranged his jeans around his narrow frame then smoothed his dark hair off his face.

Shawn said, "I think they're also using legholds."

"What are legholds?" Leena moved close to the black-haired Scotsman.

Crossing his arms over his chest, his legs shoulder width apart, Shawn explained quietly, "They're putting animal carcasses near traps, legholds, to draw in bigger animals. The word is that there are record-book heads that can sell for $30,000 to $40,000 or even more."

His tone belittling, Malone set his stocky hands on his hefty hips. He sneered as if chiding a young subordinate, "Where's your shirt, boy, what is this, a male strip club?"

126

"Vance, you are so jealous of this fine specimen of muscular hunk." Leena put her hand on Shawn's bare chest and stroked over his pectorals combing through the dark hair before Shawn snatched it off and pushed her away.

"Leena, keep your bleedin' sleazy hands off me, and you," Shawn said to Malone who was shooting hateful glares at Leena, "keep your fucking voice down."

Malone turned his malevolence to Shawn but kept his voice low, "Anyway, again, Darkonn, who cares about the poachers, it's nothing to do with us."

"Because with that kind of money at stake they might have no compunctions in killing us so we can't report them." Shawn said.

Irritated that they were talking about this in the middle of the night when he could be sleeping, Malone said indifferently, "So what, we're not going to report them."

Beau retorted, "But they don't know that. They find out we're here and they could come and slaughter us in a skinny minute."

The rest of the group was watching them talk and waiting to see what was going on. Cheri sat with her back resting against a boulder, pulled her knees up and strung her arms around them.

Shawn stood like a bare-chested samurai ready to do battle. Feeling his inscrutable eyes penetrate the dimness across the landing at her, she kept her gaze averted.

Bella got bored and crawled under Zach's blanket with him to wile away some time.

"We could be in serious jeopardy," Shawn advised the five people in his huddle. "I want everyone *tae* go stay behind those big rocks and do not make a sound. Nothing. No one moves until I come back."

"Where are you going?" Malone asked suspiciously, peeved that Shawn continued to usurp his leadership, his authority. This was Malone's deal after all and he had the highest rank of anyone there, and the convicts were under his supervision, his control, dammit. Yet they all ignored him and did whatever Darkonn ordered.

Shawn said to Malone, "I'm going *tae* watch them until they leave and I feel we are safe."

His sarcastic gaze moving up and down the bulky man, Shawn asked, "You got a problem with that, Deputy? You want *tae* come with me?" He dared the coward to follow him into the dark perilous forest.

"No, asshole, I'll let you have all the glory." Malone spat vitriol from his every pore at the Scotsman, thinking, when he's done with Darkonn it'll be a pleasure killing him, slowly, painfully, tortuously. He turned from Shawn so the other man couldn't see the galling hateful thoughts in his vile expression.

Daf said under his breath so no one but Shawn could hear, "Bro, we need to report those poachers."

Shaking his head slightly, Shawn looked over the group, their faces betrayed question and concern. "*Na.* Our first duty is *tae* keep the group safe. Human lives are more important than the poachers.

"When we are able *tae*, we will advise the game wardens of what I saw and where. I have descriptions. Right now, you need *tae* keep everyone close together and quiet."

His long legs ate up the space between them and the woods, then he melted into the trees and was gone.

Chapter Ten

It was almost an hour before Shawn returned. He emerged from the woods so stealthily most of them didn't hear him cross the grassy clearing to the boulders they were hiding behind.

Their hearing more attuned, Daf and Beau were already heading towards him. Shawn scanned the group behind the rocks to ensure everyone was still there. He sought out the sunflower hair first.

She was sitting with an empty space on either side of her, he assumed Beau and Daf had been sitting with her. The blue eyes stared blankly at him displaying no emotion.

Shawn trod over to the center of the group. They all knew by now what was going on.

He said, "The poachers are gone. I followed their lights up the south side of the mountain. Their camp is probably there. We'll go in the opposite direction in the morning. I think tis best we stay here on this side of the rocks *tae* sleep. Tis cramped, but it'll be safer. So, everyone lay your blankets back out, we need *tae* be quiet. No unnecessary talking or moving around."

Yawning and grumbling, the people set out their blankets and settled down practically arm-to-arm.

Shawn had Cheri bookended between him and Beau, Daf guarded the opening, the entrance to the hidden space behind the rocks. He would be first response if anyone, or anything approached.

The rising sun woke them slowly.

Shawn got up and traipsed back into the woodland to see if the poachers were still gone. He found no sign of them other than the disgusting traps they left with rotting meat in them.

Using a branch he tripped all the traps he could find then returned to the others.

They hiked towards the north, away from the direction he saw the poachers headed, fortunately it was the direction Shawn wanted to go in.

By noon they broke for lunch. They'd stopped near a lake.

Shawn and Beau went in search of edible plants and berries. Daf checked out the lake for fish. He was particularly adept at catching fish using a branch carved to a point making it a spear.

When Shawn and Beau joined him, in no time they had a blanket full of fresh fish. The three men carried the fish and berries back to the others, Shawn went to make a small fire.

"What about the smoke, bro?" Daf asked, as he helped build the fire.

Stacking the kindling, Shawn said, "Tis under this low cavern, it should help *tae* reduce the amount of smoke it makes. We're inside a mountain cleft, the smoke will be less visible as it rises."

On his knees, Shawn was just finishing building the fire, his gaze stroked across the campsite. His eyes narrowed to searing fissures when he saw most of the people sitting on rocks in a circle, and Cheri was perched on Beau's lap.

Leaving the rest of the fire and the fish to Daf, he tramped over to them. His hands on his hips, keeping the ire he felt out of his voice he inquired, "What's going on?" He glared at Beau who had his arms cheerfully wound around Cheri, and she was laughing.

"Hey, Shawn, laddie, we're playing Simon Says, and Cheri here is really good at it! Aren't ya lass?" Beau gave her a hug.

Her face aglow, Cheri giggled. "It's fun. Beau tells us what to do, and if he doesn't say Simon Says first, and we do it, we're out!"

"Aye," Shawn nodded, a frown furrowing his brow. He could see Beau laughing at him. He was busting his balls on purpose. "I know how the game is played."

Trying to keep the annoyance out of his tone, he said coolly, "Beau, Daf said he needs your help with the fish," he gestured to Daf by the fire, "maybe you could skin them."

Moving right in front of them, he bent and twined his fingers around Cheri's arm and pulled her off Beau's lap. He waited while Beau smirked gleefully at him knowing he'd gotten Shawn's goat and casually climbed to his feet. Passing his friend, Beau gave Shawn a taunting pat on the back.

Shawn kept his hold on Cheri and without preamble, walked her away from the group all the way out past the rocks. Leaves rustled like paper chimes around them, the balmy breeze lifted her hair making it dance in its uneven currents.

When they reached cooling shade of a rounded maple tree, he stopped and looked at her, stuffing the unfamiliar irritation of jealousy that crawled in his stomach.

"What have I done now, Mr. Darkonn?" she asked, as usual fear laced her tone but there was indignation in it too.

131

Feeling his space invaded, a bird flew out of the tree cutting loose a pointed maple leaf. The leaf fluttered down, drifted off Cheri's shoulder then swirled to the ground.

Arms folded over his chest, Shawn lowered his head to watch her expression. "You were sitting on Beau's lap."

Her brows knit in puzzlement. "Yes, you saw." Braiding her fingers together, she held them in front of her against her stomach.

"You should never sit on a man's lap that isn't your boyfriend or husband." Between the picture of her on Beau's lap with his arms around her, and trying to explain to her why it was wrong, he could feel his neck redden.

"Why not?"

He studied the completely guileless face that struggled to understand what she'd done wrong.

"Because...tis...uh...an intimate thing. Sitting on a man's lap means basically you are his, you belong to him. Do you ken, understand what I'm saying?"

Her forehead wrinkled, her lips pushed out. "No one belongs to another person. That's what got me here."

Shawn pinched between his eyes. "Uh, aye, that's correct, no one owns a person," *unless she's your woman*.

Keeping his sexist thoughts to himself, they generally weren't too popular with females, he said, "Tis not exactly what I meant. I meant you only sit on a man's lap that you have a relationship with. Like you don't let a man you're not in a relationship with touch you. Tis the same for men too, men shouldn't go around handling women that they're not involved with. You ken what I'm saying now?"

She crossed her arms and said blithely, "You had your hands, and your mouth on me, that's pretty intimate as far as I would think, and we are not in a relationship. What about that?"

132

Shawn had never in his life ever blushed before. He could feel the heat roiling up his neck and the red creep into his face. Struggling to know what to say, a pulse drummed at his temple. "Uh, you…you are right. It wasn't right of me *tae* do that."

"Why not?"

"Because- because you let me only because you were afraid of me; you were afraid *tae* say no." The guilt squeezed like vice on his heart. All this time he had worked to get her to trust him, to look to him when she was in trouble and he'd failed her the second they were alone together. What a weak fool he was.

Her lips pursed as she shook her head, the light hair swept across her back. "No. I was not afraid of you then. I mean at least not at that moment. Before and then after we got down from the ledge, yes, I was afraid of you, but not while you were…we were kissing."

The feminine face softened sultry and mellifluous, her smile honeyed and sweet as she recalled their intimacy on the ledge. Her fingertips drifted to her lips, sifting across them like they were his mouth.

Following her moves, Shawn could feel tingling start in his legs and spread through his body like a voltaic charge. He wanted badly to touch her, but didn't dare.

The urge to brush back the loose wisps of hair that tickled her cheek was insistent. He wanted to- wiping his mouth he scrubbed his fingers up and down his face.

Letting out his held breath in a hoarse shudder, he cleared his throat of weakness and tried to say strongly, firmly, "That was, uh, I was wrong. I shouldn't have touched you…I shouldn't have kissed you."

Her brows drew down between perplexed blue eyes. Tilting her head at him she asked innocently, "Why? You

133

didn't like it? Did you want Leena to be there, not me?" Her fingertips tucked into the back pockets of her jeans.

"What?" This was getting worse. He'd opened a can of worms. Damn Beau. He had done this on purpose. His face darkened, "*Aye,* I mean no, I mean I liked kissing you, I have no desire *tae* be with Leena."

Shawn couldn't believe the words that dribbled out of his mouth. He should have bitten his tongue and flattened Beau for getting her on his lap knowing it would incense Shawn.

She asked so childlike yet her womanliness wanted answers, "You liked kissing me? Do you have this...de-what is it, desire to be with me?"

Her innocence and inexperience were killing him. One of the reasons he should have kept his hands off her. He was way too old, too jaded and weathered in life experiences, too rough and tough for her, too big and hard and her so slender and petite. She could never comprehend the life he's led, the ruthless things he's done.

His mouth grit, his teeth ground together. "Cherriana, this discussion is over. I should not have kissed you for a variety of reasons. I told you, I will not do it again. Please forgive me for my boorish actions."

He did touch her then. Setting just the pads of his fingers on her upper back he moved her to walk back to the camp. Keeping his eyes straight ahead, he couldn't bear to see her bewildered and sad expression.

Her steps slow, she looked up at the stony hewn, strikingly masculine man and asked with sincerity, "You don't like me, Mr. Darkonn?"

His feet did a double take. Then he made the mistake of stopping. He looked down at her beautiful earnest face. "No, Cherriana, I mean yes, I like you, tis just..."

"Just what?"

Shawn jammed his fingers into the sides of his hair and pulled at it in frustration. She didn't deserve to suffer for his lack of control.

She lifted her hand, drifted her fingertips with the lightness of a cloud down the side of his face. "I think you are hard on the outside, because you need to be." Her fingers soothed across the hard planes of his cheek, softening the hardness with her gentle stroke.

His eyes closed against the feather caresses. Her hushed lilting voice brushed musically into his ear.

"But I don't believe you are as menacing on the inside as you try to be. I think you are brave and kind."

His head tilted into her warm palm, she stroked her fingers through the side of his hair, he moved his head to allow her, so small, to further access his height.

With ingénue in her tone, Cheri asked, "Why can't we be in a– a relationship? You don't find me...attractive, I guess."

His heavy eyes opened to a slit. The pain constricting her lovely face tore at his heart. Shawn reached and grasped her stroking hand, pulling it gently from his hair, lowered it to press against his heart.

He bowed his head to hers. "Lass, you are one of the, no *the* most bonny girl I've ever seen, with the biggest heart of gold. I wish..." emotion pulled at his voice, "there's nothing more in the world I'd rather do than be with you," he begged her to understand.

"What is wrong with me then?" she asked in a little voice.

His midnight eyes seared deep into her big blues, like he was stroking them. He said quietly, "Cherriana," *ahh...* "There is nothing wrong with you, tis the circumstances.

You are too young, actually I am too old for you for one thing."

"I understand from Beau that you're less than ten years or so older than me. That's not ancient."

"Aye, lass. But in living life, I am too- weathered, stained with the things I've done, had *tae* do. You are too pure, you deserve a young man that is sweet and kind and pure like yourself, not- not a rugged hardened man like me."

She suggested shyly, "You could teach me." Standing on tiptoe, she knitted her arms around his neck and pressed her soft velvety lips against his.

Caught off guard, Shawn had no will, his arms just bound right around her pulling her in. Feeling her curves yielding against his hard surfaces and ridges, heat coursed through him firing up every nerve like light switches snapping on so rapid fire his skin burned with crackling electricity.

How could he resist when their kiss deepened sending an intense raw flush that lit every single cell, imploding Shawn's reserve until the word *stop* disintegrated.

Rougher than he intended, he pushed her mouth open. Unsophisticated yet pliant lips parted to let him taste the honey he'd thought about constantly since the moment on the ledge.

The warmth of her skin seethed through the thin material of her blouse heating his palms. He stroked one hand down her lower back to hold her closer, the other cupped her head forcing their mouths to crush together in wild senseless abandon.

Feeling her curl so sublimely against him, filling his arms, just as the last thin strand of self-control, Shawn's code of honor, untwined in his fevered brain and as it slipped away, he garnered his strength and with a grievous groan gently set her away.

He covered his eyes with his hand so as not to look at her while he took big breaths, in, out, slow, swallow.

"Shawn?" Again the tone of what did she do wrong, rang in the one word.

His breathing steadied slightly, slowing his heart rate. He raised aching lids swollen with need for her and gazed guiltily at Cheri.

Seeing her so young, trusting naïve eyes wide and misted with passion, his gaze dropped to her small full lips trembling with feelings she'd never felt before. He had to move away from her before he swept her back in his arms where she fit so perfectly, like a curvy ball in a hard glove, and never let her go again.

"Cherriana," her name fell from his mouth in a regretful breath.

She sighed with knowing distress and shame. "I understand, it was a mistake, you didn't mean it. I get it...*Mr. Darkonn.*"

"Lass, you don't understand. I can't have a relationship with you, because of our...circumstances, which I can't explain. If, when we can clear up your situation-" his hand reached out to her but she swung out of his reach and started walking away.

Then she hesitated, her small hands rolled into tight fists. Turning back to him she said, "You're saying because I'm a criminal you don't want me. Fine. I don't want to talk about it again ever, don't you dare touch me again. How do you think it makes me feel when you kiss me then throw me away like trash, twice now. Like you tried me, didn't like it, tried again, didn't like it again. You're toying with me and I won't have it."

His Adam's apple jumped up and down furiously as he swallowed the words, fighting not to correct her.

"I can only think that you are trying to make Leena jealous using me, and," she spun back, fire in her eyes. "I am asking- *telling* you to stop." She ran off to the camp before he could respond.

Knowing he shouldn't stop her, but the hurt and shame in her face made him take a step to go after her, then, he shook his head in guilt thinking what an asshole he was losing his control around her, again.

He had to let her go.

Chapter Eleven

Beau was stuffing a last bit of fish in his mouth as he wandered over to where Shawn was putting out the fire. Licking his fingers, he said, "The lass looks like she's about to break like glass into brittle shards, and you look like you want to shove your fist through something. What have you done to her now?"

A cloud of smoke blew up when Shawn kicked dirt over the last of the flames. "Tis none of your business, Beau."

Snorting his mirth, Beau wiped his sticky fingers on his pants. "Getting your back up won't help things, Shawn. I can tell anyway. You couldn't keep your hands off her and then you ignominiously pushed her away again. Talk about mixed signals. You're not being fair to her, mate. What's the big deal anyway? She's a living doll, sweet, pure, hot, willing, the whole nine yards. Why resist her?"

Shawn dragged a sleeve over his face then combed his hair back with harsh fingers, his blank gaze fell bleak. "You know why. She is a prisoner, off *tae* trial, and I'm," he exhaled hard. "We know what I am, and we both know why tis wrong."

His hands stuffed in his pockets, Beau shook his head at his friend. "Well, you always had that stiff-necked integrity, unbending sense of duty. I have integrity too, but not as rigid and inflexible as you. As blue as the sky and her eyes are, I know she's innocent of those charges against her, and you know damned *bluidy* well that she's innocent too. Besides that pressing issue, you should stop telling yourself you're not good enough for her, that's up to her to decide."

Rolling his shoulders to loosen them, Shawn said, "It is what it is, Beau. I was forced *tae* commit a lot of…brutal, ruthless actions in the military, and, you know, later. My hands are covered in blood, my brain a mess of violent, torturous memories.

"The things I did…I can't undo. That girl is way too…sweet, naïve, for the likes of me. When we complete this…mission, we can go clear her name. But until then, it would be wrong and you know it."

"Hell Shawn, you did what you had to do, just like me and Daf. But now, your job is-"

"My job, Beau, for now, this moment, is *tae* protect her, from me too, and turn her over *tae* the authorities when we're done."

Beau stared at his friend in disbelief. "You are a hard man, Shawn Darkonn, too hard. You can't turn her over until she's cleared of the charge, you want her trapped back in prison until we do that? You know how long that could take?

"What will happen to her there in the meantime, and what, Shawn, what if we can't clear her, then what? Are you going to be prepared to break her out? Because I will be, and Daf too, with or without you and your stupid code of honor. You know we have ways. Some things just can't be left to the justice system."

Shawn didn't answer him. All of this had plagued him from the minute they escaped the crashed bus.

"Well, *ma brither*," Beau said smiling, smoothing his cropped red beard that was growing from lack of trimming. He brushed curly hair back off his temples. "If you don't want her, I sure as hell do. If you can't squash that sense of duty when you know what is right, too bad for you. Your loss.

"She likes me. Not as much as I think she's attracted to you, but she'll come around. With both our blue eyes we'll make beautiful babies. Thanks for the gift." He started to walk away, Shawn threw out a hand and grabbed Beau's arm, shoved him around to face him.

"You keep your *bluidy* hands off her, Beau, I'm warning you. Stay the hell away from her, she's-"

Beau grinned. "She's what, Shawn, yours? Is that what you were going to say? If you aren't going to claim her, bro, someone will and it might as well be me. At least I won't abuse her like the other clods here, or make her feel like shit about herself like you do."

Leaving Shawn smoldering, he strolled back to where the rest of the group was resting.

It was torture for both Shawn and Cheri to walk beside each other all day and then sleep next to each other all night.

As hard as it was on him, Shawn refused to let her out of his sight. Too many things had already happened to her. He prayed for the nights to grow warmer, but it was as if Mother Nature was punishing him for his lack of control.

After only one warm night, now when the sun set it grew chillier by the second until the nights were downright frigid.

In the beginning, Cheri had faced Shawn when they had lain down so she could fend him off if he tried anything. Which was of course laughable, her stopping him would be

141

like a flower fighting a sandstorm, if he was going to do anything to her, which he wasn't.

But, he had to keep her warm, and the only way he knew how to without more blankets or a sleeping bag, was to enclose her against his own body heat, whether she wanted to or not.

Ignoring her angry statements that she didn't care if she froze to death, and her struggles to fight him off, every night he forcefully turned the freezing young woman around, then pulled her in so her back was against his torso. Then he would encompass her with his bulky arms and hold her all night, keeping her warm.

Now, after hiking all day, night was falling, they had found a clear area surrounded by a wall of rocks to camp.

After dinner, the weary group settled down to sleep.

This night, Cheri lay down as far away as she could get from Shawn making it clear she didn't want to touch him. He just reined her in anyway.

Knowing it was futile to fight him, as soon as his hand hooked around her waist, Cheri fought him anyway, her silent way of reiterating that she wasn't willingly in the shelter of his arms.

Trying to squirm away, she pushed at his concrete block of chest with her dainty ineffective hands, then pulled at his muscled forearms using all her strength to wrest herself from his unbreakable embrace, all to no avail. His powerful hold on her was unbreakable.

Maneuvering her like she was a doll, Shawn turned her so her back was against his torso and wrapped his muscular arms around her.

His whisper a peaceful caress against her ear, "*Leamin*, you know I have *tae* do this *tae* keep you warm. I will not allow you *tae* freeze to death. Don't waste the energy that you need for hiking fighting me."

The hurt clear in her voice, Cheri muttered bitterly, "You do not need to be responsible for my wellbeing. Who are you trying to impress with your righteousness?" She gave a futile hard jerk away from him.

Fastening her arms to her body so it was impossible for her to struggle, Shawn held them down until she grew weary and finally fell asleep. Even when he felt her finally succumb to sleep, her body falling limp, he didn't relinquish his hold.

He loosened his arms but still kept her pressed solidly to him, her behind fitting tantalizing in the curve of his hips. Tucking his knees under hers, he pulled them up drawing her closer to him into an intimate spoon.

Inhaling her hair's sweet perfume, Shawn told himself he kept her curled close to his body only to keep her warm.

With that thought in his head, he slipped a hand under her relaxed elbow moving to place his palm flush on her stomach. Savoring the flatness of it, his hand so big his fingertips just touched the gentle jut of her supple hip.

With Cheri warm and protected in his embrace, he compartmentalized his arousal that came as natural as breathing when he was in contact with her. Submerging it in the far recesses of his mind, Shawn fell into fairly comfortable slumber.

The next day, when they stopped to eat, Cheri hung with Beau and Daf, the trio telling stories and laughing at jokes while Shawn scouted the perimeter to stay on the right trail and look out for danger.

It was better than standing idle fuming stupidly while Beau audaciously flirted with Cheri, finding every excuse to touch her. Shawn's gaze burned at Beau's hand lifting one of her bright spirals letting it curl around his hand like a lazy snake before setting it behind her shoulder, and deliberately brushing her shoulder with his hand.

Loud enough for Shawn to hear, Beau had suggested to Cheri that she could use his body warmth at night. Shawn turned on him with wordless rage in his eyes. Beau grinned at him, deliberately tormenting and provoking his friend.

Hiking deeper into Big Sky Country, they reached a beautiful valley, a satin sash of green landscape etched by magnificent mountains, and studded with maple, birch, cypress, elms and oaks.

Honeysuckles' flared lobes of orange blossoms scented the entire valley with their sweet fragrance. Under any other conditions it would be a paradise to some. To this weary, bored group it was yet another area to trudge across.

The good news was, the land was level. A gurgling stream bordered the north side drawing them to its cool freshness.

Dropping packs off their tired backs, everyone hurried to refill their canteens.

Leena and Bella dipped their hands in the delicious liquid and washed their dusty faces. Getting their fill, they sat back leaning against a couple of regal oaks.

Yawning, Leena said, "So, Bella, you and the un-jolly blond giant still an item?"

Bella chuckled at her description of Zach. The man she spoke about drew Bella's attention over the soft wavering grass. As usual, he stood by himself smoking a cigarette staring off into nothingness.

She sighed, plucked a dandelion and twirled it aimlessly. "If you call violent bestial sex an item, then yes. If you're talking about anything else, that would be a big resounding no. I've tried every which way to draw that man out, but his lips are glued together."

Now Leena chuckled. "I bet they're not *always* glued together, honey."

Bella frowned at the twirling dandelion. "No, you're wrong there, they are always glued together. He doesn't kiss me, and he certainly doesn't do anything else with them except bite sometimes. Make that a lot of times. Most of the time."

Her words drew Leena's attention to Bella's arms. She couldn't stifle her gasp and reaction fast enough. "Oh, Bella," she cried, seeing the bite marks on the officer's toned arms, neck, even one on her face. "Why do you let him-"

Bella scoffed sardonically, closing the dandelion in her hand but not crushing it. "Girl, no one lets or doesn't let Zachary Stockton do whatever he wants."

"Then stay away from him," Leena suggested firmly. "He's supposed to be locked up all the time anyway."

Bella's mouth pulled in, drooped. "Yeah, well, first, I don't want to stay away from him. I've always dug the...uh...rough sex. Although I admit he often goes well over the edge, but I'll live with it, it's worth it.

"Second, since Shawn threw Ritchie out, the only ones big enough to really hold him even cuffed are Shawn, Daf, and Beau, maybe Malone. But they aren't going to be chained to the crazy goliath. Shawn needs to scout ahead and he wants his guys free to protect us or whatever," she trailed off with a shrug.

"Yeah," Leena agreed. "Look even now, poor Tomas Trent trying to cuff Zach to him. He shouldn't have let him loose in the first place."

"Zach doesn't like anyone watching him pee. Tomas doesn't want to be alone in the bushes with Zach, he's worried he'll sling the chain around Tomas' neck and strangle him."

"What about the cuffs? He'd still be chained to Tomas."

Bella giggled at the sight. "Honey, Zach could chew that chain off if he wanted to."

Leena laughed with her at the picture of giant Zach leaning over small dead Tomas and gnawing at the metal cuffs. Or more likely he'd chew Tomas' arm off first.

"So," Bella sighed, "what about you? You missing Ritchie?" She watched Leena's eyes narrow as they travelled over the grass to where Cheri was talking with Beau.

"Hmm. Yes, I was growing quite fond of him. I worry that he's okay. I haven't spoken with him since I slipped him his blankets and food. Sometimes I catch a glimpse of him way back. He's following us, he has to. There's no way he would ever find his way out of this wretched wilderness on his own."

Her glare frothed in murderous waves at Cheri, the girl was blissfully unaware of the officer's hateful wrath.

"It's her fault," Leena said hatefully. She seduced my guy. It wasn't his fault. I'm sure she led him on and when he refused to screw her, she complained to Shawn. Being the big protector of women and children, Shawn had to exile him."

"Geez, Leena, if looks could kill-"

"Oh, honey, she'd be dead as a doornail right now and buried." The two women laughed together watching Beau and Daf leave Cheri to wander downstream to see if there were any fish in the water.

One arm draped around her knees, Leena brushed her palm over the grass feeling the blades' soft raggedness. She pulled her backpack over and took out a pack of cigarettes, tapped one out and lit it. Bella automatically shook her head when Leena habitually offered her one. "What about Zach?"

"Huh? What about him?" Bella wiggled the dandelion under her chin, tickled the tip of her nose with it then aimlessly twirled it.

Leena took a drag, blew the smoke away from Bella's direction. "You think Zach would do the girl?"

"Really?" Bella snorted, waving at the smoke that managed to waft in her face anyway. Her shoulders twitched, she tried to act like it didn't bother her but the resentment shown in the downward slant of her almond shaped eyes and the corners of her turned down full lips.

The brown eyes shifted from Leena to Cheri who was now sitting by herself cross-legged on the grass. Throwing the yellow weed on the ground, Bella said glumly, "Leena, he would have done her the second we were off the bus if it weren't for Shawn's protection. He'd have easily blown off any pathetic objections Malone would have made."

They looked up when a shadow loomed over them. Bella said tiredly, "Hey, Shawn."

He replied, "Hey. Listen, you shouldn't linger by the water. Tis probably a source for most of the animals in this area, like bears and coyotes." Saying this, he trod back up the grass to where Beau and Daf were skinning fish. He glanced over once to see where Cheri was.

She had gotten to her feet, sauntered over and was now talking with Tomas who looked unhappy as he prepared to hook Zach back up to him.

Shawn presumed she was seeing how his wound was healing. Tomas hadn't had any trouble walking, and didn't complain about any pain. So Shawn figured it was healing properly as was his own shoulder. Cheri was quite the healer.

Since Trent's attack on Cheri the night she sewed up his leg, Shawn was leery to have her anywhere near the guy. But she insisted vehemently on checking on his wound to the point that he gave in.

Caleb for once was strolling around instead of plopping down the second they stopped for anything.

Shawn reached his friends. They had several fish lying on a towel in the grass. "Looks like success so far, *ma brithers.*" he said joining them.

Knives in hands ready to continue skinning, the three men stared intently at the water looking for flashes of silver, the more fish the better.

Across the lawn from them, Caleb quietly called out, "Hey," to Tomas and Cheri who had wandered quite a ways down the valley, "come look, way cool." He pointed beside a mesh of bushes. They were rigid, broad-leaved starworts \covered in clusters of white flowers and pink-flowered vervain.

Cheri and Tomas were curious, Zach was bored, all three came to see what had finally excited the nervous disgraced accountant.

"What is it?" Cheri asked, enthused to see anything new in nature.

"There, so adorable, aren't they? Shh, they're sleeping," Caleb whispered softly, in awe for once.

Tucked just inside the shrubs were two tiny, baby cubs. Bear cubs. The hair stood up on Tomas' neck, he backed away.

"What's wrong?" Cheri and Caleb asked in unison.

Tomas stuttered, "Where- where there are babies, there's- there's going to be-" a horrendous roar drowned him out, "a mother-" he blurted, then screamed, "*run!*"

148

The flat-headed, short-snouted grizzly stood up on her hind legs making her well near six feet tall. Her mouth open big and wide revealed all her meat ripping teeth. She roared again then dropped on all fours and came barreling straight at them.

The roar got everyone's attention.

Shawn dropped the towel of fish he was just picking up and raced towards the sound with Daf and Beau on his heels. Hurtling over a small rise, Shawn's blood ran cold, almost stopped entirely.

A bear, at least 300 pounds was raging straight at Cheri, Tomas and Caleb! Zach was already yards away running in the opposite direction.

Grabbing the shotgun, Shawn pulled it down off his shoulder as he raced across the valley holding it in both hands.

In his fright, Tomas' feet churned without moving, then he gained traction and turned and ran into Cheri knocking her to the ground. He didn't stop- just took off as fast as he could. Cheri scrambled to her feet as the bear closed in.

Caleb stood frozen like a block of ice.

Roaring again, the bear reached them and slashed at Caleb. Cheri pushed him out of the way just as the bear swung. Cheri screamed, "Run Caleb!"

Instead of running towards the camp, Cheri ran the way Zach had gone.

Caleb still hadn't moved a muscle. Behind his glasses his eyes as wide as spinning wheels he stood in shock, and awe, fascinated at the enormous creature.

A deadly clawing monument on her hind legs with her arms bowed out only feet from him. Her mouth open exhibiting every tooth huge and glistening, the bear tipped

149

her head back and roared again, then dropped her head to Caleb. The only thing small on her was her round ears.

"Run, Caleb! Fucking run!" Shawn yelled, cocking the shotgun as he tore towards them. He couldn't shoot the bear, Caleb was directly in front of it. With the bear towering, falling to a crouch then towering again bullets might hit Caleb.

Then it was too late. The massive bear slashed her powerful paw out again and literally clawed the look of awe right off Caleb's face.

The accountant still stood. The bear pounced on him, taking him down, then clawed, ripped and bit and chomped and stomped the little man.

While in its frenzy destroying Caleb, the grizzly caught site of Cheri running, her bright hair like a matador's cape flapping.

The sow left Caleb and thundered after Cheri, the hump between the bear's shoulder blades a mass of rippling muscles in the sunlight. The bear cut her off, charged right in front of her so fast Cheri almost ran into it.

On its hind legs, like a howling monolith with teeth, the grizzly raised its arms, all ten claws spiked like steel spading forks-

Cheri stood paralyzed as if her feet were in cement.

"Down Cherriana!" Shawn shouted still over fifty feet away. "Drop to the ground, now-*drop*!"

She dropped and Shawn shot, and shot and shot again. The bear bellowed as the bullets slammed into it, then, its arms drooped, it swayed.

Shawn yelled, "Roll lass roll!" He kept racing head on towards her.

Beau rushed around one side of the bear, Daf the other, their guns aimed at the wobbling grizzly. Then she toppled like a building hit by a wrecking ball.

Directly under the falling mammoth, Cheri rolled like a log, covering her head with her hands as the 300 pound bear crashed to the ground, mere inches from the terrified girl.

Shawn pounded to her, threw his gun down, grabbed Cheri up off the ground and slammed her against his heaving chest and dashed away from the bear.

Beau and Daf rushed to the grizzly, their guns trained on it, watching to see if she was dead.

Hearing Cheri gasping for breath, with shaking hands Shawn lowered her to the ground, but held onto her.

She clung to him, white with fright and shuddering all over. Breaths like little panicked squeaks, her eyes polarized on the bear waiting for it to leap up and come back after her.

His arms around her like bands of steel, Shawn spoke huskily through the lump in his throat, "Tis all right now, baby, you're safe." He stroked a still shaking hand over her downy hair.

Daf went over and checked Caleb. He came back not looking too well shaking his head bleakly to Shawn's questioning look.

The others arrived to see what had happened.

Leena and Bella were holding each other's arms they were so scared.

Malone stood off to the side. He had only one, make that two interests, and a dead bear and deceased male prisoner were not one of them.

Jim Vega stood with his hand over his mouth. He was supposed to have been cuffed to Caleb.

"The- the- the babies," Cheri stammered, tears of terror and relief clogging her throat. "The- cubs," she pointed to the shrubs Caleb had discovered them in.

Shawn put his hand around Cheri's head and laid it against his shoulder, still stroking her hair.

With his gun raised, Beau strode to the bushes Cheri indicated. He was there only a moment before coming out and joining the couple. Shaking his head sadly, he said, "They're dead, at least a day."

"Oh no…" Cheri cried, pressing her face into Shawn's shoulder.

Shawn set the side of his face on her head, patting her back. His eyes on Beau, he murmured, "Tis better that way, lass. They have no one *tae* care for them, they would have died anyway."

To Beau he said quietly, "Thank God, we would have had *tae* report them if they were alive. We couldn't leave them-" seeing Beau's head shake slightly, he realized what he was saying and shut his mouth.

After taking a few moments to calm and catch their breaths, Shawn said, "Let's go back *tae* the campsite, we need *tae* regroup, decide what *tae* do about Caleb." His arm clutched so hard around Cheri's shoulders he feared he'd crush her. He had to force himself to keep his grip loose.

When the group returned to where they'd left their things, everyone just fell to the ground exhausted with terror from the horrifying attack.

"Well," Jim Vega said brightly, "the good thing is the bear is dead, and-"

Releasing Cheri, Shawn stomped over to the officer and got in his face. He snarled, "Oh yeah? That's good?" Shawn's face was so black and enraged, Jim backed off a few steps.

152

Shawn said through grit teeth, "Caleb is dead. The damned bear is endangered. I killed a fucking endangered animal you idiot. And we were this close," he held his thumb and finger a hair apart. "*Tae* losing," he looked at Cheri, his skin paled, voice dropped, "her."

"You had no choice to kill the bear, bro," Beau told him.

"I know," Shawn grated, still glaring fiercely at Jim. "We have a dead bear and a dead man. What's good about any of that, huh?"

Jim wiped his mouth, twice, stuck his hands in his pockets then pulled them out and nervously crossed them over his chest. "Well, uh, like, the girl is okay. You saved the, uh, girl."

Furiously, Shawn jerked his head at Cheri.

She was looking at him like she thought he was going to do damage to Jim.

The fury drained right out of him. He stalked over to a grove of trees and lit a cigarette. Beau and Daf followed him.

"Shawn," Daf said quietly, "we have to get word, we have to let them know about Caleb."

Shawn nodded, sucking insanely on his cigarette.

Dragging his hand again and again through his hair he said, "First we have *tae* wrap him the best we can and we'll have *tae* bury him. The animals will find him eventually but it'll slow them down. We need *tae* get away from here, the dead bodies will draw every beast within miles and then some."

Stamping the cigarette out in the dirt, Shawn said, "After we bury him, I know where *tae* go. It'll take some time. You guys stay with," he hesitated.

Drawing a shaky breath, he wiped his arm across his forehead. His gaze like a magnet remained unwavering on Cheri. "Stay with them. Keep everyone in a tight bunch.

Come with me." He led them to the hills opposite the stream and showed them the trail.

"Keep on this today for at least an hour. I know it will be slow going as usual with this group of inexperienced hikers but you need at least an hour away from here. Tomorrow, and the next day, stay on it heading north for six or seven miles, or as far as you can get them *tae* go. I'll find you, it'll be two days. Okay?"

The two men nodded soberly.

Tying his dark blue, long-sleeved shirt around his waist Shawn tucked his white t-shirt back down inside his belt.

They trooped back to the others. After retrieving some tools they had taken from the first cabin, the men dug a hole which was backbreaking difficult in the hard packed rocky ground. Then they wrapped Caleb in his blankets and buried him.

Without a word to anyone, Shawn took off over the closest hill.

Cheri sat on a fallen tree, her hands folded in her lap, watching Shawn's black hair disappear over the crest.

Beau came and sat down beside her. "He has to go, Cheri lass, he has a duty to fulfill. I can't explain it to you, maybe later after all this is over. He didn't trust himself to talk to you before he left. I can't explain that to you either." His cheerful grin apologetic.

She turned to the bearded redhead. "Beau, I may be green, but I'm not stupid." A rueful grin tugged the corner of her mouth remembering Shawn calling her that the night she ran from Ritchie. Then her smile fell remembering the rest of that night. Shawn's amazing kisses, then his rejection.

Sighing, she said, "Anyway, there's something going on here, we're not just a group of prisoners that happened to roll down a hill in a bus and crash and are trying to find our way

154

out of this wilderness. You, Daf, and...him," she couldn't bear to say his name, "the three of you are not what you say you are, and you're definitely up to something."

Cheri had the satisfaction of seeing the effect of her words tumble across Beau's freckled face.

She also saw his jaw clench in resolution. He wasn't going to tell her anything. She already figured that. Her gaze drifted back to the hill Shawn had disappeared over.

Pulling her feet up on the tree, she wrapped her arms around her knees and recalled the sight of Shawn terrified, *for her*, racing to her, killing the grizzly to save her.

Remembering too, when he had hurtled through the dense brush and threw her up in his arms to keep the wolves from getting to her.

She rested her chin on her knee and tucked the memories away.

Chapter Twelve

The group did as Shawn instructed, hiked as long as they could staying in a tight knot.

Beau and Daf noticed Zach had not returned after the bear attack.

Tomas came back with his tail between his legs, but even as they left the next morning, Zachary Stockton was a no show.

Malone looked unconcerned. The blond Hulk gave him the willies. He hoped he'd fallen in quicksand or something and was gone for good.

Bella wiped at tears all day and night.

Daf and Beau knew if Shawn was still there, one of them would have gone after Zachary, but with only the two of them they knew they had to stay with the group to protect them.

The evenings had grown several degrees warmer, much to Beau's chagrin. He had hoped to be the bed warmer for Cheri in Shawn's absence.

Alas, it was probably for the best, he decided. He already liked her a lot, and although Shawn denied it to hell and back, he had staked his claim on her. She slept on her own sandwiched between him and Daf.

After the second day, they woke to find Bella missing.

Staying within sight of the camp, the rest of the group searched and called for her, but she was gone.

Seeing her backpack was gone too, Leena said, "I bet she's with Zach." They considered this and everyone agreed Bella had run off to be with her beastly lover.

At the very end of the second day as the lead, descending part of the mountain on a crisscrossed trail, Daf rounded a corner and came to a horrible halt. He saw buzzards flapping around a few feet into the brush.

Telling everyone to stay put, he slung the shotgun off his back and into both hands. Leaving the group, he crept through the tall grass into the web of shrubbery.

Everyone jumped at the shot he fired.

Leena shrieked at Beau, "Well? Aren't you going to go see what happened?"

"*Na,*" Beau replied calmly, but he had his gun drawn. "Only one of us leaves at a time. I stay to protect the rest of you."

In minutes, Daf came out of the brush, his brown face ashen and tight in disturbed strain.

Beau asked, "What is it, *brither?*"

Daf glanced around at the group, he was unable to disguise his distress. They would all find out eventually anyway. "It is…was…um…Bella."

"What?" Malone spouted, gripping Daf's arm in disbelief. "What the hell are you saying, Jamieson? You shot her?"

"Leave off him, Malone," Beau warned, stepping closer to the men, his gun still in his hands.

Knowing he was giving shocking news, Daf didn't slam the deputy for touching him. He just said with sadness filling his voice, "*Na,* she was dead. I shot a round to run off the vultures." His bleak eyes found Beau's stunned blues. Malone released Daf's arm like he'd been burned.

Everyone was shocked into silence. Tomas was so stricken he looked like he was having a heart attack.

Jim Vega uttered, "How?"

Shoving his shotgun up and bracing it over his shoulder, Daf said, "I'm not positive. She had…uh…a lot of bruises. It looks like, ah, her neck was broken." A collective gasp again burst from the group.

"I think maybe she was killed then tossed off the side of the mountain which would explain how she got here before we did."

Seeing a vulture sneaking back into the bushes, Daf said, "We need to, ah, see to her."

Looking around behind both his shoulders, Jim whispered, "I bet it was that freak, Stockton." He didn't need to hear the verbal affirmations to know everyone agreed with him.

They were all shaken. Everyone's eyes darted nonstop around the area ready to flee if the blond giant suddenly came charging at them.

Daf, Tomas and Jim went and took care of the task of burying Bella. Once they finished throwing the last bit of dirt on the grave, they left a mark at the site and on the trail so it could be found later.

On the fourth day, everyone was voicing their concern. Where was Shawn? Were they lost? What's going to happen to them? Was Zach out there stalking them, going to kill them off one by one? They were tired of fish and berries.

Then they came to the end of the trail.

Daf announced, "We'll stay here and wait for Shawn."

Tomas snorted sitting on a stump. "Come on. Face it, he's dead."

Shrugging at the women's sharp intakes, trying to stuff his gnawing fear, he continued harshly, "Or he skipped out on his own leaving us to die out here."

Everyone glared at him. He huffed, "Admit it. Beau said Shawn would be back in two days. It's been four." His gaze stretched across to Cheri who stood biting her fingernails to the nubs.

Off to the side, Vance Malone was in a bad flux. He needed that damned Scotsman to get him to the Grand Crest. What if he didn't return? Maybe the bastard made a run for it after all. Maybe he's going for the gold himself.

Out loud, he groused, "Fucking Darkonn, leaving us out here alone with that psycho running around out there somewhere. Just like in those slasher movies, the Mohawk monster is probably going to take us all out one-by-one. Bella was the first."

Ruffling the hair on the back of his neck with nervous fingers, Malone wondered out loud, "Maybe he killed Darkonn…"

Cheri cupped her hands over her mouth to stifle her cry.

Beau shot Malone a dirty look. "Maybe you should keep your *bluidy* thoughts to yourself you fucking *idjit*."

Clearing the scowl from his face, tanned from years of being outside it still freckled, Beau took Cheri's elbow and moved her to sit on a fallen tree.

He sat down next to her and put his arm around her shoulders drawing her against his side. "Come on *lassie*, don't give up the faith. Our Shawn will return. I promise, *wee hinnie*." Hugging her, he separated a lock of her hair, wrapped it around a freckled finger then watched it unravel.

Dropping down on the other side of Cheri, Daf pulled out a rag and wiped his forehead of dust and sweat. Stuffing the rag back in his pocket, he clinched his fingers together and set them on his knees. Giving Cheri a steady smile with strong assurance in his voice, he said implacably, "He'll be back."

"Tis heartwarming to hear such trust, *ma brither*s." Shawn's steely deep voice suddenly stirred the air.

They all looked up.

The black-haired Scotsman materialized in the middle of the clearing. He entered the area slowly, in dusty jeans, shirt sleeves bunched up over the solid forearms, hands on his hips even leaner than a few days ago.

Like a buccaneer without the sword, his dark eyes probed Beau's arm wrapped around Cheri and his fingers in her hair. Shawn couldn't look directly at her, after four days the sight of the beauty made his knees buckle.

Grinning at him, Beau hugged Cheri tighter. Then seeing Shawn's brows rake down and his skin darken, he let her go, got up and trod to him.

Daf was already slapping Shawn on the back, whispering in his ear, "We were getting a bit concerned bro. Glad you're okay."

Beau and Shawn fist-bumped then hugged, now Shawn did look at Cheri over his friend's shoulder.

Tears gleamed in her eyes making them look huge and bright. Like before when he climbed in the hole after Caleb fell in, he wondered if they were tears of relief he was safe and back, or tears of disappointment he'd returned.

"We need *tae* talk," Shawn said curtly and stalked off to where they could speak privately but keep an eye on the group.

The three men huddled by several shading trees. Daf told him, "Bella's dead, Shawn."

Surprising them, Shawn said, "I know. I was half down the mountain when I saw the vultures. I got close enough *tae* hear you found her then double-backed *tae* report it. That's why it took me so long."

Beau said, "We think it was that whacko Zachary Stockton."

Staring at the ground, his hands in his pockets, Shawn nodded in agreement. "Aye." The earlier morning air had been cool, Shawn threw his long-sleeved shirt on over his t-shirt. He scanned the surrounding area like he was looking for something.

"I tried *tae* find him. His tracks were good, he's so big he snaps branches and smashes the dirt and grass like a stumbling ox, so he's easy *tae* trace. Then he got *tae* a river and the tracks disappeared into the water. He's a sociopathic thug but he's canny.

"We have *tae* keep a watch out for signs of him as we go. Like Marx, he's probably following us. We need *tae* make sure everyone understands *tae* not be alone ever. The women can go do their *preevat* business together as they've been doing, but we need *tae* stand guard relatively close *tae* them."

Shawn shot a quick glance back at the camp. Malone glared with wrought suspicion and relief at him. Jim and Tomas and Leena looked downright thrilled to see him.

Cheri moved over to where Leena was sitting near a sprout of wild purple hyacinths and white clover, they spoke quietly, but both of their eyes were on Shawn.

Although she tried to mask it, Cheri's expression was of sad aching rather than disappointment.

Shawn caught her emotion. Her face was like an open book. It pained him to see that she ached as much as he did, yet he couldn't fight the way it warmed his heart.

Back to his mates, he said, "One of us has *tae* stay awake and guard at night, we'll take turns, and during the day we have *tae* take extra precautions."

The other two men nodded with him.

Daf said, "The trail ran out, Shawn, we had to stop here." Sounding concerned that they'd missed the rest of the trail, he lifted his Stetson off to drag a rag across his head and face and down his neck.

Tucking the rag back in his pocket, huge biceps contracted with his movements. He set the hat back on, tugging it down low over his forehead to keep his pony-tailed dreads loose.

His black boots were dirty from the trail, and there were hand prints on his black jeans where he'd been wiping his dusty palms. Eyes dark and smooth as mink waited for his friend's response.

Shawn grinned, and clapped him on his brick hard shoulder. "I know. Don't worry, I still know the way. Let's catch all the daylight we can get." He moved to where Cheri was sitting and held out a hand to her.

She hesitated, he was getting used to that so he waited. Then, she put her hand in his and he pulled her gracefully to her feet.

Leena suddenly jumped up in front of Cheri and threw herself into Shawn's arms, shoving Cheri back and almost knocking Shawn over. "Oh, tall, dark and hot we were so worried, I'm soooo glad you're safe!"

Her arms wrapped around his back, she pressed her breasts staggeringly hard against his chest and smacked her mouth right on his.

Shawn reached behind his back to get at her wrists to untangle the tight grasp of her hands. He had to pull them apart roughly because she wasn't letting go. Jerking his head back from hers, he pushed her away, wiped his mouth with his sleeve.

"Fuck off, Leena, how many times do I have *tae* tell you *tae* keep your hands off of me." His gaze swept to Cheri, her eyes like shocked bluebonnets watching in bitterness.

She suddenly swiveled and strode away as fast as she could to where Beau and Daf were waiting, grinning like village idiots.

Beau shook his head and said joking, "Poor Shawn, the women are always throwing themselves at him."

"You're jealous," Daf teased, elbowing him in the side laughing.

One shoulder hopped, Beau grinned. "Sometimes, right now not so much." The blowsy Leena was nowhere near his cup of tea.

Daf elbowed him again then gestured with his head to Cheri as she joined them.

Her mouth was a firm line, the stress of keeping her expression unreadable made her skin stretch taut. With a face that showed everything, she wasn't succeeding anyway.

"Lass," setting a giant paw on her shoulder, Daf said gently, "trust me, he doesn't want her. He likes to do his own choosing, and believe me, she is not the one he wants."

Winding her arms around her body, Cheri shrugged with studied indifference. "Who cares? I don't. We all have way more important things to be concerned about and focus our attention on than teenage drama."

The two men smothered their knowing smirks, she was already embarrassed and hurting, they didn't want to make her feel worse. They watched Shawn berate Leena.

She only smiled and nodded, tried to touch him, he swatted her hands away like she was a fly that was trying his patience, and he was clearly losing his grip on trying to remain a gentleman and not crack her one.

Stalking away from the grasping officer, Shawn strode angrily right to his friends. He spoke to them all but looked at Cheri, his voice impatient and cold he ordered, "Let's go."

When it didn't look like she was going to move, he curled his fingers around her arm and pulled her next to him.

"Daf," he said to the Black bruiser, "you lead as soon as I find the trial."

Daf saluted him and took his place behind Shawn until Shawn indicated the trail then Daf moved ahead.

At their break, Shawn went over to Malone. Since he didn't do that very often, Malone watched him warily, one brow arched in leery suspense.

"What is it, Darkonn?" he asked, his florid face set. Expecting the worst like Shawn was going to tell him he really didn't know where the crest he sought was or something like that.

Shawn stopped a couple of feet from the deputy. He hated getting too close to the despicable man. "We're near."

Malone's brows shot up, then lowered in suspicion. "Near what?"

His crooked grin mirthless, Shawn replied steadily, "Grand Crest."

Malone's brows jammed up again in disbelief but distrustful hope. "Where? How far? You're not teasing me are you, Darkonn, because if you are-"

The side of Shawn's lip pulled up drily, "I would not *tease* you, Malone." The fact was the guy made him so sick he never spoke directly to him unless he had to. He swung his arm up and arced it towards and up the mountains.

"There. Tis not all that far from here but will be really difficult *tae* get *tae*. We have *tae* go up that mountain and tis steeper than it looks. It'll be another day or two before we reach it."

Greed and glee struck Malone's ruddy face. His eyes lit up and he smiled for the first time since leaving the bus. "No kidding? We're that close?" Visions of gold dancing in his head he looked excitedly up the mountain. The setting sun streaked his face making his flaccid skin look jaundiced.

His reverential gaze still on the mountain, he said to Shawn, "Well, let's go. What are we waiting for?"

"We're staying here for the night, there's a body of water nearby. We can all finally get a soak and we want *tae* do it before sundown when the animals will be around. Like I said, it will be a difficult trek. We have *tae* do it in full sunlight. Even so it will be strenuous and dangerous. We'll start out right after dawn."

He turned away from the deputy who was disappointed to have to wait, but his small brown eyes still gleamed greedily.

Shawn moved back to the group that was shrinking almost by the day. "We're staying here for the night. I can tell you with fair certainty that we should be back into civilization in less than a week."

"A week!" Tomas blurted. "We're stuck in this primitive hellhole for another week? You've got to be kidding."

Shawn said mildly, "We were way out in a range of mountains in the middle of thousands of acres of nothing when the bus rolled a half mile down the slope. With a vehicle it would have taken some time *tae* cover this uninhabited land, on foot..." He shrugged a shoulder.

His mouth pushed out, Tomas grumbled, "Yeah, but another freakin' week."

"What would you expect? We're damned lucky *tae* have been able *tae* secure the supplies we came across." Of course Shawn couldn't tell them they would have been out long ago if it wasn't for the gold bars Malone was after.

Daf and Beau took off straight for the water to hopefully catch some fish.

Vega and Trent gathered wood for a fire while Cheri and Leena broke up the smaller branches. Shawn built the fire,

Malone sat on a big rock like a lump watching everyone work.

Sitting around the fire the group ate and chatted quietly. They didn't need the fire for warmth this night, it was warm enough without one, but they made a small fire to cook the fish.

Shawn left with Jim Vega for a smoke away from the others. When they returned, he kicked dirt on the fire putting it out.

Shawn hated to draw notice from anyone in the area with the smoke, but they had to eat. At least it wouldn't be there all night to point to their location.

With the fire out, some of the people had already laid out their blankets and settled down on them.

Cheri was sitting on a log between Beau and Daf deliberately not looking in Shawn's direction, even when he started towards them.

Beau had told him earlier that Cheri thought Shawn had the hots for Leena. That she believed Shawn had used Cheri to provoke Leena's jealousy.

Shawn's lip curled up in a 'you're funny, ha, ha smile' then saw by Beau's obnoxious grin that he was serious. The redhead had reminded him that if he didn't want the girl then Beau sure did.

"Tis time for bed. Come with me, Cherriana." Shawn held his hand down ignoring the sophomorically winking, semi chagrined look on Beau's mocking face.

When Cheri put her hand in his, Shawn pulled her gently to her feet and led her to where he had laid out their blankets.

Without a word or fuss, Cheri knelt down and slid under her blanket. A shuddered rolled through her when she felt Shawn climb in his next to her, and she held her breath.

Though it was warm enough, Shawn still stretched his arms out, looping them around her and pulled her to him.

She didn't resist.

He tucked one long arm under her neck and dropped the other over her waist pulling her against his torso, his knees curled behind hers.

God, he had missed her. All he could think about when he was climbing the mountain was Cheri. Only a few days gone, and his body and mind had ached to hear her lilting voice, take in her bonny face, feel the softness of her body meshed against his, safely enveloped in his arms that had panged to hold her.

Hearing her sigh out her held breath and relax in his embrace, Shawn nuzzled his chin, just touching her hair.

Savoring the flume of her sweet essence, he slept like a baby.

Chapter Thirteen

They used the mountain-fed lake again to clean up before heading out in the morning.

Shawn remonstrated severely how precarious their travel was going to be. "Follow the person's moves in front of you. Don't deviate at all. The mountainside isn't incredibly steep but tis a good steady incline. Watch for loose stones, keep your packs square on your backs so they don't shift and pull you *tae* the side. All right, let's go."

Shawn went first. He had wrapped a rope around Cheri and tied it to Daf. He told Daf to stay behind Jim and Leena and keep Cheri in front of him. If she slipped, Daf could catch her.

Stalwart Daf could hike a mountain like a goat. He and Shawn and Beau had climbed some of the biggest mountains in the world. For the three friends this was just a hill compared to those.

It was slow going with people who had never hiked before this trek much less up anything steeper than a hill.

The worst was Vance Malone. As eager as he was to get to the crest, he also was the most out of shape. He was huffing and puffing and wheezing before they'd gone a half a mile. Beau was at the bottom so Malone was slowing him down.

Shawn had to tamp back his speed to accommodate the hefty red-faced deputy. He didn't want any of them to get too far from the rest of the group.

Besides the danger of the mountain, psycho Zach was still on the loose somewhere and probably still trailing them. Ritchie was behind them as well.

Occasionally, Shawn would spot the deputy. He wasn't unaware that Leena left things on the trail for him, but he was surprised Zach hadn't taken Ritchie out yet just for fun.

They had to stop and take a lot of breaks.

Shawn led them to a wide expanse of tree dotted valley strung between two mountain peaks like a hammock. Fluffy cotton balls of clouds like sheep hung languidly in the blue bandana sky, thankfully veiling some of the blinding sun.

Everyone shrugged off their packs and dropped on the ground. Malone, Tomas, Jim and Leena flopped right on their backs and laid there.

Shawn untied Cheri from Daf. While winding the rope around his arm he muttered to her, "Go with Leena, *tae* you, know..."

Cheri glanced over to where Leena was lying down and headed in her direction. Shawn wandered over to where Beau and Daf were conferring about where they were and how much longer to reach their destination.

Cheri took off her backpack and set it on the ground, removed her biodegradable toilet paper and helped Leena get back up so they could go relieve themselves.

Shawn called out to them, "Don't go further than a few feet in the brush!"

"Yes, papa," Leena yelled back impishly. Straying far wasn't a problem, neither of the women enjoyed the scaly scraping of prickly bushes or the bugs that lurked in the undergrowth waiting to pounce. After the bear episode they were reluctant to even leave the men at all.

Leena, Tomas and Jim all had guns issued to them for the transport, but Leena had never had to use hers before other than target practice, which she wasn't very good at, and she was anxious about having to possibly fire the weapon at a charging attacking animal.

Figuring Malone would probably shoot him in the back the second the gold was located, Shawn had taken his weapon from him right off the bat and instructed no one to give him one of theirs.

Quickly conducting their business the women hurried back to the group.

A lunch of edible plants and the survival packaged food sustained them. The entire group was so exhausted, Shawn allowed them an hour or so to nap. Happy about that, they all took the opportunity to rest.

An hour of rest, the sun at its highest peak, they stretched and yawned, refilled canteens switching back and forth to ones that had bleach tablets in the since the last stop for water.

After throwing water on their faces, they gathered together to start trudging towards the cleft that Malone envisioned the rocky sides studded with gold bars, he was barely able to contain his glee.

Suddenly gunshots rang out!

Not able to tell at first where they were coming from but hearing a bullet hit a tree near him, Shawn brought his shotgun down off his back and yelled, "Make for the trees, back by the mountainside! Keep your heads down!" He grabbed Cheri's hand and ran with her to the mountain wall.

More bullets banged in the air and whizzed by slamming into trees.

Shawn rushed back to a small cave they had just passed. Dodging screaming bullets everyone ran to where they saw Shawn heading, except Daf and Beau. Drawing their weapons, they split off, moving silently and swiftly out to opposite directions staying in the cover of trees.

At the cave, Shawn darted in to make sure there weren't any animals in there then he told Cheri to get inside and tossed his backpack in.

When Leena arrived, he quickly told her to stay inside the cave by the entrance. "Leena, let me see your gun, I want *tae* make sure it's loaded."

She nervously handed him her weapon. Turning slightly towards the light, Shawn opened it then closed it a second later and handed it back to her. "Okay Leena, if anyone but one of us comes near, shoot him. Don't give a warning, just shoot."

Her face white and hands shaking, Leena nodded and hurried into the shelter of the cave.

As the others ran up, Shawn said quietly urgent, "Jim and Tomas, leave your packs, draw your weapons and come with me." The two men looked nervous but did as he said.

Malone demanded, "Give me a gun, Darkonn, you're going to need all the help you can get."

Not sparing him a glance, Shawn replied, "No way."

Malone argued, "Darkonn, don't be an ass, I can help." He held his hand out for a weapon.

Shawn ignored him and turned to run back out. Cheri hurried over to him. "Wait! Shawn, I can help! Show me how to use a- a gun and I can help! Or I can throw rocks or give me a knife and I-"

He smiled down at her, then his expression turned serious. "You stay here. Do not leave this cave. I can't do what I need *tae* do if I'm worried about you. I can't have the distraction. Please." He bent slightly, grasped the back of the head and held her while he kissed her, hard.

Then he grabbed the shotgun and jogged off with Jim and Tomas yards behind him.

Keeping low, Shawn raced along the mountain wall to a thicket of trees. He could hear a constant barrage of gunfire all around him as he ran.

Without warning, a man sprung up in front of him, his grin as evil as the pistol aimed at Shawn's heart.

"Don't move you fuck! Raise yer hands an turn aroun'." His cocky voice glottal and dumb, he waved his gun at Shawn motioning him to turn around with his back to him.

He looked like he sounded, husky and uneducated with teeth missing and unintelligent eyes. "Yer goin' ta take me to the others. You got women, we seen 'em. Get movin' before I plug ya."

"All right, take it easy," Shawn said calmly. He raised his hands shoulder height and went to take a step. But he didn't actually take the step, he faked it, but the clod was already walking assuming Shawn was moving, he plowed right into Shawn's back.

As soon as he hit Shawn, Shawn rolled causing the man to roll too and stumble. In a flash, Shawn was behind the thug shoving one arm around the man's neck in a half-Nelson, but the man whipped out a huge knife and jabbed it back towards Shawn's belly.

Shifting his stomach in a flash to the side, the blade missed by a hair, Shawn grabbed two of the man's fingers bending them back so the man was forced to lean in that direction. When his fingers snapped with audible cracks, Shawn released them.

The man's howls reverberated through the forest. Shawn grabbed the man's other arm that he still held the knife in, jerked it up and back, breaking his shoulder. Then he swiveled the thug around to face him.

Ignoring the man's screams, Shawn bent his arm, pushing it down, forcing the knife back, then with a hard fast thrust he shoved it straight into the guy's gut.

The man's eyes wide with shock, he looked down at the knife sticking out of his gullet then to Shawn. Shawn gave him a little shove, he dropped like a sack of mud.

Taking the man's gun and yanking the knife out of his belly, Shawn tucked both weapons in his own belt. Wiping his hands on his jeans, he scanned the area until he saw a blotch of blue flannel behind the cover of trees and shrub up the mountain.

He darted from tree to tree until he reached a pile of boulders that jutted dozens of feet up in the air. He heard Tomas and Jim's footsteps pounding after him.

His voice on the edge of panic, Jim whispered, "Shawn, Shawn, where are you?"

Both men jumped a mile when Shawn whispered right beside them, "I'm here, let's go."

He started towards the cover where Beau was and whispered to Jim, "You go right over there behind those rocks, keep your head down." As Jim took off, Shawn turned to Tomas and pointed in the opposite direction. "Tomas, go over about twenty feet and up about ten."

Tomas stood frozen.

Shawn gripped his arm and shook him. "Come on, Trent, man up, get over there."

The deputy just stood with his eyes unblinking and mouth open, sweating bullets.

Sighing with disgust, Shawn said, "Go back *tae* the cave, warn them ahead that you're coming or Leena might shoot you."

Tomas still didn't move until Shawn gave him a little shove with a brusque. "*Go.*" Tomas took off running like he was being chased by a mountain lion.

Shawn had debated taking Trent's gun but figured with only Leena armed, Trent might pull through if direct danger threatened.

Climbing towards the blue flannel, he whistled then called in a loud whisper, "Beau-"

Seeing the redhead pop out and grin at him, Shawn climbed over and behind some boulders to reach him. He had to lunge the last few feet as a rush of bullets rang and bashed, chipping the rocks following him.

Hitting the ground, Shawn scrambled quickly to his feet and in a crouch ran over to Beau. Beau had his shotgun braced on a boulder with one hand, and his pistol next to it.

"Who is it?" Shawn asked. Sticking paper in his ears, he propped his own shotgun on the rock and lowered his head to squint through the scope.

After shooting several rounds, Beau said, "I think tis those trappers you saw. There's one with a t-shirt that says 'I'd kill for a brewskie' on it, you had mentioned seeing that."

Cupping his hands around his mouth, Shawn yelled out, "This is the police. Lay down your weapons and come out with your hands on your heads." His words were met with a volley of gunfire.

His mouth pulled in, he shrugged one shoulder. "It was worth a try."

Seeing a light flash down by a grove of trees, Shawn fired repeatedly at the light. After a second he saw a man stumble out from behind a tree. Holding a hand over his chest, he staggered a few feet then fell.

"Nice one, bro, I've been trying for him forever," Beau crowed.

"Where's Daf?" Shawn's keen eyes searched the area for evidence of other shooters. Seeing flashes, he shot back.

Beau mumbled while firing his own weapon, "To the right, that bunch of rocks and trees up the mountainside." Still shooting, he motioned up with his head.

Then he cheered quietly, "Yeah! Got one!" A man tumbled down from a 50-foot high stance up the mountain. His body banged and bumped hitting rocks all the way to the ground.

"Do we have any idea how many there are?" Shawn asked, shooting at a man that was running a dodging crooked line and shooting wildly. He missed him, then the man dove from a rock into high brush.

Shawn shot as he was airborne, the man dropped like a dead duck. He didn't get up but Shawn couldn't see if he was actually dead or alive because of the tall shrubbery.

Slowly the shots grew further and further apart until the return fire stopped completely. In the distance they could hear engines turn over and roar away. A cloud of dust rose up in a plume quarter mile away.

Lowering his gun, Beau wiped the sweat and dirt off his face with his shirttail and said, "Dunno how many. You got two, I got three."

Standing up but staying bent over, Shawn said, "I left another one down just past the cave. Let's check the rest of the area out." He whistled short and sharp, then he and Beau cautiously crept from behind the rocks.

Scanning the area as they moved, sweeping up the mountain, down it, over to the trees and rocks and back again. Hearing a noise behind them they both swung around with their weapons raised.

"It's me," Daf said, approaching them from cover.

"Could you see anything?" Shawn asked him.

"Some," Daf answered. Setting his shotgun hooked to a strap over his shoulder, he lowered it down his back to the side of his backpack, his shirt dragged up with it.

Releasing the strap, he tugged his black t-shirt back down and wiped one sweaty hand on his jeans. Still grasping a gun in his other hand, he switched it to his free hand to dry that palm on his pants.

"You guys took out five, but we need to check on the one that fell in the grass to make sure about him. I got two, and I think three more made a run for it in a couple of jeeps."

His eyes surveying the area nonstop for any movement, listening for any sound, Shawn said quietly, "*Ma brithers, we need tae go check the bodies, see if there's ID on any of them.*"

Pushing his black hair out of his eyes, he looked up to where Jim Vega had gone. "Jim," he called out. He could see movement, a swatch of plaid showed and some leaves rustled.

"Come down, carefully, keep your head down," Shawn told him.

It took Jim a few minutes to climb down from his perch. The fright of the shootout was evident in the way his eyes, light brown and round like hazelnuts were sprung wide. But there was swaggering pride in his walk as he came nearer to the other men.

"You did great, Jim," Shawn praised the smaller darker man. He clapped him on his strong but twiggy shoulder.

"I didn't hit any of them, Shawn," Jim said, sounding disappointed in his part. He bowed his head slightly, plucking at a tear in his plaid shirt with spare knobby fingers.

"Doesn't matter," Shawn replied. "You were courageous and did as you were told, and you fired. That made them know there were more of us and we were armed. We didn't really want *tae* kill anyone, tis unfortunate that they forced us *tae* defend ourselves."

Holding the bottom of his shotgun, Beau slung it over his shoulder and commented, "I hope they're gone for good."

Daf remarked ominously, "I doubt it."

"Why?" Shawn asked him. Rolling up the long sleeves of his dark blue shirt that covered his white T, he straightened the strap that crossed his chest which held the shotgun over his back.

Using the side of his boots, he pushed down the legs of his jeans that had ridden up when he had climbed the mountainside. Wiping his hands on his pants, he set his palms on his hips, his strong fingers curving around the lean sinew.

The men looked at Daf in question. "I'm pretty sure I saw a bit of a yellow Mohawk," Daf answered.

"Shit," Shawn spat. Eyes narrowing, he scanned the area, his lips set in a tight grim line.

"Yeah," Daf agreed, and Beau nodded with him.

"Okay, let's go check the area out, make sure they're gone and look after the dead men. But I think we should stay together now." Shawn strode quickly but cautiously through the grass.

The men fanned again leaving around ten feet between them as they scoped out the scene. They located all of the dead men, dragged their bodies to one place and checked them for ID but as they had expected they had nothing on them. They took their weapons and ammunition.

"Do we have to bury all these guys?" Beau asked, casting a baleful eye on the group of deceased men.

"*Na,*" Shawn replied wearily, dragging his hand through his hair then let it drop to the side. "I'll have *tae* leave again and report this." He may have felt reluctant to have to go on the rigorous trek again to make a report but he would never say it or show it. "Let's go back *tae* the cave, they must be frantic by now."

As they neared the cave, the men called out announcing their presence so they wouldn't get shot by a nervous Leena or panicked Tomas.

Cheri poked her head out first. Seeing them, she ran out and straight to Shawn.

She didn't give a darn if he cared for her or not, she'd bitten her fingers almost clean off sitting there listening to the nonstop shooting and picturing the black-haired man falling dead to the ground.

Chapter Fourteen

Cheri hurled herself at him.

Grunting from the impact, Shawn's arms swung right around and held her tight. He turned his head to lay it on top of hers. Feeling her chest hitching, he knew she was crying.

Relishing her closeness for a moment, he tipped her chin and tilted her head up to see the tear filled blue eyes.

Embarrassed that she was crying all the time, Cheri closed her eyes and tried to pull away. She never was this weepy before, her weakness shamed her.

The others emerged from the cave, everyone was staring at them.

Leena, grateful she hadn't had to fire her gun, gave Shawn and Cheri a doleful look then shrugged as if saying, *whatever*. She traipsed over to ask Beau what happened.

Malone came out and sat on a rock. Plunking his elbows on his knees, he set his chin in his hands and sulked.

"Where is Tomas?" Daf's low heavy voice disturbed the quiet.

"Huh?" Shawn tore his gaze from Cheri's to quickly search the area. Before he could go inside the cave to check there, Cheri said, "He left."

Shawn's raven brows rounded in shock. "What do you mean he left?"

Standing next to Beau, Leena told them, "When Tomas returned, his face was white as snow, then after a minute it turned bright red. He wouldn't look at us, you could tell he was humiliated and ashamed because of his cowardliness."

"But where did he go?" Shawn asked, first Leena then he looked at Malone then down at Cheri.

Cheri answered him, "We don't know. He stood by the door for a few minutes. He looked so jarred from the gunfire, so terrified, we all were." Shuddering, she put her hand on Shawn's chest. Shawn covered her hand with his own.

Malone muttered, "He mumbled something about fish in a barrel. I think he was afraid the bad guys were going to come here and kill us."

Leena nodded in agreement. "Yeah, I think he felt safer out there than trapped inside the cave. He just left."

"We'll check the perimeter," Daf said, lifted his chin to Shawn while tapping Beau's shoulder for him to follow. The two men took off to look for Tomas.

Letting out an uneasy breath, his arm still around her, Shawn led Cheri away from the remaining group over to the side of the hard wall of the cave where they couldn't be heard.

He didn't miss Beau's grin though as the redhead started to search the trees on right side of the cave for signs of where Tomas could be.

Moving Cheri so she was leaning back against the rocky wall, Shawn faced her and set a hand on the rock near her shoulder. "What is it, lass, why are you crying?" His brows drew down in sudden anger, he ground out coarsely, "Did that fucking Malone-"

"No!" She quickly put two fingers on his mouth to hush him. "It's nothing." She clasped her hands in front of her and bowed her head.

Surprised when she touched his mouth, Shawn had unconsciously opened his lips to kiss her fingers or lick them, but she pulled them away too soon.

He put his thumb and finger to her chin and lifted it to make her look at him. "You don't fear for Tomas do you? Are your tears for him?" Shawn inhaled quickly then exhaled his jealousy out. "Tell me, Cherriana, why are you crying?"

Peering up at him through wet lashes, she spoke so softly he almost couldn't hear her. "I was...worried...about...you, you jerk..." her words trailed off as her eyes dropped. "I'm feeling...relieved."

Reassured and thrilled, Shawn brushed his knuckles across the side of her face, then slid his long fingers along her delicate jaw cradling it.

His thumb stroking her cheek, he said quietly, "You didn't need *tae* worry, *nesh leamin*, we are experienced..." he left off, 'we know what we're doing.' "But," he couldn't help it, lowering his head, he said, "I shouldn't say it but I am pleased that you cared."

His mouth covering hers, he muzzled the nagging voice in the back of his head that told him to stop and walk away.

The fortitude he'd sworn to himself to not kiss her again disappeared like a snowflake in the hot sun. Fiercely locking his mouth on hers, Shawn spread her lips apart, enticing her to respond to his tempestuous intensity.

Wanting to feel her body touching his, he slid an arm around her, swung her around so he was now leaning against the rock and pulled her in close between his spread legs continuing his mouth's ardent pursuit of hers.

Cheri tugged her head back a little, "But Leena-"

Shawn splayed a large hand on her slender back drawing her closer, imbedding her soft womanly curves into his hard masculine body. With his other hand still behind her head, he urged her mouth back to his.

Against her lips, he murmured, "There is no Leena, there has never been a Leena except in Leena's mind. There's only you, you and me," and he kissed her.

Pulling back slightly, he whispered, "I tried, *leamin*, I tried *tae* stay away from you. Resist my feelings for you, tis too late now."

Sliding a hand under her long hair, he lifted it off her shoulders then pushed the thick waves to flow down her back. He shifted his legs further apart so he would be lower and even out their height.

His hands returned to span her waist and draw her in tighter against him, pressing her so he could feel those lush curves contact every part of his torso.

Her torn and stained white blouse with its frilly collar and few remaining tiny pearl buttons was tied at her midriff. Shawn moved his hands to between the blouse and her jeans to feel the warm fine skin on the curve of her waist.

Smiling at her tiny shiver, he fused his mouth on hers, groaning at the fullness of her soft as velvet petals. Prodding them apart, he grazed the inside of her lips with his tongue. Sliding his tongue across her teeth, he then thrust in to taste and tangle and stir her tongue.

She was ready to learn. Tentative at first, she eagerly followed what he did.

Massaging the breadth of his shoulders with exploratory fingers, Cheri shyly yet brazenly unbuttoned the top buttons of his shirt, pushed the lapels apart. When she lightly ran her fingertips along his collar bone his rough intake of breath was an audible groan.

The moment he had touched her, he grew hard. He had every time since the second he laid eyes on her, even a glance would do it. But he had labored to keep that part of him away from her, even when they slept with their bodies coiled together. Feeling the heat of her tentative shy hands even on just his shoulders was exquisite torture.

His thoughts flashbacked to when he had wanted to grab Malone's head with his hands and rip it off his neck that first day when he watched the deputy handcuffing her. Restraining her in that vulnerable and helpless position on the bus with her arms trapped up, and was climbing all over her like a horny swine.

Chained himself, he had been impotent to help her other than call Leena's attention to Malone's actions. Shawn told himself he was no better than the deputy. Look at him, now he had his hands all over her.

Yet, he was not forcing her against her will, *she* came to *him* and tore away his last shreds of resistance, and she was willingly it seemed, enjoyably touching him.

She fit perfectly to him. Her breasts wedged succulently on his broad chest, her body all cuddled up in his arms. At the rate they were going, there would be no way to keep her from feeling his arousal as he had her soldered so tightly between his legs and plastered against him.

Shawn moved his hands to her shoulders to hold her back, away. But she fought him. Still, he pulled away from her lips. "Listen, Cherriana, we need *tae*, uh, you don't know what you're doing,"

Her hands flexed along his strong wide shoulders then slid to his chiseled chest that was so hard it felt like a marble statue under her fingers yet still yielding.

The caresses she made with her little hands crazed him. Shawn wanted to pull off his shirts and feel her warm strokes all over his flesh.

Her voice started out timidly as she wasn't used to talking about such things, but then it grew firmer. She stared levelly at his dark eyes and said, "Shawn, I may be inexperienced but I am an adult. I'm not totally ignorant of what goes on between a man and a woman. I'm not asking for you to drop me in the grass and, um, make love to me, at least not now."

She smiled at him, sliding her hands up and around his head pulling it back down she leaned into him. "But I do want to feel the length of you, all of you, for once not in anger. Please don't push me away."

His breath expelled, tickling wisps of her hair around her face. There was no way he could continue to repel her, not anymore. They were obviously aroused by each other but they cared about each other too, a lot.

He thought he would die when he'd seen that bear going after her, thinking he wouldn't get to her in time like he had with the damned wolves. Her tears of concern and relief for him while in the shootout told him she cared too. How much, he didn't know. She probably didn't even know herself.

Giving up, Shawn pulled her back into his breathless embrace. Feeling every soft feminine inch of her against every hard sculpted square of him, he kissed her like a dying man.

She melted into him like she had been made to fit his body, only his body. He drank her up as long as he could until his duty broke through the entrancing cloud of passion.

Hating to with all his heart and being, he had to hold her away. Looking at her, skin glowing, eyes almost closed with just a hint of blue showing, her puffed lips dewy but starting to frown.

"*Leamin*, I have *tae* go."

She peered up at him confused. "Go? Go where? Can I come with you?"

"*Na*," he said. He had actually considered it but knew he would be moving way too fast for her, and his stamina was ten times what hers was. He had to leave her here.

"Remember when Caleb was killed and I had *tae* leave those few days?"

Blinking perplexed, she said, "What does Caleb-" Understanding started dawning. Realizing he was leaving again, she started growing upset. Brows drawing down, eyes glinting frantic and angry, she begged, "No, Shawn, no, please don't go away again, please."

She didn't realize she was hitting him, her small fists like flies hitting the solid wall of his powerful chest.

Unhappily, he captured her fists and kissed each one then held them. "I can't explain what I'm doing, but I have *tae* go. I don't want *tae*, baby, believe me. I want so badly *tae* be with you. Tis hell for me *tae* leave you here." He dropped a gentle kiss on the top of her head. "Daf and Beau will watch out for you-"

In a rush, her words blurted, "Take me with you!"

Shaking his head somberly, still holding her hands he rested them on his chest. The square jaw firmed, reluctance rang clearly in his dark eyes. It hurt to watch her finally declaring her feelings for him then him instantly dashing them. He released her hands. If only they had more time.

Cheri splayed her fingers, spreading them on his chest. He laid his hands over hers. "I can't."

He didn't explain that he would be moving fast and hard without taking any breaks. The last time he took off he hadn't slept for almost four days. No way could she keep up. She would only deny it and insist she could. "You will be safe with my friends."

"I'm not worried about me you lunkhead, I'm worried about you. There're many of us but only one of you." She slipped a hand out from under his and caressed his roughly handsome face. Brushing the satin pads of her fingertips across his full masculine lips, he opened his mouth and she slid them in.

Watching intrigued while he sucked and licked them like he had wanted to moments ago, like they had that day in the cave, she felt a flush start from where her legs joined her body. It was unfamiliar, but she wanted more of the swelling heat it struck.

His fiery eyes glazing, the pupils burned black seeing hers mist with passion. Swallowing his ardor with tremendous difficulty, knowing he didn't have the ability to spend another moment alone with her without losing his senses, Shawn grasped her hand and slowly pulled her fingers out of his mouth, then he kissed them.

"I have *tae* go, *leamin*, now. The sooner I go the sooner I'll be back." Her woebegone expression ate at his heart, but he had a duty to do. Taking her hand he brought her back to where the others waited.

Everyone was sitting.

Daf and Beau got up when they returned.

"Stay here," Shawn said to Cheri releasing her hand. He motioned for Beau and Daf to follow him. He took them out on a path and pointed up the mountain.

"At first light tomorrow, follow this trail north for, about," he thought back to when he was last there. "About five miles. It continues *tae* incline steadily but not steeply. See the line of pines?" He indicated a dense column of pine trees to the west.

At their dual nods, he said, "Continue with them on your left until you come *tae* a triangle of boulders. Go around behind them and you'll see a small, enclosed clearing where you can stay tomorrow night. If the trappers return they won't be able *tae* find you. Don't make a fire. I will meet you there. I may even be able *tae* get back before morning."

The two men nodded again.

Knowing he could trust these men with his life, his voice dropped low and husky, Shawn said firmly, "Daf," he gestured to the darkly huge man with potent hunks of muscles defining his back, shoulders, arms, even legs, wielding powerfully against the black T and jeans.

"Don't lead, let Vega do that and keep Cheri tied *tae* you like before. Keep an eye out for Tomas, Marx and Zachary, and the trappers."

Daf nodded. "Aye."

"And you," thumping Beau lightly on his blue flannel covered chest with a knuckle, Shawn pierced his broad-shouldered friend with a joking yet severe look. "Keep your freckled fingers to yourself. Tis warm enough, she won't need your furry red body heat. Keep her away from Malone, Vega too for that matter. And keep her between the two of you when you sleep tonight. Got that?"

"You're referring to Leena, right *brither*?" Beau teased his friend.

Not answering, Shawn looked heavenward seeking help that he didn't pop his friend in the head for his jokes.

Taking in Shawn's flushed face, and his glazed and shining eyes, tussled hair and the unbuttoned shirt, Beau's taunting grin stretched his freckles across his face. "Aye, you gave in then, didn't you?"

Shawn didn't respond.

Daf smiled too. "Tis okay, Shawn, everyone can see you have it bad for each other, we can see the way you watch each other when the other is looking away." He laughed at Shawn's surprised expression.

Daf said, "Get on with you, *brither*, right from the beginning, you were all about protecting her the minute they brought her on the bus. You're a man, she will understand your violent past, the things you had to do. Get over yourself with this crap about your experience compared to hers. The man is supposed to teach the woman."

Shawn started to speak but Beau jumped in. "We'll clear up that business with her charges and that will clear things for you to," treading lightly he said, "continue seeing her when we're back home." His raspberry red brows arched in question. "Are you thinking about that or is this a one-shot-wilderness-deal?"

A smile flickered across his lips, Shawn said, "Tis none of your business."

Beau clapped him on the back. "Okay, be that way. Keep in mind, if you foolishly let her go, I will snap her up." He laughed out loud at the thunderous face Shawn turned to him.

"Oh, aye, she's got you good." Beau hee-hawed at Shawn's broad back as the black-haired man started back to the cave.

Again, he didn't tell the others he was leaving or what he was doing. However, this time, Shawn went to Cheri. Grasping her upper arms, he pulled her in, gave her a deep, devouring, head-spinning kiss and abruptly let her go.

He turned and swiftly took off down a winding dirt trail.

Watching him leave, his long sturdy legs moving easily over the rocky terrain, his broad shoulders looking strong even against the backdrop of the formidable mountain, the sinking sun shining on the ebony hair, Cheri stood with the back of her hand pressed against her lips.

SHAWN'S PRISONER

A shimmer of worry misted her eyes as he disappeared around the mountain.

Chapter Fifteen

The dwindling group started right out early in the morning knowing they had to cover many miles before it was dark, and they were eager to put distance between them and the trappers if they returned.

Even Malone who hated Shawn was apprehensive when the powerful, wilderness savvy guy wasn't with them. He felt a lot less secure about their safety, make that *his own* safety. Of course he mainly worried that if something happened to Shawn and he didn't make it back, he couldn't take Malone to his treasure, and all of this researching, planning, scheming, all this traveling hell would have been for nothing.

The group spoke very little now, concentrating as the trail wound and backtracked like a skinny craggy paperclip up the side of the mountain.

It was a struggle to navigate the hairpin turns with a steep drop off on one side of them and a mountain wall on the other.

A column of pines bordered on their left, but only a smattering of trees sporadically thatched the rest of the mountain. Links of grass covered sketchy trails bordered with scrubby brush and stones scaled up and down and around.

Malone fell back to walk beside Beau who always brought up the rear where he could see everyone and catch any threat coming from behind. He was tying a blue bandeau around his red head to keep the sweat out of his eyes.

"What are you, boy, a fashion plate?" Malone barely had the energy to be disparaging, but he still managed to.

Beau glanced down at his blue flannel shirt then canted a look at the heavier, older man wheezing beside him, his filthy, sweat-stained shirt sticking to his flabby chest.

Beau closed his eyes and scarcely shook his head letting the deputy's idiot words pass. "What do you want, Malone?" His affable voice was layered with an undercurrent of cold aggressiveness.

Sweat pilled across Malone's forehead, it ran down his temples, over his nose and under his eyes, pooling on his thick chin. The armpits of his shirt were soaked, the material darkened in wet blotches across his chest. A cube of sweat covered his back funneling to his belt.

He dragged his arm across his face managing only to smear the sweat, getting salty excretion in his eyes. "Yeah, I want to know how you, actually Jamieson who's up front, knows which track to take."

Blinking rapidly at the stinging salt burning his eyes, he gestured, his arm stretched and rolled indicating the vast landscape. "The damned paths crisscross like crazy."

One hand tucked in his pocket, the other loose at his side, Beau said coolly, "Not to worry, Deputy, we know what we're doing."

"Harrumph." Deep in his throat, Malone's crass grunt suggested disbelief and distrust. Regardless, he had no choice but to stay with the group even if he was dubious that they knew where they were going. Smearing more salty moisture in his eyes with his sweaty hand, he mumbled a snippy, "Sure," and strode ahead.

Grinning contemptuously at the deputy's sweat soaked back, Beau muttered, "Good riddance soon enough, asshole."

Another mile passed then, "Hey, look," Jim said. "Check that out-" he pointed up at a bighorn sheep that was perched miraculously a hundred feet straight up. It easily and comfortably balanced on a tiny rock that jutted out from the mountain. His head moved in their direction at Vega's shout, in an instant he was gone.

"That was pretty cool, huh?" Jim asked the others.

Her lip curled, brown frizzy hair draping over one eye, Leena snarled, "I have had enough of the stinkin' damned wildlife. He was just showing off knowing we can't just dash and prance and sail over this wretched mountain like he can."

Malone snorted distastefully. "I'm sure he didn't give you a second thought, honey. He probably smelled you a mile away, I sure can."

"Shut up you stupid horrid man. This is all your fault, Vance." Leena got up in his face sputtering like a mill wheel in the water, "If it wasn't for your stupid driving you stupid ass-"

Malone stopped in front of her making her halt abruptly.

"I've had about enough of your whining and sniveling, Leena. You don't gotta stay with us. Why don't you go find your lover, Ritchie, or that freak psychopath and hang with them you cow?" Sweat sprayed and dripped on his shoes with his vigorous movements.

Wiping his flinging perspiration from her face, Leena shrieked, "Don't you dare talk to me like that- you- you-

dirtbag!" She swung her fist at him- he knocked it away effortlessly.

Sneering and spitting at her, he sniped, "Kiss my ass you bitch," and shoved her.

Leena stumbled backwards then fell landing hard on her butt. Opening her mouth to curse the deputy, she happened to glance over to her right and saw the steep drop-off she was inches from. Her mouth dropped open like an oven door and her skin drained of all color.

Then red flushed her face, her nose dripped. Tearing her eyes off the edge of the cliff, she wiped her hand across her nose and climbed to her feet. Her hands curled like claws, she shrieked like a banshee and went to hurl herself at the deputy-

Jim Vega jogged back from up front of the line and scurried over to get between the two of them.

Holding his hands up at them to keep them apart, Jim yelled, "Come on now, we have to-"

Both Malone and Leena pushed him out of the way- The path was extremely narrow, he was so close to the edge he screamed as he went over.

Then Leena screamed. Malone stared at the empty space in horror.

Hearing the commotion, Daf took Cheri's hand and hurried back to see what was going on. They couldn't see until they came around a sharp bend.

Beau had witnessed the entire horrible episode but had been too far away to prevent it.

"What is it?" Daf asked, as he reached them.

Leena had her hands clamped over her mouth, her eyes wide and freaked out over her hands.

Malone was white as a ghost, panting and sweating buckets like he'd run ten miles. Neither one said a word.

His dreads tied back in a ponytail jostling, Daf grabbed Malone's flaccid arm and shook him. He asked harshly, "What is it Malone? Tell me or I'll-"

Vance Malone pointed a quaking finger towards the cliff edge. "It's- it's- it's- Vega-"

Leena stuttered with him, "He- he went over the edge! It wasn't our fault, I mean we didn't do anything, I mean-"

Malone shook his head nonstop like a cat's head on a spring in a car window. "No- no- not our fault!"

Beau reached them.

Daf spurted, "What the hell?" Daf and Beau rushed to the edge of the trail, dropped to their knees and peered over.

Jim Vega was down, way down, lying on his stomach. His leg moved, then it stopped.

"Vega!" Daf cupped his mouth and yelled, "Jim! Talk to me!"

The deputy didn't move.

"Vega!" Squinting down, the ground was hard dirt, rocky and covered with low scruff. Daf could see the mashed trail Vega had made bumping and rolling down. His drag marks in the dirt until he'd flown off over a sharp jut and landed on solid rock. Daf strained to see if he moved again but he was too far away to tell.

"Holy fuck," Beau muttered next to him. "Is he dead?"

Cheri stuffed her knuckles in her mouth to keep from screaming. Her eyes tacked wide like harrowed blue moons over her hand.

Daf shook his head slowly. "I don't know. I saw him move and now I can't tell. We have to go get him. He might still be alive."

"Aye," Beau agreed. "Let's go."

Daf untied his rope from Cheri, uncoiled the rest from around his arm and waist and wound it around the nearest tree.

The mountain area was mostly rocks and pebbles and dirt packed so hard it was like cement in some places. Tree coverage thickened as it crept up the mountainside from where they were standing.

"I'll go," Beau said, tying the end of the rope around his waist. "You guys help lower me."

Suppressing his despair, his shoulders rigid, Daf said tensely to Leena and Cheri, "I need you girls, ladies, to please stand back, away." He drew them up the path where it was wider and the steepness of the mountain sloped less.

"Here. Stay here, right here until we get him back up." Seeing the devastating alarm on Cheri's face, he patted her arm then gently squeezed it. "It will all be okay, just..." He took a deep breath. "Stay here, don't move." He jogged back to the men.

Daf and Malone grasped the end of the rope, wound it around the tree and let it slack slowly bit by bit as Beau went over the edge and slowly, carefully, repelled down to Jim.

It took a long time, the two men up top struggled and strained to hold the rope taut enough so Beau wouldn't fall, but loose enough so he could keep moving down.

When he finally reached Jim, the redhead gratefully put his two feet on sturdy level ground. Letting go of the rope, he scratched his beard with both hands observing the prone man before him.

He knelt on one knee next to him feeling for a pulse. He already knew it was to no avail judging by the large pool of blood that was pouring out of the big crack in his head.

They were going to have to leave him there, no way could Daf and Malone pull Jim up without the officer helping by climbing.

Beau took Vega's gun and stuffed it in the back of his jeans. Shaking his head at Daf who was peering over the side, he cupped his mouth and yelled, "Bring me up."

It was arduous work for Daf and Malone to pull Beau up as well as tough going for Beau climbing the sheer mountainside while they pulled him.

Jamming his steel-toed boots into the hard dirt between rocks, searching for crevices, he dug his fingers in holes and cracks, gripping rocks and vines helping to pull himself up.

It seemed to take forever. If he weren't an experienced mountain climber it would have taken much longer.

Daf breathed a sigh of relief when he saw the top of the red hair, and bent over to grasp Beau's arm to help hoist him up and over the edge.

Beau threw himself down on his back, his diaphragm pumped in and out with shallow quick breaths.

Daf and Malone bent over with their hands on their knees catching their breaths as well. The exertion had Malone totally sodden in perspiration.

Recouping in a few minutes, Daf held a hand to Beau to help him up.

When the big Black man pulled his friend to his feet, he let go of his hand. Clapping him on the shoulder, he said, "A bit torn up, *brither*, but you made it." He indicated Beau's hands that were scraped and burned from the rope.

Both knees shone through the torn jeans, and a pocket was ripped off his shirt. The ends of his sleeves were now ragged.

Beau smoothed his scraped hands over the flannel. "Gee, and I was growing attached to this shirt." Rolling up the sleeves and grinning wryly, he wiped his hands on his pants. "Next time, bro, we go on a mission I'm bringing gloves."

He shirked at the warning look Daf shot him. Daf wasn't amused at Beau's joking. He'd feared too much while his friend had scaled the dangerous mountain. To distract from his words, Beau quickly said, "Let's get the girls and go."

"Aye, let's move on." Daf agreed. There was deep sadness in his tone. He said quietly, "Jim Vega was a good man. He tried hard, was a team player, never grumbled and always did as asked. It was a bitch that the man died in a freak accident like that."

Beau murmured, "Yeah."

Daf gathered the rope. Wrapping it around his arm, he looked for Cheri to tie her to him.

She was nowhere in sight.

His head switched back and forth and all around. Daf decided she must be relieving herself. Then he spotted Leena talking quietly with Malone. The girls never went to the bathroom alone, especially after the bear attack, and even more so after the trappers' assault.

"Leena!" he shouted shortly as he strode over to the brunette standing with her hands on her hips whispering to Malone.

She started guiltily when he approached.

Daf barked, "Where's Cheri?" Now Beau came over too realizing something was amiss.

In an annoyed shrug, Leena's palms turned up. "How should I know? Am I her keeper?"

"Daf..." Apprehension dug deeply into Beau's voice. His head pivoted all around searching for the striking hair that would have stood out against the rocky, tree-capped countryside.

Daf put his hands around his mouth and yelled, "Cheri! Where are you?" He waited, his eyes darting around then going to Beau who looked as frightened as Daf felt.

The hair on the back of his neck rose. A knot began twisting in his belly.

Both men started calling her name and walking up and down and back and forth.

She had vanished into thin air.

Chapter Sixteen

Twenty minutes earlier

Standing beside Leena nervously wringing her hands while the men worked to get to Jim Vega, Cheri wished there was something she could do to help.

However, the men had told them to stay out of the way, she didn't want to make their task more difficult so she stayed back even when Leena moved forward a few feet from where they worked lowering Beau down the side of the mountain.

A crowd of trees and bushes at her back, Cheri leaned forward to watch the men. It was taking so long. Wishing like crazy that Shawn was there, she wrapped her arms around her body fearing for the young man, Jim. *He was such a nice-*

A hand clamped over her mouth and another around her waist. She was lifted up off her feet and her back slammed against a hard solid mass, then it ran with her.

Although held as tight as wire on a spool, her body still bounced and jarred as the man holding her ran up the side of the mountain.

When he was several hundred feet away, he swung her down. Keeping an arm around her, and a hand over her mouth, he laid her on the ground. Letting go with one hand he still kept the other over her mouth and a knee between her legs to keep her down and fumbled with something in his pocket.

Her screams smothered, Cheri frantically clawed and hit at his arm holding her down. She kicked her legs out and up at anything she could connect with.

The man pulled out a jar of something liquid and a cloth. Taking off the cap, he held the cloth to the jar and tipped it. It was awkward to do with one hand and keep her held down with only his other hand over her mouth.

Horror stung her every nerve when she recognized who it was. Her blood froze solid as she recognized the maniac Zachary.

Confused and frightened, Cheri punched his arms and kicked at him trying to get away, but he was a very big, very strong man, even bigger than Shawn. Her punches didn't hurt him in the least, it was like a baby batting at an elephant. He held her head rammed against the ground so hard she was afraid he would literally squash it.

His face a blank, eyes empty of humanity sifted down her body then up to her face. It appeared her fear amused him, and apparently turned him on. A glimmer of lustful interest briefly reared savage and vile in his base smile.

Then, blinking, his face morphed back into a blank mask, he turned his attention back to his task.

After soaking the cloth with the liquid, muttering, "At least I got one good thing out of those fucking trappers," and holding his breath, he held it near her and let go of her mouth then shoved the cloth over her face when she opened her mouth to scream.

Everything went black.

Cheri wasn't aware when he picked up her unconscious body, slung her over his shoulder and moved swiftly at an angle so his trail would be harder to track.

He headed for a creek he had found on his way while following the group and strode right into it knowing it would eliminate his footprints.

Realizing Cheri was nowhere in the near area, Daf and Beau came together. They could see the anxiety mirrored in each other's eyes.

Leena approached them, suggested, "Do you think a wild animal took her?"

Daf swung such furious eyes at her she took a step back, her shoulders rose to her ears.

"You women were supposed to stay together. What happened? Why weren't you together? Why didn't you notice she was gone?" He hammered his questions at her. She kept stepping back, he marched forward.

Her back arched to bend away from his accusing wrath, her expression terrified of the huge man with cordons of muscles rippling across his back. His face swelled with outrage.

She tried to nonchalantly shrug it off. "It's not my job to babysit. I-"

Daf vehemently grabbed her arm and shook it ruthlessly, demanding, "When did you see her last, tell me!"

Intimidated, Leena's face was taut with alarm that he would strike her. His hands were so massive, covered with scars, she feared one hit and he could kill her. She turned to

Beau for help, but the redhead was staring at her just as intensely as Daf.

Daf's huge biceps bulged in his arm as he shook her harder. "Answer me, when did you see her last, where!"

Her head whipping back and forth, trying to pull away from his gorilla hold on her, Leena whined, "I don't know! It- it was, you guys were trying to get Jim. I never- never noticed she was gone until you said something."

Grabbing both her arms now in rage, Daf shook her until her teeth rattled. The stringy hair flapped back and forth over her pudgy shoulders hitting her double chin.

"You were told to stay right there," Daf gestured with his head, "You had to see what happened."

Her head shook side to side, the filthy hair now swatting her in the face. She cried, "It's not my fault I didn't see anything, it's not my fault!"

Beau said in a low desperate voice, "She can't tell us anything, Daf."

It took everything he had to not string his big rough fingers around her neck and squeeze until she puked. Daf let Leena go and turned away from her as if she made him sick.

He said to Beau, "Let's search for trace." The two men parted and walked the area more carefully this time looking for evidence of what happened to Cheri.

Malone and Leena sat on the ground and waited.

A little while and Beau called out, "Daf, here."

When Daf reached him, Beau pointed to the ground. It was near where the two women had been standing when the men had gone after Vega. Daf took a few steps in, then crouched down, nodding.

Standing up, he trawled his arm raggedly across his forehead. "It's mashed down, too much for that slight girl to make."

Beau nodded. "Aye, she was taken." He said miserably to Daf, "How are we going to fucking tell him-"

Daf cut him off. "I've got a feeling tis Zach. We know he's out there. Marx doesn't have the balls knowing Shawn would rip them off and feed them to him if he tried anything again with Cheri. No one else would have a need to take her. And why take such a chance just to have the woman?"

Thinking about it, Beau stuffed his hands in his pockets, peered sideways at his friend. "Aye, but you don't know. Could be anyone in these mountains saw her. A sex-starved mountain man or one of those trappers and just went for it. She's such a softly striking beauty."

"Aye, she is that. Listen," Daf said in a quiet tone. "It won't take Shawn as long as last time to get there and back to us, we're much closer to the station than we were before. I'm going to try to track whoever took her, he has to have left prints and more.

"You take them," he jerked his head at Malone and Leena, "to where we're supposed to meet up with Shawn. He should be back by late tonight or early morning. Maybe we'll be blessed and have her back before he even knows she's gone."

His mouth was a curve of hope, but the dark eyes betrayed grave doubt. Beau had the same expression.

"Sure. Okay, go on, hurry, don't waste any more time talking," Beau urged the big man. "Watch your back, *ma brither*." He clapped his friend on the shoulder as Daf nodded and took off to follow the trail of whoever abducted Cheri.

Up the side of the mountain, the shrubs and trees grew more densely. There were patches of tall grass dotted with boulders and sometimes piles of shale, fallen rocks lay scattered from landslides.

Going back to the disturbed ground where Daf believed Cheri was snatched from, he saw scuff marks in the dirt and a trail of mashed the grass from footprints that led up the mountainside.

Daf rapidly hit the trail, moving stealthily. His eyes stroked everywhere, constantly inspecting the ground for clues, looking for broken branches and perusing the trail trying to see ahead to where it led.

Not knowing how long a head start the abductor had, Daf moved as fast as he could.

Beau ushered Malone and Leena to move urgently along the path to where they were to wait for Shawn. Ignoring their grumbles and whines, Beau said callously to them, "Keep up or don't, I don't *bluidy* care. I'm not slowing down for either of you or stopping. If you get lost it's on you."

He kept a hustling pace almost a jog. The more thoughts of what could be happening to that wee lass filled his mind the faster he moved. He wished he could leave these two *amadans* and join Daf in the search for her.

Feeling useless, he hustled along, his only job was to get to where they were to meet Shawn.

Just over an hour they reached the destination. Now they could do nothing but wait.

Beau couldn't sit or stay still he was so gripped by agitation at having no way to help, or to know what Daf was doing. He paced in a circle around the boulders and out of them and back inside, and out and in.

Malone sat on the ground with his back resting against a tree stump, one knee up, his arm resting on his knee. Bored silly, he twirled a long piece of grass watching the torn fuzzy end go round and round.

He tried to ignore Beau stomping back and forth scraping his hands through his thick curly hair then dragging his fingers through his short beard muttering to himself.

The deputy couldn't stand it anymore. Annoyance raising his voice, he said, "Man, you're making me dizzy, can you stop with the pace-"

With a low grating growl Beau burst over to the deputy. Crouching down, he put his furious face, his skin drawn and haggard, blue eyes stark with worry for Cheri, so close to Malone's the deputy could count his freckles.

His hands itching to punch something, Beau crunched them into fists and snarled, "You best keep quiet you fucking *bastart mahoun*, this is all your *bluidy* fault. If it wasn't for you that wee lass wouldn't-"

Leena stood up and interjected soothingly trying to keep the peace, "All right, all right, simmer down, Beau, honey. Just 'cause you have red hair doesn't mean you have to be a hot head."

Hoping to distract him, she reached over and petted his short springy curls. "Such nice hair you have, Beau, what say you and I-"

Beau roughly slapped her hand away and stood up. He had nothing to say to these loathsome freaks. His hands deep in his pockets, shoulders rounded, he stalked off to continue pacing.

"Whew," Leena slid down and sat next to Malone who turned paralytic like a wood stump when Beau had gotten in his face, and was now letting out his held breath.

"He's as bad as Shawn with that short fused temper," Leena remarked, picking her hair off her sweaty face. "You need to watch yourself, don't set him off."

"Oh shut up, Leena. I don't need him, I only need Darkonn. If I thought I could, I'd take out both that ginger-haired heathen and that big black asshole."

Leena sighed into her hand then crossed her arms over her chest resting her hands on her pudgy belly. "Well, you can't take the chance. Besides, you don't have a gun. What're you gonna use, your bare fisties?" She raised her own fists up punching the air mocking the deputy.

Leaning back, she tilted her head to look up at the sky and babbled, "Speaking of heathens, I thought I could get it on with Shawn, but he won't let me near him. You know, I wouldn't mind taking on that Daf, his dark skin is so smooth I'd love to run my hands along those enormous arms or that rocky chest. He's a huge beast of a man, I bet all of him is huge."

She sighed again, her droopy chest rose then fell with resignation. "But he never even acknowledges me, looks right through me like I'm invisible."

"I told you, you stink," Malone said maliciously. "And you talk too damned much."

Leena punched him in the shoulder. "Asshole."

They settled back to wait.

Daf knew it was Zach. He'd seen the footprints, larger than his own and an almost invisible patch of torn cloth on a twig. He recognized the olive green material he'd last seen the giant wearing. He was able to track Zach for miles until he reached the creek.

"Damn that fucker." Slamming his fists against his sides, Daf spewed his frustration and fear when he realized he could not track Zach any further.

He had found strands of Cheri's hair on the ground a few miles back. Half relieved, half afraid, it indicated he was going in the right direction to find them.

But the strands were on the ground were half covered with dirt. That meant she was lying on the ground. The thought sent shivers through his body and chills across the back of his neck. He didn't want to think about what that could mean.

Not wanting to go back and face Shawn when he returns, Daf decided to follow the stream in one direction for a while to see if he could catch where Zach left the water for solid ground again.

Remembering the way Cheri had greeted him after the shootout, Shawn's feet moved swiftly. Looking so forward to seeing her, his heart light, he seemed to fly right over rocks and holes and heavy underbrush.

He'd made great time, the sun had long set, he'd brought back a flashlight.

Not sure how he was going to explain it to Malone, he might not need to. Malone never questioned when Shawn left the group for the couple of long periods of time. He must assume Shawn was only scouting.

Shawn decided he'd tell him he found the flashlight, that maybe one of the trappers dropped it. He didn't dare bring back anything else like a phone or tracking device, Malone could not be trusted and Shawn didn't want the deputy to find anything on him that shouldn't be there.

He could already tell something was wrong before he got there. He felt an agitation stirring the air. Plus, Daf and

Jim Vega weren't present. Perhaps they were taking a piss, somehow Shawn doubted it.

Malone and Leena jumped, their heads bobbed up guiltily as he materialized in front of them. The couple sank back as if expecting to get slapped.

His body wound tight as if waiting for a bomb to explode. Face a mask of stoic impassiveness, Shawn spoke without inflection, "Where is everyone?"

"Uh," was all that came out of Malone. Leena huddled next to the deputy her mouth a tight straight line.

Shawn took a menacing step towards them, his brows rigid and low like an eagle's, skin darkening, fists clenched, he had a wretched feeling in the pit of his stomach. "Malone, where-"

"Shawn," Beau came out from in front of the boulders as Shawn, not wanting to be detected right away, had gone in from behind. The two friends faced each other. Shawn's stomach pitched at the look on Beau's face.

"Where is she?" his voice a bare rasp fearing the worst, Shawn moved near to Beau.

Swallowing his own frightened panic, Beau's freckles stark against his pale face, his voice shook, "*Brither*, she, uh…"

"Beau!" Shawn stuck his fist in his friend's shirt and pulled him. His voice dropped, "Tell me." He was now noticing Daf and Jim were gone too. Maybe they were all together and everything was all right, no- the look on Beau's face said it was bad.

His blue eyes, the pupils mere pins, expressed his anguish as he said bleakly, "She's gone. She's been taken."

"Tell me," was all Shawn said, releasing Beau's shirt.

Beau explained about Jim Vega falling, and then Cheri going missing during that time. That their suspicions it was Zachary Stockton, and Daf was out searching.

The dark sheen drained from Shawn's face, sweat popped up around his hairline. "Show me."

Beau turned immediately and headed out of the clearing with Shawn right on his heels.

"Hey!" Malone stood up shouting. "What about us? What about my gold? Get back here!" His demands fell on deaf ears, he plopped back down next to Leena.

When they reached the area where Cheri was taken, Shawn and Beau followed the trail Daf had deliberately made to the creek. They saw Daf's footprints leading downstream. There the two men split.

Shawn went in Daf's direction knowing what a powerful tracker the man was, and told Beau to go in the opposite just in case. Whatever happened, they would meet back at the boulder triangle.

His head dizzy with dread, Shawn stared blindly at Daf's prints. He moved woodenly trying to follow the fading prints with blurred vision. Shawn told himself to snap out of it, he would be no good to her acting like a mindless tool. He was trained for this.

Compartmentalizing his despairing thoughts to the recesses of his brain, he took a deep breath allowing the clarity to return. Moving quickly but slow enough to follow the tracks with the flashlight and scan the area at the same time, he traveled along the stream.

The way Daf's prints were elongated he could tell Daf had also moved fast but he had started when the sun was still out. Shawn allowed a thread of hope to seep in, he had Daf and Beau, the best of the best, they would find her.

Daf's movements so stealth a bird wouldn't have heard him coming, had to slow way down. His only light now was the meager silver glow of the moon that shimmered over the water.

Thank goodness it was a clear night, no clouds to block any of the precious light. Stretching his neck, he turned his head from one side to the other, then shook his beefy, rock solid shoulders to loosen them.

Miniscule glee bubbled at the bottom of his stomach. He had found Zach's prints coming out of the stream. They emerged several miles downstream and Daf now had a handle on his current tracks.

Zach might have a head start but he was carrying Cheri, that would slow him down at least a hair. Especially navigating the steeper land and climbing over big rocks. Now that it was dark Zach would have to slow to a snail's pace, Daf hoped.

He was sure Zach was carrying her because his left footprint was a pin's breadth deeper than his right, not from the weight of the slight girl he carried but from leaning to the left to balance carrying her over on his right side.

The damned tracks circled around and around then came back on themselves, then out again. Following them a distance when they circled again, standing in a total quandary, Daf thought, *what the hell was the bastard doing-*

Daf was standing in a portion of low grass around twenty by twenty feet when he spotted some broken branches on a thick bush and went to investigate.

Crouching to see if there was anything caught in it like hair, torn clothes, a button, he peered in the dark struggling to see by the meagre light of the moon and the brilliant infinite stars.

He heard him just in time to dodge the huge branch that swung at his head, but it threw him off balance.

Like a fired cannonball, Daf rolled across the grass! As he was rolling and scrambling back to his feet, Zach stormed after him like a blond bull snorting and grunting, cursing and swinging the branch like it was a warrior's club.

He swung it hard at Daf. Daf hurled to the side and the branch more like a tree trunk, slammed down with a bang on the ground just missing him. The thick branch sounded hard as steel.

As Zach swung it again, Daf struck out with his fist punching the psychopath in the solar plexus. Yanking his hand back and ducking again, Daf shook his fist, it had been like hitting an iron wall.

Zach hardly grunted at the punch and kept coming like an out of control charging locomotive. Swinging the club, he missed Daf's head by less than an inch, the wind from the club whizzing past blew his dreads back.

Tossing his backpack, Daf threw himself to the ground and rolled again. The strap holding his shotgun snapped and the weapon flung off his back.

Zach came right after him like a wood chipper- chop-chop- chop with the club. Swinging it back and forth like a pendulum forcing Daf on the ground to scuttle back and forth on his palms and feet with his back to the ground. He tried to get his gun out but he needed all his limbs at the moment.

In an awkward roll, Daf yanked his gun out but Zach was right there and smashed the gun right out of his hand like a baseball bat striking a ball.

Daf sprang up and tried to get another punch in but Zach kept swinging that club like he was Thor with the hammer, and coming at him so fast Daf backed into something so hard it about broke his back and tripped him to his knees.

In the dark, he'd run into a wall of boulders that had avalanched down the mountain at some point in time. Now they virtually blocked him from moving in any direction away from Zach.

The maniac chortled at his luck in getting the other man down and trapped. Daf was a tremendous opponent but with the wall behind him, he was dead meat. He had to make a try for the giant's knees while avoiding the club-

Grinning hugely, fiercely triumphant, Zach raised the club over his head. His back muscles straining the back of his shirt, biceps pumped outrageously huge and deadly, his maniacal laughter rang through the trees as he brought the club down fast and hard directly at Daf's head-

Out of nowhere- Shawn launched himself from the invisible darkness at the blond monster, hitting him in the middle and knocking him down.

Both men tumbled to the ground. Landing hard and skidding, Shawn's shotgun was knocked off his back. He shrugged the backpack off as he rolled. Finding their bearings instantly, both men jumped to their feet.

Still holding the club, Zach raised it to the side again like a baseball bat, his face red and angry. He shouted, "Where the hell did you come from, Darkonn?" He scowled, then the scowl slid into a wicked smile. "No worries, I will enjoy killing both of you and keeping the pussy."

Shawn stood in a boxer's stance, his arms bowed, hands raised mid-body, ready. Aware that before he could get his gun out of his pocket Zach would bash him with the club, he asked, "Where is she, Zach?"

Knowing the beast wasn't going to reveal his intentions or Cheri's whereabouts, he wasn't surprised when Zach stood grinning like the insane psychotic that he was.

"That's for me to know and for you not to find out, bitch," Zach snarled at him, swinging the club.

Shawn jerked in his stomach in and raised his arms as the club swung almost slicing him in the gullet.

Zach goaded him, "I knew you would be coming looking for her. So I tied her up and stashed her, she can't get away and you ain't finding her. I'll take care of you then go back and get her free and clear.

"You manage to take me out, which you won't, you'll never find her and she will die. You lose either way, so fuck you." Zach came at him swinging the club back and forth like a gigantic bat.

Shawn ducked and spun and jumped out of the way of the deadly weapon all while trying to spot his own shotgun in the tall grass in the almost pitch dark.

As Zach brought the club up to bash it on his head, Shawn leaped and rammed his shoulder into the big man's knees, taking him down. The blond fell furiously hard. Instantly Shawn jumped on him, wailing with his fists at his head as fast and as lethally as he could.

Dropping the club and trying to get to his feet, Zach punched at Shawn, one blow from his massive fist almost knocked Shawn out.

Daf raced over and kicked Zach in the head snapping his neck, flinging his head back. Shawn swiveled and kicked his heel catching Zach a stinging blow to his jaw knocking him back down.

On his hands and knees, the giant shook his head. Blood spewing in all directions, he lashed out at Shawn with a colossal blow to his shoulder knocking him sideways. Shawn crashed on the ground.

Zach turned as Daf swung- and blocked his right uppercut but didn't see the left hook, a powerful punch it dazed the blond for a half a second. Quickly shaking off the punch, with a roar, the vicious prisoner vaulted at Daf smashing into his ribs, bashing him back against a tree and punched a glaring blow to Daf's temple.

With superhuman strength, Daf shoved Zach with both hands as hard as he could.

The blond stumbled backwards and Shawn jumped in the air as Zach was falling backwards and slammed the side of his steel-toed boot into Zach's neck like a rocketing missile, instantly crushing his windpipe and fracturing his neck.

The giant's eyes popped and then he just dropped, crashing like a toppled tree to the ground, landing on his back spread eagle. Shawn and Daf ran over and stood on either side of him with their fists raised ready.

When the giant didn't move, Daf knelt and touched his neck. Zach was looking up at him with sightless eyes, the orbs already turning opaque. Panting and sweating, Daf wiped his mouth and gazed up at Shawn. "He's dead."

Every ounce of tension fell out of Shawn. He relaxed his stance, pulled out his shirttail from his jeans and wiped the sweat and blood out of his eyes.

Climbing wearily to his feet, through heavy hard breaths Daf huffed dismally, "Bro, now he can't tell us where she is. She could be anywhere in these thousands of miles of goddamned wilderness."

The dark night loomed vast and empty over them. The land stretched on forever with treacherous mountain terrain, tree shrouded foothills, deep wide valleys that went on for miles.

Still panting, Daf said what they were both thinking, "It would be like searching for a tear in a rainstorm."

Shawn nodded, the black locks flopping on his wet brow. He leaned over with his hands on his thighs to catch his breath. "I know," he wheezed. "I know."

Chapter Seventeen

After finding their weapons hidden in the darkness and the flashlight that had popped out of Shawn's his back pocket when he launched at Zach, they stood pondering their next move.

The two men came to attention at a rustling in the nearby stand of trees. Both melted back silently into the shadows and watched. A sharp, short whistle blew briefly through the thicket.

Standing in the pitch black, boots damp with dew, Shawn called out, "Beau."

The redhead came crunching over the bushes, shoving aside fat leaves and stomping on twigs. He glanced down at the dead giant lying on the ground spread eagle, his neck caved in and his face a smashed bloody mess, hardly recognizable.

Nodding his head briefly at Zach, as Beau went over to them he said, "Your work, Shawn, I assume?"

A flicker of a grim smile shuttled across Shawn's mouth. "Aye. Both of us."

"The lass?" Beau was afraid to ask since he didn't see her there. Leaves clung to his red springy curls and blue flannel shirt. A streak of mud slashed across one cheek, he rubbed absently at it with his palm.

Wiping his sleeve across his sweaty bloody face again, Shawn stared down at the ground. His voice was unemotional but it scraped out, "He said he's stashed her somewhere. She's bound."

"What are we waiting for, then?" Beau asked, his hands on his hips.

Daf laughed a faint hollow sound, said, "We're thinking."

Beau stared at them momentarily, then understood what he was saying. They couldn't go running off hither thither, the chance of finding her would be like a billion to one. They had to reason it out. Shuffling to stand closer to each other they spoke softly.

Shawn said, "He circled and backtracked a few miles back a bit after he came out of the creek."

Daf nodded remembering the confounding tracks. "Aye." He turned to Beau, his brows in question. "How did you find us so quickly?"

"The part of the creek I was following eventually turned into a waterfall and there was nothing around it but straight up bone mountain, or straight down bare drop. He had to have gone the other way.

"When I got near this area you three were making enough noise to wake the next state over. Sounded like three bulls in a china shop." Beau grinned at the other two. Daf cuffed his shoulder grinning back.

Shawn said, "Let's head back *tae* where he circled, he could have been trying *tae* mislead us, which I'm sure was part of it, but it could also be where he put her. Let's go."

He hoofed back the way they'd come in with the other two right behind them, none of them spared Zach a glance.

217

Shawn led the way sweeping the flashlight ahead in the gloom. They tried to walk quietly but their footsteps still crunched leaves and they kicked pebbles, branches tore at their clothes and thwacked them in the face and scraped their hands.

A mile or so and they found the tracks where Zach had circled and gone back and forth and up and down.

Shawn stood silently, scanning through murky darkness, dew was settling on the grass and trees.

When they stood still they could hear things moving around them. Small nocturnal animals scurrying about, flickers of eerie eyes flashed from the dark shroud of scrub like lightening bugs.

Shawn listened intently for larger animals, mountain lions, bears, but mostly he listened for crying or breathing, or the sweet lilt of a beloved voice. He heard nothing but the breeze rifling through the tops of the trees and the bushes stirring.

Daf and Beau stood mutely, also listening and letting Shawn think. Still glancing all around, Shawn searched his memory.

Zach indicated he planned on keeping Cheri, so he wouldn't have left her out in the open where the animals could get at her or she could escape or the men could find her. She had to be inside something.

He pushed away the paralyzing thought of Zach burying her alive in a box somewhere and planning to come back later to retrieve her when they were gone.

Inhaling a long breath, he wiped a hand over his eyes. Zach wouldn't have had time to dig a hole, or possess a box, thank God.

Suddenly he started running.

Startled, Daf and Beau dashed after him.

Crashing through the thick underbrush, Shawn shoved aside wicked branches cutting like knives and flew over rocks and fallen trees. His footsteps pounding the hard ground made up of packed dirt and rock.

Less than a half mile and he reached it. He slowed as he approached a mound almost invisible in the trees and pressed against the mountain. He heard Daf and Beau racing up behind him.

"What is it?" Beau asked scarcely breathing heavily. The men were used to running long impossibly tough distances at high speed.

They stood in front of what looked like a bunch of big rocks piled along the mountain.

"There's a cave here, it used *tae* have a wide yawning opening. He's hidden it, masked it. Look for fresh tracks, movement, scrapes in the boulders," Shawn explained, quickly pacing around the area.

His head moving up and down while shining the flashlight as he searched for anything looking like it had been recently trod upon or moved.

"Got it!" Daf called out. The other two ran over to him.

"There," he indicated with his hand. The rocks left trails in the dirt when Zach had pushed them in. He had tried to smooth the trace of tracks and threw leaves over to hide them.

Moving closer to the rocks, Shawn muttered, "Help me."

The three men heaved and pushed and grunted and groaned. Aggravatingly tediously slowly, they moved the boulders aside, enough for them to cram their bodies past the blockade into the hidden cave.

Shawn stepped inside, swinging the flashlight. His heart sank, it was dark, cold, and empty.

The damp pungent smell of dirt clung in the air. The emptiness closed around Shawn's heart like a coffin. Not giving up, he moved to the wall and edged along it. Daf went to the other side and Beau trod down the middle.

Shawn called out, "Cherriana, Cherriana!" He thought he heard something and walked towards the sound. Now he could see that the wall curved around. He stepped around it-

There she was.

Bundled in a blanket tied all around with a rope securing her so she couldn't move a muscle, a rag was tied over her mouth. With her weak struggles, the rag had pushed up completely covering her nose and mouth.

Lying on her back, her eyes closed, under the gag it sounded like she emitted a feeble moan but it was actually an exhalation of death's last breath.

The sound making his ears bleed, Shawn rushed to her. Dropping to his knees, he slid an arm under her head and jerked the rag down. His heart squeezing in gratitude, his husky voice plaintive in duress yet faintly jubilant, he rasped, "Baby, tis Shawn, we're here, you're safe now."

She made no sound, not even of breathing. Her chest was as still as the rocks surrounding them.

Shawn swiftly laid her back down flat, tilted her head up, pinched her nose, pressed his mouth to hers and blew in his life saving oxygen.

Watching her abdomen rise, twice, three times before he felt her breathe on her own. Her precious life air exhaled, barely a wisp on his scruffy face.

Her lids lifted like they weighted a hundred pounds, Cheri tried to look to him but her glassy eyes wavered. Peering at him through feeble slits, unable to focus, all she could see were blurry shapes, she couldn't hold her head up.

Pulling a knife from his pocket, Shawn cut the binds and then loosened the blanket. His voice shaking with rage and stifled panic Shawn swore, "If that fucker wasn't already dead I'd *bluidy* fucking tear him limb from limb, crush his skull with my bare hands." His hoarse threat softened as he took her in his arms.

Keeping Cheri wrapped in the blanket, Shawn stood up with her. He said curtly, "Let's get the hell out of here." He handed the flashlight to Daf.

Daf went first to make sure it was all clear, they didn't know if Zach had compatriots lurking. He stepped cautiously out of the lightless cave into the dark forest, moving quickly to stand next to the mountain wall so as not to be seen in case someone was waiting for them.

Daf waited a minute for his eyes to adjust. Inside the cave, the beam of the flashlight had lit the small area, but outside with the flashlight off, it was pitch black.

The canopy of trees made visibility almost nil, the moon had risen and being so far out from civilization the billions of stars helped illuminate the sky. Hearing not a sound, not even the rustling of leaves, Daf turned the flashlight on and let out a short whistle.

Beau appeared then Shawn emerged carrying Cheri.

With Daf leading the way with the flashlight sparsely lighting the trail, they moved deftly through the woods. It was too dangerous in the dark, damply bone-chilling cold, and rife with wild animal to linger in the forest.

They trudged a few miles before exiting the dense woods and hitting the original trail.

Making quick work of the miles to where Malone and Leena waited, they didn't want to tarry in the area where there might be others waiting to pounce from the protection of the darkness.

Shawn wanted to get to where they had a bit of a fortress, albeit a rocky one, a buttress between them and whoever else might be out there lurking, seeking to harm them.

So high on adrenalin energy, Shawn he had no problem carrying Cheri the distance. Daf and Beau both offered to take turns carrying her, but Shawn just cradled her high and tight against his chest and strode silently ahead.

Malone and Leena never heard them coming, they were sound asleep curled next to each other.

Shawn gently set Cheri on the ground. Kneeling beside her, he pulled the blanket back to see if she had any life threatening injuries.

She was either unconscious or asleep, she didn't make a sound or move. Her body was dead limp, but she was breathing. Shawn ran his hands down her arms, then her legs, pressed his fingers carefully along her ribs, then lifted her to check her back.

Setting her down again, he cupped her face turning it so he could check both sides, and the back and top of her head. Her clothes were intact, belt buckled, it didn't look like Zach had, had time to sexually assault her.

Sighing his intense relief that she seemed relatively unharmed, other than whatever drug Zach had given her and bruises on her arms from where she apparently tried to fight him off. He must have forced her to swallow something, Shawn could see more bruises like huge fingerprints on her face.

Shawn would have been proud of her for fighting the psychopathic giant but Zach might have hurt her more for not cooperating.

However, even Zach, as he had obviously planned on keeping her, couldn't foresee that in her struggles to get free the gag had moved up to cover both her nose and mouth and thereby snuffing out her breath.

Zach knew Shawn would come for her, so he had waited in the dark to ambush him. If Shawn was dead, Zach assumed the others wouldn't come looking for Cheri, at least that's what the fool would have thought.

He didn't know Beau and Daf well, so he wouldn't realize the pair would never have stopped searching for her. And, if Zach had managed to kill Shawn, they definitely would have gone after Zach. The blond freak thought everyone was as narcissistic and sociopathic as him and wouldn't care if one of them went missing.

Wrapping Cheri back up in the blanket, Shawn sat down with his back braced on a rock. He pulled her over his lap and held her across his chest. Beau and Daf stood over them like proud parents.

"Thank God, Shawn, thank God," Beau murmured. A tranquil grateful smile laced his lips, he dashed at his wet eyes.

"Aye," Daf choked, his eyes shimmered with tears too. The same salty liquid gleamed in Shawn's own dark eyes as he gazed down at Cheri.

Beau and Daf settled down next to them. Exhausted, the pair fell asleep almost immediately.

Shawn sat the rest of the night holding Cheri, staring at her, watching her chest rise and fall, thanking God she was breathing.

Occasionally her lashes would flutter over her pale cheeks. Her breaths would cut into frightened whimpers.

Shawn would hug her tighter and whisper in her ear, "Shh, baby, you're safe, *ma nesh leamin*. You're safe in your Shawn's arms," and rock her until she fell peaceful again.

Chapter Eighteen

"**S**o," Malone's cynical voice sifted into Shawn's groggy head, "you got her back. How'd you manage to do that?"

With great reluctance, Shawn pushed one sluggish eyelid up to squint at the deputy. Without answering him, he gazed down at the bundle in his arms. The harsh lines etched around his eyes and mouth softened, his lips turned up in the barest of smiles.

Still wrapped in the blanket, Cheri was sleeping peacefully in his arms. He couldn't help stroking her cheek with a gentle finger. When Shawn ignored him, Malone huffed and stalked away.

Daf and Beau were also closed mouthed when questioned.

"But we need to know if that psychopath Zachary is still out there waiting to take us out, we have the right to know," Leena whined at them.

"Something happened, boys, you," she pointed at Daf, "and Shawn are covered in blood. Your clothes are ripped and filthy and you're cut up and bruised. Your fists look like they went one-on-one with an 18-wheeler. Tsk tsk," she shook her head at them.

Shooting a quick glance at Shawn, Daf got to his feet dusting the dirt off his black jeans and shirt. He'd slept on his blanket not the bare ground last night but the fight with Zach had taken a toll on his clothes. He looked ruefully down at his shirt and pants.

Nodding painfully, he had a residual headache from some of Zach's punches that had landed true and hard. "You're right, Leena," Daf acknowledged. "I sure feel like I duked it out with a gargantuan truck and it ran over me. More than once."

Stretching and cracking his neck, Daf turned slightly towards Shawn seeing he was still concentrating on Cheri, Daf said to Leena, "I can tell you with all certainty Zach will not be bothering us again. Ever. Now, he might be giving the devil shit as we speak, but he won't be hassling us. I'm hungry." He walked away from Leena to go search for something for them to eat.

Closing her mouth when Leena got the hint that Zach was dead, she watched Daf walk away from her like she didn't exist. She seethed, annoyed at being treated like crap by these men. All they cared about was that bitch with the unnatural hair.

Looking over at Shawn, she could see the candlelight colored locks swirling out of the blanket and waving against his chest while he looked down at her like she was a precious porcelain doll.

Blech, makes me sick, glaring at them, she wandered over to Shawn and said crassly, "Will you wake her please, I need to go to the bathroom." She was holding to the decree that Shawn had made that the women don't ever go off alone.

At Leena's strident voice, Cheri's eyes flickered then she opened them vaguely surprised to be looking up at Shawn. She struggled to sit up.

"Here," Shawn said helping her, "take it easy *leamin*." He lifted her up off his lap and settled her so she could lean against the rock, then crossed his legs and moved to face her.

Peeling back the blanket, Cheri blinked and put a hand to her head. Her entire body wobbled, she set both hands on the sides of her head to hold it still.

"I'm so woozy," she mumbled. Rubbing her eyes, looking like her head was stuffed with cotton wool, she tried to sit up straight.

Shawn moved closer to her in case she fainted. Picking up her hand, he held it loosely with both of his hands and asked softly, "Do you remember what happened, Cherriana?" He observed her, carefully watching for signs of distress.

Her eyes drifted closed. Pulling her hand from his, she set her palms on the ground beside her to brace herself, letting the dizziness pass.

Leena still stood waiting, a little less impatient than a moment ago.

Cheri moved her legs stretching them straight out. If possible, her skin turned whiter, her lip trembled, the blue eyes turned up hazily at Shawn. Then she glanced at Leena who was studiously watching her. Cheri looked back to the man who was staring so intently at her his eyes darkened to hot round coals. He set his hand on her leg.

Replying quietly, "Yes," Cheri looked up at Leena again. "We were standing near the bank of the mountain where Daf told us to wait. After a few minutes, you," she said to Leena, "started slowly meandering over to where the men were working to rescue Jim."

Her brow creased as she struggled to recall the sequence of events. Her eyes widened then suddenly narrowed somewhat in accusation. She exclaimed, "After you and Deputy Malone pushed him off the cliff."

Leena yelped angrily, her mouth turned unpleasantly down. "How dare you, we did not push him, he fell, it wasn't our-"

"Anyway," Cheri continued smoothly, rubbing at an eye. She sat up straighter as her head cleared more. Crossing her legs, she pushed her long hair back then combed through the thick locks with her fingers to detangle them.

A shudder rippled through her, dread seeped into the planes of her face that were sharper from losing weight. She was growing more waifish by the day.

Struggling to push back the terror of the abduction, gulping a few deep breaths, Cheri said grimly, "I was watching the men trying to get to Jim when suddenly I was grabbed from behind.

"He covered my mouth with his hand and picked me up like I was nothing and ran for a while. Then he laid me down and put a- a cloth over my mouth," she put both quivering hands to her lips as if reliving it. Her eyes crinkled up recalling when she saw that it was the psychotic Zach looming over her.

His hand still on her leg, as her voice grew higher, fright seeping in, Shawn patted her softly.

"He- I saw it was Zachary. He held the cloth so hard over my mouth, he's so big," she wrapped her arms around herself and shivered. "He leaned on me so heavily I thought he was going to crush my head into the ground."

The terror was taking over her face, it pulled her eyes wide and thinned her lips. Remembering groggily waking in the dark cave, bound and helpless, thank goodness he had drugged her, if her wits weren't severely dulled by the drugs Cheri would have died from sheer mind-screaming fright.

Her breathing hitched rapidly, gulping shallow breaths, the panic rising, Cheri's hands trembled so hard she held them together.

Shawn quickly gathered her in his arms. Pressing her against his shoulder, stroking her head, he soothed, "That's enough, you have no more *tae* fear, *ma leamin*, Zach is dead. He can't hurt you ever again. God led us *tae* you in time."

Later, it would be Beau who would tell her how they found her and the life giving breaths Shawn had delivered to her empty lungs.

Cheri worked to get herself calm. Her heart raced and her body was shaking like tremors after an earthquake. Gritting her teeth, she repeated weakly, a faint echo, "He's dead?"

"Aye," Shawn assured. Pulling her onto his lap, he hugged her. "Daf and I..." he glanced down, broke off his words. She didn't need to hear the grisly details it would only stir up her fear of himself again if she heard what they'd done to take Zach down.

"Just leave it at Daf and I took care of him. It was a necessity, *leamin*, we had no choice."

He tucked her under his chin and laid the side of his face on her hair. Normally smelling of fresh cherries, now the tresses were scented with earthy woods, dried leaves and dew. He inhaled and relaxed, she smelled endearingly alive.

Her mouth turned up in a strong smile accepting his explanation. This time out in the wilderness was definitely making her mature fast. People could be dangerous, and she needed to learn to look out for herself.

Smiling more broadly, she said, "As long as he's gone for good, and you and Daf are okay that's all I need to know."

Shawn stroked her hair, her face, her neck then lifted her up so they could lock lips. He held her lightly, kissed her gently, to him she was as fragile as spun sugar and he'd almost lost her.

His own body quaked from holding himself in check, he wanted so badly to crush her body against his, his mouth cried to ravish hers. Pent up with fear and relief he was wired, his muscles so jacked up he was afraid of his own strength, afraid he would hurt her.

Cheri pulled back, looked him in the eye and said gravely, "Thank you, Shawn, for coming for me, for finding me. I remember when I saw you in the cave, I thought you were in my mind, a delusion."

Wincing from the memory, the wince turned to quiet joy. She went on, "Then you picked me up, carried me, for miles. I was dopey but had periods of vague lucidness when I realized you were real. The relief, the reality, you. You pulled me back from the brink of death, Shawn, I'm alive, Shawn, alive, because of you."

Her face paled but she held a hand up when he went to say something. She reached her hands up to clutch the back of his head and bring it down to her. "Now kiss me like I'm a woman, not a piece of gossamer."

Startled at first then grinning hugely, he acquiesced. Stroking both hands around her head and with scorching heat, he crushed her lips with his.

"Really?" Leena's ghastly voice broke into their romantic moment. "I *have* to go *pee!* she wheedled, standing over them watching them make out.

When Shawn felt Cheri had recovered enough to travel, he gave the okay to start out. They were down to only six of them now, they moved more quickly getting used to the hiking after doing so much for a while now.

Shawn led them around the mountain until he found where he knew they were getting close.

They came to a mountain pass that was virtually invisible from ground or air. Shawn guided them through to what seemed like the veritable inside of the mountain. It was like a vast carved cradle, solid chains of bare rock mounds went on for some distance.

When they took a break, smoking a cigarette, Shawn went to sit on a boulder next to Malone and asked him, "How will you know where the gold is exactly? I can take you *tae* the crest but that's it."

Knowing he might need help in finding it, Malone reluctantly told him, "We'll be looking for a part of the mountain wall that would be flat, like it had been sheered. Within twenty yards or so of that on the west side would be a crack in the wall, a wide crack, as tall as a house.

"Next to the crack will be a rock jutted up against the wall. Behind the rock is a hole," he raised a palm up, "and there you go."

Tossing the cigarette, Shawn nodded, pushed back a flopping lock of pitch black hair. "I know where that is."

Malone looked at him in shock. "How the hell could you possibly know that?"

Piercing Malone with a slated gaze Shawn informed him, "If I've been *tae* the crest *tae* show you where it is, it would be understandable don't you think that I would know where the crack is? Tis a big fissure, Malone, you can't miss it. Tis more of a vertical crevasse up the mountain instead of across the ground." He stood up, pushed off from the boulder.

230

"Okay, okay, whatever, let's go." Malone motioned impatiently with his hands and climbed awkwardly to his feet.

"Sure, we'll head right out," Shawn placated the man. Calling to the others to ready themselves to leave, he moved towards Cheri.

The area was broad enough they could all walk together and not have to stay in single file. Shawn asked Malone, "So, how are you going *tae* get that gold out of here? You have nothing *tae* transport it with. You can't carry it."

Malone tossed a sly smile and haughty glare at Shawn. "Don't you worry. You have your job, that's all you need to do."

"Whatever," Shawn muttered, and held Cheri's hand as they traipsed over and across the vast rocky mounds.

Suddenly Malone whooped, "I see it! I see the crack!" The deputy in torn, filthy clothes jumped up and down showing the first bought of energy he's had since getting off the bus.

He scampered over and stood looking up at the slit in the mountain. It was at least a story high, but barely wide enough for a man to fit into. Eagerly, he bounced sideways searching for the rock that was supposed to jut out.

Leena hurried up and joined him. She exclaimed excitedly, "Did you find it? Did you find it?" Jouncing around with Malone, her shirttail flapped wildly around her jiggling plump hips.

Shawn, Beau, Daf and Cheri stood back watching the pair run a few paces then back again. For a few minutes the two were out of sight. The Malone came back into view and said, "Come on, I need your strength, the three of you."

The men strode over to where Malone was gesturing.

"There, there, back there, help me dig it out, it's wedged in. There's a boulder that must have fallen, I tried but I can't move it," Malone said, directing them to go inside a small cutout in the mountain wall. Like a cave it went back a bit. They had to remove their packs and bend their heads to get inside.

"In the back," Malone told them waving his hands at the hole.

While the three men were inside the cave, Leena sauntered over to Cheri and said with unusual friendliness, "It's going to be awhile, I saw some shrubs over there on the other side of that gulley. We can take a quick pee. Let's go."

She grabbed Cheri's arm before the girl could respond, and hurried her off towards the gulley.

As soon as they reached the other side of the gulley, Malone sprang out from nowhere. "Hey babydoll," he grinned salaciously at Cheri. His hand snaked out fast and snatched her arm before she could run.

"What are you doing, Deputy?" Baffled and rattled, Cheri yanked her arm to free it from his painful grasp.

At that moment, determining the fissure was completely empty, suspicious, Shawn, Beau and Daf shuffled back out. They halted when they saw Malone, Leena and Cheri across the gap.

Malone wrenched Cheri against him and put a gun to her head.

Chapter Nineteen

Shawn muttered, "He's got Leena's gun."

It looked to Shawn that Leena had just now given it freely to Vance Malone because she stood smugly beside him, without any trace of surprise.

Of course it hadn't dawned on Shawn until this very second that Leena had known about the gold.

The deputy dug his fingers in Cheri's hair to hold her head up and he wrenched it back, arching her spine so her slender body was pressed so hard against his thick torso, she couldn't move.

Holding the gun to her temple, Malone barked at the men, "Put your fucking weapons down now! All of them, including the shotguns and the others tucked in your pockets and behind your backs."

When they hesitated, he jammed the gun into Cheri's head. "I can just as easily shoot off an ear, won't bother me, they aren't one of the main parts of her I'm interested in. So, drop them now or I start shooting." He shoved the gun brutally hard against her temple, forcing Cheri's head to bend painfully to the side.

Having no choice, the men did as they were told, removed their weapons and set them gingerly on the ground.

Shawn called out, "What the hell is this, Malone?"

Triumphant elation lit the deputy's jowly face. "This, Mr. Know-it-all, duh, is a double-cross. It wasn't gold I came for you dim-witted prick, it was-"

"Money from an armored car robbery," Shawn interjected calmly, moving towards the gap.

Malone's eyes popped, his forehead wrinkled with his mouth dropping open. He sputtered, "How the hell did you fucking know-"

Shawn took another few steps forward.

Malone pushed the gun viciously against Cheri's temple making her head bend on the edge of breaking her neck, her cry of pain arced across the gap.

Snarling his threat, Malone ordered, "You need to stop right there, hero. Tell me what the hell is going on here? How did you know?" The elation deflated from his bearing, and the smugness fell right off Leena's face.

Around twenty-five feet separated Shawn from them.

"I am," Shawn motioned to Beau and Daf, "we are, Federal Agents, special weapons and tactics officers. We were put on the bus *tae* help you find the stolen cash. More than 30 mil they say."

The color draining along with his triumph, Malone stammered, "But- but- how did you know? How could they know?"

Setting his hands on his hips, Shawn told him, "Since the robbery five years ago, the Feds have kept feelers out waiting for word about the money. None of the sequential numbers ever hit the market so it was assumed the people that did it were incarcerated for other crimes. The law laid low and waited. For years nothing hit, until, you."

Shawn moved his long legs closer with a nod of his head at Malone. "You started suddenly asking around about the

Grand Crest. The armored car that was robbed was out in this vast area. But of course up on the main road, not down the mountain where we were. A known bank robber, Tai Brand, blabbed to some people while in prison, your prison, about the robbery and that the cash was hidden in Grand Crest.

"None of the other prisoners believed him, thought he was a storyteller. But you, a corrupt junkyard dog, got wind of it, believed it and started asking around trying *tae* find someone *tae* take you here."

The more Shawn spoke, the paler Malone's face turned. Even the knuckles on his hand whitened he held the gun so tightly.

Leena was easing away from the deputy. Finding out Shawn and the others were cops changed the whole sphere of the scheme.

"Listen, Shawn," Leena worked a shaking smile, curving her lips provocatively while trying to look innocent. "I had no idea about any of this. It wasn't until just recently that he told me about the money."

She shrugged nonchalantly, gazing brazenly at Shawn while blatantly perusing his body from those long legs up to his phenomenally dark and secretive eyes.

Moving a step further from Malone, Leena simpered, "I thought, you know, what's the big deal now that we're already out here and all…I mean," she turned away from the deputy a little so she could look coyly at Shawn. "Really, who would have figured you dangerous, hot looking hunks were cops?"

Dismissing Leena as if she hadn't spoken, Shawn said to Malone, "We get it right, Malone?"

The shock of them knowing his real agenda still apparent in his slack jaw and pallid complexion, the corrupt deputy took a deep breath then exhaled slowly. It didn't matter what they knew anyway, he was in charge now. The thought bolstered him, a scornful grin spread across his face.

"Yeah, Tai Brand was gonna be in custody for a long time. Two of them pulled off the heist, the other thief was caught right away and was killed months later in a jailhouse brawl. Brand started worrying about his own safety so he was not that reluctant to give out information.

"He wanted a new lawyer soon for appeals. I talked him into telling me where the money was, promising to help his family and get him another, better lawyer. Told him we'd split the dough."

Remembering what he was holding besides the money, what he considered his prize, Cheri, Malone took his hand out of her hair, stroked it down the side of her head and across the front of her neck.

Inclining his head slightly, he sniffed her hair. "God that's so nice, makes my legs...harden." He slid his hand sensuously across her breastbone to her shoulder. His arm a band across her, he jerked her possessively, roughly against his torso.

Her elbows bent, she clutched at his arm desperately pulling at it. The deputy ignored her feeble efforts to get free of him.

Watching his every move, although his eyes burned his fury, Shawn stood casually, said calmly, "You were telling us about the money."

Broken out of his revelry, Malone kissed the side of Cheri's face so sloppy he left her skin wet. Still holding her tightly, he lowered his arm to wrap around just below her breasts holding her arms against her body, totally immobilizing her.

He moved his hips back and forth rubbing his erection against her bottom, forcing her to feel his arousal.

Cheri grimaced in disgust. With Malone's arm around her holding down her arms, she couldn't lift a hand to wipe her face or even move an inch from his disgusting body.

"Yeah," Malone went on, using the hand holding the gun, he dabbed at the perspiration on his forehead. "Anyway, he could only tell me where the money was once I was here, but not how to get here. He had hidden it and ran and hid out as far away as he could get for months before getting caught.

"Brand had thought he would remember the location, the crest, yet he tried to come back and find it just before he got arrested and discovered it all looks alike out here. He had no clue how to find this place. But how did you, I mean, I don't understand..."

Shrugging his wide, solid shoulders, rocking side to side like he was thinking, Shawn inched another step closer.

He said, "Once the Feds heard about you asking around, everyone knows there are no secrets in prison, there were flags all over the robbery, they put other feelers out too and found out I'd lived out here a few years back.

"They put me in jail with you and let out some rumors that I had lived here and that I knew every nook and cranny. You thought you were being subtle when you asked me about living here and if I'd ever heard of Grand Crest. The Feds knew you would arrange *tae* have me lead you here." He nodded at Daf and Beau.

"The Feds replaced the real prisoners that were being transferred with my men. They were sent along of course *tae* ensure nothing went wrong. There wasn't supposed *tae* be anyone else on the bus except the driver and Vega. Somebody fucked up and had other prisoners and therefore additional corrections officers on board."

237

Shawn put his hand over his brow to hide the grief in his eyes. "We hadn't planned on you crashing the fucking bus, and getting half of the people on it killed throughout this messy horror of an extraction."

He looked in physical pain thinking about the men, and Bella, who had died for no reason other than Malone was dirty and greedy.

"When Caleb, Bella, and then Jim were killed, I had *tae* go *tae* the ranger's station *tae* report their deaths, as well as the bus driver's and the other deputy. They had *tae* be made aware that Zach was on the loose, and Tomas was missing too, and the trouble with those trappers."

His eyes on Malone, he motioned his head at Cheri. "The last thing we expected you piece of shit was that you'd have women on the bus."

The deputy leered a nasty grin at the girl he held powerless, he squeezed her. "Oh yeah. As soon as I saw this," he gave her another hug and a kiss then sucked on her face leaving it wet and red.

Laughing crassly when she tried to wipe her repulsed face on her shoulder, he said, "I had to have her. I was thwarted every time I made a move in the prison. It didn't matter though, this worked out better. Now I can have her as often and for as long as I want. Right, baby?"

He nestled his cheek on her head, hugging her until she was breathless, any harder and he'd break her ribs.

It took all of Shawn's formidable effort to stand still and not launch himself at the repulsive deputy, rip off his arm and beat him to death with it. "Malone, you-"

Malone shot a sideways glance at Leena trying to sneak away. "Leena," he said. She stopped and looked at him.

"Thanks for the gun," he said with a grin then shot her in the head.

Cheri screamed.

Leena's eyes bulged, then she looked straight at Malone like she had expected it, and collapsed to the ground.

"Dumb bitch, you outlived your usefulness to me," Malone sneered at the dead woman lying face up. A line of blood trailed out of the hole in her head, poured down the side and started pooling around her.

He smirked at Shawn. "Brainless gullible bitch. I told her if she gave me her gun I would cut her in." He noticed Shawn had inched closer during the distraction.

Furiously, Malone quickly moved the arm he held Cheri with and stuck his hand in her hair. Grabbing a fistful of her locks, he yanked her head back and knocked the gun against her head hard enough it clunked on her skull.

"Not a step closer you son of a bitch, or I'll shoot her. I want her, Darkonn, but I want the money more. I'll shoot her then all of you before you can get to me."

He tightened his grip on her hair, pulling her so she was forced to arch against him. Exhaling a harsh, wet gravelly sound, he grinned heinously. "As you see," he nodded at Leena lying on the ground, the blood darkening a strip of her hair. "I have no problems killing in cold blood." The gun pressed harder against Cheri's temple.

Everyone froze.

Daf and Beau had been moving unperceptively to the sides, separating themselves so Malone would have a harder time shooting all of them. Unfortunately, there was nothing to hide behind, not a tree or a rock. They were all out in the open.

"So," Malone's voice came back snarky and bold now that Leena was out of the picture, she had been a dismal drain on his senses. His exhilaration was returning. "This is the plan," Malone wanted them to know what he was going to do, to rub it in. "I have the money."

He indicated a large case at his feet. "When you were searching the crevasse I pulled it out from a tiny cave hidden beside the slit." At Shawn's look of chagrin, Malone said with a smirk, "You didn't think I'd tell you everything did you?

"Now, I am going to kill you three, and I must say with profound pleasure. I am so tired of you men I could cry. Especially you, Darkonn, you bastard. I would have done it while you three were in the crack just now but Leena wouldn't give me the gun then."

Shawn stared impassively at the crazed deputy. Stalling for more time, he asked curiously, "How involved was Leena really?"

Enjoying having the upper hand, keeping the strong as shit agents under his control, Malone couldn't help gloating. A corner of his lip pulled up cagily making him look ever the sinister Joker.

He snorted gleefully. "That was great. We staged the fight on the mountain hoping to knock one of you off to occupy yourselves with the rescue, just as you did, so Zach could snatch Cheri, just as he did."

"Why? Why involve that maniac?"

Malone shrugged ruefully. "Didn't actually have much choice, as you said, he's a maniac. He thought if he held the girl hostage he could make you do whatever he wanted, force us take him to the money and then have you get him the hell out of here.

"That's what he said anyway. We met secretly when I disappeared a few times along the way for a piss. I think he just wanted her," he licked Cher's face again. "And the money too of course. He had forced me to tell him why we were really out here."

Malone winced at the memory. "Wasn't as retarded as he looked. He was cunning, he'd figured out the whole crash scene and shit was a ruse. He knew something else was going on and forced me to tell."

"What happened, what'd he do *tae* you?" Shawn asked, to keep him talking.

His face turned ashen, Malone suddenly looked old and weak. He glared blankly at Shawn, his body involuntarily shivered recalling what the depraved sadist had made him suffer through until he broke and blabbed everything.

With an aggrieved blink and a shake of his head, he flicked away the unbelievable pain Zach had wrought on him to make him spill his guts about the money.

The men remained still, watching Malone struggle to bury the sickening horridness of his brief time alone with the murdering Zach. Shawn started to say something but Malone shook his head.

"Never mind. Regardless, he had figured something was wrong about the whole thing. The bus rolling, and it taking us so long to get out of this fucking wasteland, why I was letting you run the show. Anyway, that was one time you wily asshole did me a favor, you got rid of that bloodthirsty hulk. I know his real plan was to kill everyone, except for her."

He yanked Cheri's head sideways and kissed her cheek delighting in the distaste wrinkling her smooth skin.

"Leena met with him too, she believed the freak when he told her he was going to keep her too. That he wanted to get rid of everyone else and hide away letting the police think he was dead, that everyone on the bus had died out here. He figured they'd assumed the wild animals did us in."

"What about Marx?" Shawn questioned. Casually tucking his shirt in, he carefully rolled the sleeves up, acting like they had all day to chitchat.

It was warm on the rocks in the direct sunlight, if it wasn't for the breeze it would be stifling. Daf and Beau kept silent, not drawing attention to themselves.

"Yeah," Malone appeared slightly regretful about that. "Zach told Leena he killed Ritchie and tossed his body in the river a few days back. Ritchie wasn't a bad guy, really, never gave me any trouble, went along with whatever I said. The rest of them, Vega, Bella, Tomas Trent, I could have cared less about. Whatever."

He waved the hand holding the gun like they were nothing, then knocked the gun back against Cheri's temple smirking when he heard the pained gasp she tried to stifle.

"Anyway, Zach would have double-crossed me for sure. So, thanks for that." The deputy smirked at Shawn knowing he would never deliberately do Malone any favors.

Still stalling for time, Shawn said, "So Leena was as duplicitous as the rest of you." His hands rolled in loose fists rested lightly on his tapered hips, he occasionally pushed back a lock of dark hair that the wind blew in his eyes.

"Bitch would do anything for money, or good sex," Malone snarked.

Shawn said, "Why don't you just let the girl go, I brought you *tae* your money, I held up my end of the deal, you still need me *tae* get you out of-"

Laughing at Shawn's inability to do anything to stop him, Malone said, "You're a cop, Darkonn, you'd never let me walk away. Anyway, it's done. I can see towers in the distance from up here. We're near enough to civilization that I can find the way out if I stay up high. I am taking her." He shook his fist in Cheri's hair making her yelp from the pain.

An unexpected sexual thrill from her cries of pain swarmed up his legs, striking his groin and flooding his belly with lewd hunger. Malone gasped in surprise at the sudden kick of carnal heat.

Shawn cringed at the blatant red blush of lust that lit Malone's flaccid face. Something had apparently struck the deputy, excited him, a sick eroticism cooked in the small brown eyes. He had stopped rubbing against Cheri.

He moved the hand with the gun against her hips, now forcing her to rub against him like he was using her entire body to masturbate in front of them.

Masking his repulsion, Shawn desperately tried to think of something to say to further stall the deputy, hoping for a sudden distraction to happen so he could make a move.

Malone grinned triumphantly at the men. "I got the money, I outsmarted you smartheads, and I got her." Tightening his grip on Cheri's hair, he tugged down forcing her back to flatten against his thick body.

He pulled back harder, stretching and arching her neck, and kept wrenching her head back more until she was facing the sky, her mouth was forced open.

Never taking his eyes off the three men, one of his hands still clutching her hair, the other holding the gun against her pelvis, Malone pushed her back and forth against his erection.

Deliberately inflicting pain, he brutally razed Cheri's lips, kissing her with such rabid ferocity he was getting off on her smothered cries and futile struggles. Her hands now free she frantically pulled at the arm that clutched her hair trying to make him let go.

Hearing Beau growling his wrath a few feet away, Shawn hissed "*Beau*," warning him to be quiet. They had to keep their cool to rescue Cheri and get them all out alive.

243

The more the men and Cheri reacted to Malone's assaulting her, the more sadistic he became.

Slobbering all over her, Malone lashed Cheri against him as hard as he could. His erection burgeoned even more knowing he was hurting her, and antagonizing the men.

Overpowering her even with his mouth, Malone crammed his tongue down her throat. Not expecting it to turn him on so intensely, guttural groans rumbled out, erupting repugnantly against her prone lips. In a sudden lustful haze, his eyes fell from watching the men and dropped down Cheri's front.

Arched back like she was on a torture machine, the torn blouse having no buttons left, was tied just under her breasts. From him jerking her around, the knot had loosened and her breasts were almost fully exposed mounding out of her bra.

Distracted, licking his lips, the deputy let go of her hair to slide his hand over one of her luscious globes- As soon as he let go, Cheri twisted and socked him in the eye as hard as she could.

Shrieking, Malone slammed a hand over his eye. Cheri shot her leg up and kneed him as hard as she could in the balls. His scream sucked in with the agony, he doubled over.

She crouched down, grabbed up stones and hurled one after another after another at him while he wailed clutching his privates.

Chapter Twenty

*T*he men made their move while Malone clutched his groin and writhed trying to fend off the stones Cheri flung at him.

Shawn bolted head on and sprung in the air tackling Malone. The deputy bounced hard on the rocky ground with Shawn on top of him.

They were still rolling when Shawn started wailing away nonstop at the deputy, blow after savage blow like a killing machine, blood spurted everywhere.

"Shawn, stop, bro, stop, ya can't kill him!" Daf shouted, grabbing one of Shawn's arms.

Beau wrestled the other, and using all their might, the two pulled the raging Scotsman off the sobbing deputy, who had curled up in a ball and was trying to cover his head.

Daf and Beau dragged Shawn away but he continued stomping and kicking at the deputy until they got him clear.

Trying to hold his murderous friend back from pounding Malone until he was pulverized dust into the ground, Beau gasped, "Shawn, get a grip. It'll be better that he goes back and faces the music than he dies here." He and Daf held Shawn tightly until they felt the fight finally diminishing from him, then they let him go.

Heaving and huffing, sweating and shaking with fury, Shawn yanked his handcuffs off the back of his belt and tossed them to Beau. "Cuff him." He saw Cheri standing with a rock in each hand, staring wide-eyed at him.

It was what he'd been afraid of, that she would see the vicious, ruthless, unrelenting man that he was. If his friends hadn't stopped him he would have killed the bastard.

Hurting her, mauling her, what Malone would have done if the men weren't there to protect her, livid red struck his face firing him up, working him back into a blind rampage. He started towards the deputy with his fists up.

Beau and Daf jumped in front of him.

"*Na Brither*," Daf said softly.

It was enough to clear Shawn's head. He stopped and glanced at Cheri. She had dropped the stones and had her hands over her mouth staring at him like he was a monster.

His head lowered in shame at being such a crazed animal, not able to control himself. Shawn had known from the beginning that she was too refined, too delicate, too pure to be with a brute like him.

He'd been kidding himself that they had a chance of finding happiness together. His knuckles cut and bleeding, he unrolled his sleeves then dragged them across his face to wipe off his sweat, and Malone's blood.

Beau and Daf cuffed the deputy and hauled him to his unsteady feet. His bruised and bloodied head bobbed and spun, mouth hung open, drool and blood leaked out and from his nose. He couldn't talk with the concussion Shawn had beaten into him.

They looked over at Leena lying in a pool of blood then to Shawn. Beau asked, "What are we going to do with her? It was her betrayal that almost did us in." His gaze slid over to Cheri who still stood immobile, her hands now in fists, still covering her mouth.

Shawn said, "We'll wrap her, cover her with rocks. The ranger station isn't that far away." He smoothed his tousled hair back, dusted off his shirt then his jeans. With Cheri obviously shaken by his violent behavior, he felt awkward for the first time in his life.

He didn't regret beating Malone, he just wished she hadn't been there to see it. Looking away from her, he muttered, "Let's get out of here."

After wrapping Leena up and piling rocks on and around her body, Beau and Daf half-carried half-dragged Malone over the flat rocks.

Shawn carried the case of money. Cheri walked slightly behind him. Shawn deliberately slowed his step so she would move up next to him. He shot quick little glimpses at her, trying to read her thoughts, but her face was stoic.

After a few miles, he couldn't take it anymore. He stopped, set the case down, grasped her hand to stop her and swung her around to face him rougher than he meant to. She recoiled from him.

Already worried that she saw him as a cutthroat barbarian, Shawn let go of her wrist and held her upper arms loosely, yet forcefully to keep her from walking away from him.

He was still amped up with aggression and adrenalin racing through his veins from what had just happened. Knowing he could easily hurt her, he had to strain not to squeeze her too hard in his agitation. A pulse beat crazily at his temple, sweat dripped down the sides of his face.

"Listen, uh, Cherriana, I'm sorry, that, you had *tae* see, I mean…" he really didn't know what to say. He just badly wanted her to say something.

247

Shawn waited, his eyes skimming the beautiful albeit roughed up face for...well, he didn't know what for. She refused to look at him and remained mute. The breeze shuffled her hair across her face.

He pushed it back without touching her, murmured ponderously, "Say something, Cherriana..."

Still she remained quiet. He was about to pick up the bag and start walking again, when she took in a raspy deep breath and exhaled the weight of the world. He let go of her arms.

Her face pinched and pale, there was a cut over one eye, bruises under both, and scrapes across the side of her jaw. Her arms were scratched all over and still showed evidence of the bruising from her struggles with Zach.

She untied her blouse. Shawn's brows arched and his lips parted, his face flushed as his body quickened. She was only retying it tighter, it had loosened in her struggle with Malone.

Feeling like a randy teenager, Shawn averted his eyes and hoped she didn't notice his body's reactions to her movements.

Her hands clasped in front of her, her head bowed, Cheri said in a small tight voice, "I understand now why you kept saying you couldn't have a relationship with me."

He lifted his hand to touch her, stopped, his hand dropped to his side.

Her words filled with shame and misery shook. "Because you're a policeman, and I'm a...a...criminal. You will be taking me back to..." Her throat closed up swallowing the lump of realization that there could never be anything between them, and she was soon to be locked up again. The blue eyes filling with humiliation lowered, she turned away from him to go.

Shawn suddenly grasped her arms again. "That was what kept holding me back, Cherriana, besides your…youth. It wasn't that you are a criminal, it was that you were a prisoner and I was a cop. It was wrong, unethical for me *tae* have any kind of a personal relationship with you.

"It would be a terrible conflict that wouldn't be accepted by the superiors. There would be accusations that I took advantage of your situation having authority over you, like a teacher with a student. As a Federal Agent and you a prisoner, it would appear I'd forced or coerced you and you had no choice."

She twisted to get out of his grip but he held her fast. Her voice clogged with pain she barely eked out, "It doesn't matter, I understand. You have to take me back to…" The tears fell as she struggled to get away from him. Lifting her hands, she tried to jerk out of his clutch.

"*Na*, baby, you don't understand." He pulled her combative body close so she couldn't push or hit him, lifted her chin and gently kissed her lips. "I am not taking you back, not yet. I have a place *tae* keep you, hide you until we clear your name. Beau," he chuckled remembering their argument.

"Well, Beau was quite adamant we don't let you go back *tae* prison while we work *tae* clear your charges." He tried to kiss her again but she turned her head away.

It tore him up inside seeing her so distraught, hopeless. He had already basically lied to her by not telling her he was an agent, she wouldn't trust anything he said now. With soothing movements, he trickled his fingertips across her cheek, his thumb drifted over her bottom lip.

She turned from him, yet at the same time unconsciously leaned her head against his hand.

249

Holding her jaw lightly, Shawn firmly moved her so she had to look at him. "Cherriana, I agree wholeheartedly with Beau. Nothing has been on my mind since we left that bus but trying *tae* figure out how *tae* get you out of the trouble you're in.

"I didn't believe for a second that you were guilty. Why do you think I was so tough about keeping you close *tae* me? I was terrified you'd run and get injured or killed. I had *tae* keep you by my side *tae* protect you from the other immoral males with us as well as from yourself doing something crazy."

Her head down, she shook it sadly, barely audible mumbles slipped from her plush lips. "You have to take me back, Shawn, it's your job." The wretched agony knowing for sure what her outcome would be reflected bleakly in the gaze that rose tearfully to him. "Either that, or you look the other way and you let me go now."

Vehemently shaking his head, he ground harshly with a shade of anger, "*Na.* Neither of those are options. You are not taking your chances out here. As we've already seen, you wouldn't last ten minutes alone. And, I can't bear *tae* have you in that- that- place, jail."

His face flushed thinking about her alone and helpless against a myriad of conscienceless criminals. And, as they learned by Malone, Ritchie and even drunken Tomas, she was in danger of the law enforcement officers too. "You're already a fugitive, hiding you out a little longer isn't going *tae* hurt anything."

She pushed against him. "You can't clear me, Shawn, my blackmailer has evidence. It's hopeless. I would wish that you could take it upon your heart to just look the other way while I disappear over the-"

He shook her so hard her head switched up and down. "Stop it. I am not leaving you in this wilderness, I've told you that from the beginning. You will for once do what I say. It is way too damned treacherous out here. In fact, the sooner I get you out of this area the better I'll feel.

"We will take Malone *tae* the rangers, they're already involved. You figured by now I'm sure, that's where I've been going when I've left the camp. Then I'll get you out, hide you, until tis done…and you are not going back *tae* jail. Worse comes *tae* worse, we let them believe you died out here too and obtain a new identity for you."

Furrows crossing her forehead, she said, "No, Shawn. Beau explained to me that you have tremendous integrity and honor, that it would eat you up if you didn't do the right thing. Please let me go-"

He shook her again and got in her face, said with vehemence, "The law is designed *tae* protect people. Tis wrong for you *tae* be in custody and I won't let it happen, it has nothing to do with my honor. My duty is *tae* see that justice is served. It'll be all right, I promise. Trust me, *ma leamin*, please trust me."

His eyes pleaded with hers to connect, see, believe his sincerity. Put her trust, her life in his hands.

Cheri slanted her head back and squeezed her eyes shut tight to keep in the mortifying tears she kept releasing this entire journey like an infant.

"Besides all the legal ramifications, Cherriana, I have no plans *tae* give you up. Ever." He slid his fingers across the side of her face, combed her hair back. "I want a life with you, baby, make that a lifetime."

He cocked his head at her, watching her expression while combing his fingers gently through her hair and letting it sift through his fingers and sail down her back.

His stomach twitched when her baby blues stroked his face, shined at his dark eyes. He said softly, "I think, I hope, that you feel the same way." His fingers combed through her tresses one more time, then he threaded his fingers around the back of her head. "Tell me that you do," he pleaded tenderly.

"I," she hesitated with her lips parted. Her gaze went from his black orbs glossy with blatant desire for her, to his very masculine lips turned in a lopsided smile.

Taking his opportunity, Shawn dipped down and took over her lips, reveling in their plush softness even as she remained wooden.

Angling his head for a tighter fit, he drove her lips open. Tantalizing her with his handsome mouth, he worked his tongue around those sensuous lips, teasing her tongue to respond. Dipping in and out, he dredged every cushy supple bit of her like a backhoe excavating a succulent chasm.

Melting like butter in the oven, against his mouth she whispered, "Oh, Shawn, I do feel the same. I don't want to leave you, I never have."

Her lips clung to his, moved with his, he felt so fine her head clouded in lustful bliss. Cheri wanted him to know she believed him, trusted him, desired to touch him and be touched by him. She unbuttoned his shirt and caressed his chest.

Pressed against him, she could feel his body change. It hardened yet still yielded to her body and her hands. At her touch, Shawn's kiss deepened, he fervently sucked her lips, kissed the side of her mouth, her jaw, her neck. He sucked and nibbled and kissed as if he would gobble her up.

Pushing his shirt back, she ran her hands all over his chest, her fingers dragging through the dark hair then stroking over his shoulders. She scraped her nails down caressing his arms. And his hands stroking her, so tough, she thought, yet so gentle. She could feel his feverish growl deep down in his chest.

Cheri remembered her fierce jealousy when Leena had her hands all over his incredible cut pecs. Stroking up his massive muscled chest, she moved her hands back to feel his unbelievably strong arms, the heat of his skin burning her palms. The picture of Shawn beating Malone came unbidden to her mind.

The violence didn't excite her, but watching every one of Shawn's muscles working, in action, the sinew of his arms bulging and pumping, the way he clenched his huge fists.

The way he held onto Malone while he pummeled him, his taut muscles rock hard flexed with every lightning fast punch he threw. A moan trilled from her, she'd never seen a man so strongly, so beautifully built. Weaving her hands up around his neck to clutch the hair on his head, she pulled him more urgently to her.

Shawn was absolutely mindless to everything except her lips on his and her hands on his body. His heart hammered in an excruciating rush to tear her clothes off, and his, and lay her down on…his brain shouted back- *No- not the time or the place-* they were so entwined at this point all he'd have to do is slide his arms under her knees and her back and gently set her-

"Shawn!" Beau called up at him.

It was enough to splash a little cold water on their fiery embrace. Shawn set his forehead on Cheri's, they locked eyes. Hers were ablaze with passion, the blue irises bright and intense with desire like a thunderstorm about to start crackling.

He whispered, "Tis okay baby, we'll pick back up when we're in a safe, comfortable, *private* place when we can take our time *tae* do what we want…If you want, there's no pressure baby, please know that."

Her hands behind his ears she drew him back to her lips and purred, "I want you, Shawn, all of you, with all of me. Where doesn't matter."

"*Oh God*," Shawn groaned, drawn right back into her spell. Until Beau called out again, with less patience.

Shawn waved at Beau. Beau and Daf were waiting way down the path, still holding Malone up between them. He took Cheri's hand and picked up the case and they started down the trail.

After a few steps, he said, "By the way, Cherriana, I was so proud of you the way you took charge and courageously attacked that bast- uh, fool."

Next to him she smiled. "Yes, I listened to you. I kneed him like you said I should have done to Ritchie, and it worked!" The smile dribbled into a fearful frown. "I was so scared he would shoot you guys, especially after I kicked him. I was afraid that would really make him mad and he'd kill you."

"Uh," Shawn swung her hand lightly between them. "I have a confession."

Her head swung to him. "What? No more, I can't take anymore-"

"*Na, na, ma leamin*, nothing like that. Tis just, the day we fought the trappers, Leena gave me her gun *tae* make sure it was loaded. Not trusting her, I took out all but one of the bullets. I left one in just in case a trapper got past us she could still shoot him. That one shot would have run off any others. Once Malone shot Leena with her gun, I knew it was empty. The guys and I weren't in any danger at that point."

She stopped abruptly, went to tug her hand from his grasp but he wasn't letting go. "Then why didn't you act? He was touching me, pawing me, hurting me. He was *kissing* me shoving his filthy tongue down my throat for heaven's sake! Why didn't you-"

Shawn stroked her face, couldn't help himself, he pulled her in for a short sweet kiss smothering her protests. He said mildly, "Aye, you're right *we* weren't in danger, but when Malone would eventually shoot and realize he had no bullets and that he couldn't kill us as he planned, he might have snapped your neck to spite me before we could have gotten to you or thrown you off the side of the mountain. I had *tae* get close enough *tae* him to grab him before he could seriously hurt you."

He nuzzled her still intact neck, then leaned back to look at her beloved face. The anxiety he had felt while she was in Malone's repulsive clutches grimly tightened his features.

His voice turned harsh, all the frustration, anger, and fear for her rolled out, "Cherriana, you have *tae* know how it killed me *tae* have *tae* stand there and watch him do that *tae* you. But I had *tae* wait, it was way more important *tae* me that you were alive."

The smile curved back on her face, she squeezed his hand. "I understand. Thank you Shawn, for rescuing me, saving my life, again." The smile turned to an ingenuous leer. "When we are ever alone again," she said over Beau's shouting in the background, "I will show you my gratitude."

Shawn lifted her hand and kissed it. He said seriously, "I don't want your gratitude, *ma leamin*. I want you, *tae* only want me, of your own free will. No gratefulness, no strings, no pay back, I want you *tae* just want me."

Ignoring Beau's impatient hollers down the way, Cheri slipped back into his arms. "Have no doubt, Shawn, my valiant hero, I want you."

Chapter Twenty-One

$\boldsymbol{J}$t took the rest of the day to bring Malone to the Rangers.

Taking custody of him, Ranger John Roberts offered Shawn and Beau to stay the night at the station. But they had Cheri hidden nearby with Daf, they couldn't let the rangers know she was with them.

Shawn shook Roberts' hand. "Thanks, Ranger, appreciate it. But we've been out in these woodlands for long enough. We're eager *tae* get on our way."

"Sure sure, here, let me show you the car that's been rented for you." Ranger Roberts led the two men to the car out in the parking lot.

After the ranger went back inside, they collected Daf and Cheri and they were off.

It was a big car but hardly big enough for three huge men. Daf could not get in the back seat, and the leaner Beau had to sit sideways as it was. So Shawn drove and Cheri had to share the back with Beau.

Helping her into the car, Shawn leaned in and kissed her. "I wish I could sit with you but Beau is the only one we can squeeze in back there." He nuzzled her neck. "I can't wait until we're-"

"Uh, do you mind, Romeo, it's hardly comfortable squashed back here," Beau complained.

Shawn laughed at him. "Good. That way you'll be forced *tae* keep your *bluidy* freckled hands *tae* yourself." He gave Cheri a quick kiss and helped her climb into the back. Daf slid in the front seat to ride shotgun, and Shawn climbed in behind the wheel.

They drove for hours until they reached a tiny private airport. Shawn had arranged for a pilot to take them out.

Another couple of hours passed and they landed, then got in another car for another few hours of driving. They only stopped to refuel and grab something quick to eat.

It was necessary to stop at a safe house for a couple of days. They were so bleary with exhaustion, no one argued when they heard the place was full of other people, and the men would all have to bunk in with other men.

But, Shawn kicked up a fuss when he learned Cheri would be housed with females in a different building.

"No fucking way I want her out of my sight," he bellowed at the Federal Agent in charge. "I'll take her somewhere else, a hotel-"

Daf grabbed his arm, whispered, "Shawn, she will be safer here than anywhere else, let it go. Don't attract attention to her, we don't need them discovering she's a fugitive."

So furious he was shaking, Shawn shrugged out of his friend's grasp. "Daf, I can't have her alone again, you know that." He felt a small hand slip around his arm. His face reddened, he looked down at Cheri's sweet slightly battered face.

"Please, Shawn, everyone is beat, don't make your friends suffer for your fear for my safety. Please. I will be fine." She smiled winsomely up at him, his face softened into a reluctant and loving smile. He had to give in.

It was two days before he saw her again.

The men were waiting for her at the car.

As soon as Cheri emerged from the women's quarters Shawn strode over to her. He scooped her against his chest and dropped his mouth on hers before anyone could say a word.

"Come on, Shawn," Beau whined pitifully, trying to sound like a little girl, "the sooner we get on the road the sooner you guys can have some privacy."

Cheri giggled against Shawn's mouth. They broke apart.

He cupped her chin smiling, and drew a knuckle down her cheek. "You look a lot better, *leamin*, the bruises and cuts have diminished a bit." He kissed her lightly then brought her to the car, they all squeezed in and took off down the highway to their next destination.

They drove for a few hours until the car turned onto a two-lane, roughly paved road, then after a couple of miles they diverted onto a one-lane dirt road.

Shawn followed the winding road densely lined on both sides with green forest for a dozen miles before turning off onto another dirt road.

After a few minutes, he stopped the car. Daf got out to unlock a gated fence and disarm the sensor alarms.

As soon as they drove through the gate, Shawn stopped again and Daf locked the gate, reset the alarms then hopped back inside.

A few more minutes of driving and the car pulled up in front of a light-grey ranch styled, very large house with a wrap-around porch. The back of the house overlooked a lake glimmering blue under a bright lowering sun.

Parking the car, Shawn climbed out and hustled over to the passenger side and yanked the door open.

His grin big and toothy, Daf joked, "Hey, bro, I didn't know you cared! Gimmie a big kiss on the smacker, honey," he teased getting out.

"Yeah, I'll give you a smack all right, get the hell out of the way." Shawn gave his friend a mocking push out of the doorway. Shoving the top of the seat back, he stuck his hand in to Cheri.

She slipped her hand in his without hesitation and he helped her out and into his arms. His lips found hers immediately and he about sucked her whole face into his mouth.

"Okay, sure, don't worry, bro," Daf teased, "we'll get the luggage."

Beau cracked Daf on the back with a laugh. "Duh, we don't have any luggage, just a couple of bags with a few crappy clothes in them. Hey Shawn, you want me to wash up a pair of jeans for you, bro?"

He laughed at the black-haired man when Shawn's arms didn't move from Cheri, or his lips from hers.

Daf and Beau were long gone inside when Shawn drew away from Cheri. He slipped his hands through her hair sifting it off her shoulders.

"Your eyes, baby, are so dusky with passion the blue is blurry." He smiled and kissed the lips he had already made dewy red and plumped up with his lustful kisses.

She leaned back in the arm he had circled around her, her smile a blend of sensuous tenderness and love.

Clasping her hands behind his neck, her tone shy but her voice happy, she said, "I just want you to know how happy I am to be here, anywhere, with you Shawn. Thank you for taking care of me-"

He swung her around. "Listen, Cherriana," he said seriously, "I want *tae* take care of you, but I also want *tae* be with you. Okay? So don't thank me, just," he lowered his lips kissing her softly, "just be with me."

Cheri's gaze full of desire for him, her cheeks rosy, smiled. "Okay."

Another long kiss, then his voice husky with emotion, Shawn said, "What do you say, *leamin*, I'll show you around." He took her hand and they ran up the wooden steps and through the front door the men had left open.

Inside, Shawn reset the alarm then showed her the roomy living room stuffed with cushioned chairs and two sofas, television, music center, bookcase crammed with books.

He said, "There are two wings *tae* the place. Daf and Beau will stay in the west wing and you and I," he pulled up their clasped hands and kissed the back of hers, "will have the east wing *tae* ourselves."

His brows drew down seriously for a second. He set his fingers under her chin to lift her head looking her in the eye. "Make no mistake, Cherriana, I want you sleeping in my bed, sharing a room together. I want *tae* spend the rest of my life with you."

He said quickly as her lashes swept down over her eyes, "But I will not say a word if that doesn't work for you. I don't want you *tae* feel pressured *tae* sleep with me. You can have your own room, you don't have *tae* stay with-"

She put two fingers over his lips. "Shawn," she gave him such a luxurious sultry smile his knees melted. "I want to be with you. I don't ever want to ever be apart from you again."

Taking her hand Shawn whispered, "You, uh, you mean you're ready *tae*, uh…" he stopped, red tipping his ears.

Cheri laughed. "Wow, Shawn Darkonn at a loss for words. I never thought I'd see the day." Her eyes twinkled blue gaiety at him.

Shawn swung her hand up again to kiss her knuckles. "Oh baby, believe me, I have plenty of words *tae* say what I want, I am just trying *tae* think of the cleanest ones."

Cheri slid her hands up around his neck. "How about, let's make love, will that work?"

A wide grin creased across his face. He brought his mouth down on hers, kissed her hard then leaned back. "Oh yeah, that works for me." He kissed the tip of her nose.

"Come on, let me show you the rest of the house. Daf and Beau will be starving and waiting dinner on us."

He showed her the wing they would be staying in. All five bedrooms had huge beds, dressers, thirsty carpets and fancy bathrooms.

He stopped before they reached the last bedroom at the end of the hall. "We need *tae* eat first and make nice with Daf and Beau before I show you our room. Otherwise, I don't know how many days it will be before we come out again."

He grinned crookedly at her giggle. "However, we do need *tae* shower and get on some clean clothes. You go ahead first, honey. Our housekeeper brought some things for us *tae* wear for a few days. You'll find them on the bed."

"Wow, that was really nice of her. Will I see her to thank her?"

"Maybe," he shrugged. "She might be around while we're still here." He kissed her. "Come out *tae* the kitchen when you're done." He kissed her again.

"Hurry," he said with a grin watching her disappear into the bedroom then he hurried back down the hall knowing if he stuck around another second she would not be showering alone.

Fifteen minutes later, Cheri shyly entered the kitchen.

Shawn was outside on the deck talking with Daf, but he had his eyes on the screen door to the kitchen.

The kitchen was large with a long, sparkling white island and fairly new appliances. Seeing her, Shawn immediately went inside.

Her hair was wet ringlets spiraling down her back. She wore a yellow blouse and pale blue jeans and was barefoot.

He bent and gave her a quick kiss. "You look beautiful, baby. I'm going *tae* take a shower. I can't wait *tae* eat, and then," he wiggled his eyebrows at her.

Loving her shy smile he gave her another quick kiss. "Go on outside with the guys and I'll be right back."

He watched her travel through the kitchen then outside to the wide porch and stand beside Daf who was poking things on a smoking grill with a long fork.

When Daf turned and smiled his welcome telling her to join him, Shawn took off in a jog to get his shower out of the way.

Twenty minutes passed and Shawn emerged out of the kitchen to the back porch that opened to a deck. Daf was still grilling, Cheri chatted with him.

His red hair damp, Beau sat back relaxed in a chair holding a beer. His head was tipped back and his eyes were half closed.

Still buttoning his shirt, Shawn went straight to Cheri and brought her to the railing. Smiling down at her, he commented, "How's that for a view, baby?"

The couple rested their arms on the railing and watched the tranquil blue water sway from the gentle breeze.

Cheri nestled her head on Shawn's shoulder and sighed happily, "It's breathtaking, Shawn, beautiful."

He rolled an arm around her, gave her a gentle hug. "There's a boat down by the dock. When we can. I'll take you for a spin." He gazed down at her sultry eyes almost completely hidden under limpid lids.

Growling, he murmured, "God, baby, you make me so damned hot," he kissed her. "The boat ride will have *tae* be down the road sometime, way down the road."

He lowered his mouth onto hers. Once he got Cheri in his bed he had no plans on getting out of it too soon.

"Okay!" Daf barked cheerfully. "Food's ready, let's eat!" He carried a platter of charcoaled broiling steaks and roasted potatoes to a round patio table already set with salad and bread and glasses.

Beau roused himself, stumbled to the table and plopped down. Leaning back in his chair, he reached down, lifted the lid of a cooler next to the table and took out two beers and handed one to Shawn as he and Cheri approached the table.

"Thank God for Elvira," Beau muttered with his mouth already on the bottle and tipping it, he guzzled with gusto.

"Who is Elvira?" Cheri asked as Shawn pushed in her chair and sat next to her. She took a sip of the soda with ice Dap had set out for her.

Shawn flipped off the top of his beer bottle and slugged it down thirstily.

Daf set the platter down and sat at the table, he answered her, "She's the housekeeper. She got the food ready for us. The grill was already prepared and the potatoes were partially cooked. Look at those nice grill marks on the zucchini, nothing like grilled vegetables. She'll be back tomorrow to set up breakfast for us."

His eye on the platter of steaks, Beau licked his lips, "I'm more into the charred steaks than squash, bro."

"All right," Dap said, holding one hand out to Beau on his right and his other to Cheri on his left. "But first, let's say grace and then dig in!"

After existing on vacuum packed food, berries, the rare rabbit, canned tuna and beans for weeks, they heartily dug into their food, gorging, sopping up drippings with toasty bread. It was a quiet long time while they chowed to their satisfaction.

Finally, they all sat back rubbing their bellies with sated groans.

"Here," Beau handed a plate of cookies to Shawn, "have some desert."

Shawn's eyes were on Cheri, hers were on him. He stood up. "Later. I want *tae* show Cherriana the beach." He took her hand and walked her down the wooden steps off the porch and across the stone path that led to the lake.

Both in bare feet they stopped to roll up the legs of their jeans. A swirl of soft sand surrounded the deep blue lake that went on for miles. He dropped his arm around her and they strolled as the sun set and the birds swooped noisy and crazily around them looking to roost.

After walking a bit with the warm sand sifting through their toes, Shawn sat down on the sand and pulled Cheri down with him.

She set her palm on the side of his freshly shaven face. Her contented smile curving, her eyes adoring him, she said, "Shawn, I am so happy to be here with you."

His reactive smile just as content and spectacularly happy, he touched her chin with two fingers and gave her a brief feather light kiss. "There is nowhere I'd rather be, and no one I'd rather be with than you, *ma leamin*, you are my world." He cuddled her into his embrace, her head settled on his shoulder.

Their arms around each other they watched the sun setting. It was almost dark when Shawn cradled her head, his big hands spanning the back of her neck with his thumbs along her jaw, his mouth descended on hers.

Her soft lips so tender and enticing, he pushed them apart and slid his tongue inside eager to taste her.

She responded so fiercely the fire already smoldering in his loins burst into flames.

Chapter Twenty-Two

Shawn broke the off kiss and stood up. He grasped her hand and pulled her to her feet. "I can't wait any longer for you, baby. Let's go inside, okay?"

He took her laying her head against his shoulder as an affirmative. Hand in hand they walked across the soft sand back to the house.

They travelled around to a side entrance. He opened the door for her to go in and then followed. "We have as much privacy as we want, honey. Come on." He took her hand again bringing her down the hall to their room.

The door was open but it was dark inside. He let go of her and crossed the room to a table beside the bed. After he had taken his shower he had set candles up on both sides of the bed, now he lit them.

When he was done, he turned to Cheri still standing shyly in the doorway. The candlelight flickered across her making her bright hair glow like a curly halo.

Shawn's eyes, glowing black moonstones trained on Cheri, he trod eagerly back across the room to her. He rolled his hand around the back of her head and pulled her in for his kiss.

Their mouths joined, without separating from her, he closed the door behind them. Tongues tasting and relishing, Shawn moved her further into the room.

Threading his fingers through her hair, he sprinkled soft kisses along her jaw. She tilted her head with a whispered moan, exposing her neck for his mouth to freely kiss and suck her smooth skin.

He lifted her hair, his fingertips lightly touching, skimming the nape of her neck. Bending his head, he licked behind her ear, tugged on her lobe with his lips and gentle teeth and smiled at her shiver, her flesh so sensitive to his mouth.

Cheri gripped his upper arms. Enthralled with the strength of them, she murmured, "I love the feel of your, um, masculine physique, Shawn. You're so strong, you make me feel safe, cherished." She stroked her shy hands up to his shoulders.

Smiling with tender pleasure, Shawn licked and nibbled his way down her throat. She arched her neck back as he kissed and sucked down and across her collarbone leaving a trail of light pink marks on her fair skin. He unbuttoned the top button on the yellow blouse.

Moving his mouth back up to seek hers, to fuse them together, he thrust his tongue inside more urgently, tasting her sweetness with rough hunger. He tugged at her lower lip, licking it, biting it gently, feeling the warmth of her breath on his skin, and continued unbuttoning her blouse until all the buttons were open.

Their mouths still entwined, Shawn nudged her closer to the bed. Nearer to the soft light of the candles glowing orange and yellow, moving their shadows, dark silhouette flickers shifting languorously over the pale walls.

He pushed her blouse off her shoulders letting it fall to the floor. Sliding his fingers under the satin bra straps on her shoulders, his gaze dropped as he pushed the straps half way down her arms. The mellow light turned her skin to buttercream.

"Cherriana, you are so beautiful," he groaned staring at her breasts molding over the black stain bra.

Her miniscule understanding from other women about men came through in her voice of hushed uncertainty, "Shawn...I," she stiffened. Her hesitation awkward, she waited until he pulled his heated gaze from her breasts to her eyes.

"Hmmm?" He couldn't help it, he'd waited so long to see her unfold in front of him, his heated eyes flickered from her face to her breasts to her face.

"I've heard women say men only want them for their bodies. But when they are old and no longer attractive the men cheat-"

With a dimpled smile and twinkling eyes, Shawn cupped her chin. He admonished gently, "Honey, you have *tae* know there's way more between us than physical beauty. Sure, tis what initially draws men and women together, the chemistry. But we are leagues beyond that baby. When we're gray and wrinkled, you will only be more beautiful *tae* me, because I love you, Cherriana."

He grinned evilly. "I have *tae* say though, at the moment, being a red blooded male, I do crave having your juicy body so badly right now, taking you. That means you're hot, and looking at you makes me hot and I can't wait *tae* be inside you."

His kiss on her lips was just a whisper, then he gazed back into her eyes with all seriousness. "But we're not just merging our bodies with our intimacy, we're merging our minds and bonding our souls too. You understand what I'm saying?"

Her expression relaxed, she nodded.

"You're a lock baby and I'm your key," he kissed the tip of her nose. "And vice versa."

She reached for the buttons on his shirt, but he stayed her hands, "No, not yet, I need *tae* enjoy you first." His chuckle tight in his throat, he said, "You touch me and I'll be a goner."

At her tentative but trusting smile, he wrapped his hand around the back of her head and drew her close to meld their mouths. His eyes closing in their kiss, Shawn wound his long fingers around her upper arm drawing her against him.

Cheri cupped her hands on both sides of his face caressing his skin while they kissed.

Taking a breath, Shawn pulled from her lips and lowered his gaze again to her breasts. He reached around her back to unclasp the bra, slid the straps down her arms and let it drop to the floor.

"Cherriana," he whispered, drinking in the beauty of her delicious fullness. His fingers trailed up her slender arms to slip around her neck then skimmed down over her shoulders and down to cup her breasts. Filling his large hands with her plump flesh he clutched them, molding the soft globes between his fingers.

Tearing his eyes from her pale skin, he pressed his lips to her neck and sucked until he marked her. The harder he sucked her flesh, the rougher he kneaded her breasts, rumbled groans growled hungrily against her soft skin.

With a mewling cry if arousal, Cheri's spine arched thrusting her aching breasts harder into his hands. Her body undulated against his hard form in a sudden sinuous writhing storm, he was spurred to feel her naked body against his right

270

now. But he knew he had to get her to a point of mindless abandon before losing himself in her blossoming essence.

Shawn moved his mouth from her neck to her breasts. Holding her supple globes in his tightening grasp, he peppered them with kisses. Then, centering his face against the cleaved mounds, he rubbed his face over them sighing at their splendid softness.

Caressing and sucking her skin, he tugged a nipple into his mouth and bit softly. Her sensuous moan made his erection already hard as granite throb like mad.

Suckling first one nipple then the other, Shawn reached down and undid the button on her jeans then pulled the zipper down. He knelt down in front of her and looked up at the candlelight dancing across her fair skin.

Cheri wove her fingers through his hair. Closing her eyes lessened the timidity she felt at her lack of experience from feeling Shawn's firm confident hands on her.

"You okay, baby?" Shawn asked, his palms enjoying the soft warmth of her tiny waist. He was moving very slowly, letting her become accustomed to his hands on her and giving her the opportunity to tell him to stop if she wanted him to.

He smiled at the sensual curve of her lips, her head tilted back, the soft mewing sounds of delight she made.

She murmured, "Uh huh, you feel so good, Shawn." Tingles roiling through her body reacting to his stimulating fingers, her sigh slid out hot and needy.

"*Na* baby, tis you that feels good. Your mouth, your soft skin, your perky nipples taste so indescribably sweet, I can't wait *tae* see how the rest of you tastes."

She shivered not knowing what he planned to do to her. "Taste me? I uh, don't understand…"

"You will love my mouth on your body, Cherriana, trust me." On his knees, he kissed her belly then grasped the top of her jeans and peeled them down over her hips to the floor. He lifted one leg then the other until they were free then leaned back on his heels to look at her.

Her round breasts so full and creamy, the serpentine indention of her waist, the slender heart-shaped hips swathed in just a sheer bit of black satin panties, his rough exhale etched out like he was in pain. He slid his hand between her thighs to cup her sex.

"Oh!" Cheri gasped. "*Shawn!*" She instinctually backed away from his hand. But he embraced her womanhood with his palm, moving it up slightly, lightly pressed, then slid back.

With a little sound in the back of her throat, Cheri held still at first then rocked against his skilled touch.

He tugged the wispy panties down until they were on the floor and helped her step gracefully out of them.

Splaying his long fingers against her behind to hold her stable, he commanded gently, "Hold onto my head *tae* steady yourself."

When she did, he put his hand back on her core lightly squeezing and pressing her, rubbing gently. She ground at his hand and inadvertently grasped tufts of his hair.

Cheri's head dropped back, she moaned, "Shawn, I feel…ahh…your touch is magic! I'm all- all tingly."

"It only gets better, baby," he said with a loving smile. His palm palpated harder on her sex. Her body quivered in his hand.

Exhaling an unsteady hush of air, she twined her fingers in his hair, unconsciously pulling it as a hot flush seared up her body. Her tugging his hair in throes of pleasure that he was giving her, charged electric prickles over Shawn's skin. Feeling her excitement ran goose bumps up his own arms.

His voice quiet, warm, he told her, "Okay, move your legs apart, baby," he helped nudge them apart. His hand between her thighs, he drew his fingers up the tender folds of her sex, and smiled at the sudden shudder and her sharp gasp. He held her bottom tighter to still her.

In spurts of wheezy breaths, shy to be standing nude in the middle of the room and him still fully dressed, she murmured, "Why are we standing? Shouldn't we be- *ahhh, Shawn,*" she drew a ragged hoarse inhale as his thumb pressed against her, then his fingers curled around her core trickling his fingertips upwards.

Smiling with his face against her belly, he kissed over her navel. "We will, *leamin,* but like this I can see all of you, see what you look like." His eyes warmed all over her slender shoulders, her delicate waist, down her shapely legs.

"And I can touch you everywhere, like this," his big hands splayed across her back then sluiced down the curve of her elegant spine to her bottom.

"I can touch and hold every part of you this way, including your sumptuous bottom, baby." His palms enveloping her firm orbs, he grunted in delight. "Rich and so round," crushing them in his hands he pulled her pelvis to his face.

A nervous giggle gasped when he rubbed his chin then his cheek up her inner thigh. The giggle devolved into a croaking exhale when he pressed his mouth against her pubis.

Kissing her, Shawn whispered, "Cherriana, you are so damned sweet..." He held her nether lips in a purse with his fingers and kissed them harder.

Her hips pulsed against his mouth. "Um, Shawn," she murmured, clutching his hair, her head tilted back, her eyes closed.

Shawn felt her body respond to his touch. The dampness of her sex swelling against his mouth and fingers, the little breathy sounds she made, but he could also feel her stiffen and draw away before moving back against this hand.

"Don't be afraid, just feel your body, let go, trust me, okay?" His deep voice a soft rumble in the dark, candlelit flickering room.

Her weak, "Okay," came out in a scratchy breath.

He stroked her womanhood with two thick fingers, caressing her slit. When he heard her thrumming moans, he rubbed her bud lightly with his thumb. Her hips jerked so hard he had to hold her still with his other hand. His fingers were soon wet with her silk.

"That's it baby, feel good, get ready to receive me." Knowing she was inexperienced, he was slightly worried at her smallness. He leaned forward and as he took her bud in his mouth and gently pushed a thick finger just barely inside her.

"*Shawn*," the words flushed out. Her thighs pulled together in surprise, her eyes flew open.

He licked her clitoris, and pushed his finger in deeper, but she had stiffened, her muscles contracted.

He said calmly, "Trust me, baby." He pulled his finger out and reached up to caress her breasts. Then levering her thighs back apart, he sucked and licked her sweet tiny bud and pushed his finger gently back inside her.

She did trust him, he'd saved her life again and again. Shutting off her mind, Cheri let her body feel what he was doing to her. Her muscles loosened, quiet gasping murmurs spilled out threaded with tiny shudders. His hand grew wetter.

"You're hot, baby, so damned hot," he growled. Now he was concerned he wouldn't be able to hold himself back from pushing her down and plunging forcefully inside her before she was ready.

He stood up suddenly, slid his hands under her, swooped her up in his arms and carried her to the bed and gently laid her down.

She went to sit up. "What's wrong, Shawn, are-"

Setting one knee on the bed, he pushed her back to lie down. "Nothing *leamin*, I just needed *tae* move or it would be a short night."

He slid in beside her. Rolling his mouth over hers, he scorched her plush lips with a fierce ravishing kiss, his tongue bold and searching, hungry for her. She twined her hands around his neck to hold him fast against her mouth.

He seized her breast, squeezing, filling his fingers with her chubby flesh, enjoying the heaviness of it, the womanliness of her. Then he stroked down, flattening his hand against her concave belly, then lower to touch her core.

He stroked her, rubbed her bud then slowly slid a finger inside her. She was so wet, he carefully slipped in a second finger. Her sheath was incredibly tight, he moved very slowly. Soon she was writhing against his hand with hitching groans and gusting cries.

"Shawn, it feels," her voice trailed off, her lungs squeezing her breath out.

Her head tossed back and forth in the cradle of his hand. He murmured against her lips, "It feels what, baby?" He pressed the heel of his palm hard on her mound then pushed his fingers in. Curling them, he probed, feeling for when her

275

voice grew high and tight, or she ground back against his hand, to find where her super sensitive spots were.

He moved his fingers faster, deeper, his thumb stroking her nub. Her hips bucked at his thrusts, her breaths were quick and shallow, chopped hiccups.

Shawn could feel the heat of her body, her legs stiffened, she jolted at him, her spine arching off the bed.

"Shawn-" she wailed. "I want-"

Still cradling her head in his left hand, he drew back to look at her, then plunging his fingers faster, watching her eyes roll back, her hands toss against the bed.

Then she gripped his waist, pushing her fingers up under his loosened shirt where she dug her nails into his flesh. His eyes mere glistening slits still watching her, his voice already heavy with desire, it grew so gruff the words came grating out, "You want what, baby?"

Her breaths now rapid little squeaks, she gasped, "Don't know..." she thrashed against his fingers. Her hips jolted right up off the mattress, then her entire body grew rigid and her harsh exhale gushed out with a wild cry, "*Shawn-*"

His fingers tightened on the back of her neck, he had to concentrate not to squeeze too hard when he felt the thrill of her body undulating with her orgasm.

She knifed up as her channel strangled his fingers. She pulled so wildly at his hair, Shawn grinned knowing he was losing some locks, and it was so worth it. Then her body came to a shuddering slow tremor, she gasped, a flush covered her heaving chest.

Falling back on the mattress, Cheri's unfocused eyes sought his tender bemused gaze. Her voice quaking through spasms, she panted, "That was...I mean..."

She gulped for air, scraping her fingers through his chest hair then she flexed them on his shoulder blades. Finishing on a gush of air, she huffed, "Awesome, Shawn, it was awesome!" Her wobbly smile a haze of erotic shudders.

He kissed her for a moment until her body stopped trembling then he got on his knees and moved between her legs.

Feeling him leave her, Cheri rose up on shaky elbows. Her eyes bulged out of her head when she saw him with his thick manhood in his fist. He was positioning himself to her opening.

"Shawn, I don't think, uh," her eyes were fixed on his long hard, really thick length, her legs pulled together.

He put his hand on her chest and gently pushed her back to lie down. His lips sought hers, he gentled her with a soft kiss.

As she settled back tuning into his passion, he kicked it up. Strumming his tongue over her lips and inside her mouth with such intensity he roused her back to fiery desire.

When he felt her tentative touch on his erection, his body jerked with intense shock and pleasure. "Uh, baby, that's- *ah*," a deep groan growled in his chest when he felt her tentative exploring hand wrap around his shaft.

Shuddering, he grasped her wrist and pulled her hand off.

"What's wrong, Shawn? I want to see what you feel like too."

Her pretty voice a sexy lilt in his ear, Shawn sucked in a painstaking breath then exhaled to calm his raging body. "*Na*, nothin' tis wrong." His brogue thickened with emotion.

"Believe me *leamin*, I am dyin' *tae* feel your hands on me. But," he sighed out a heavy shiver. "I need *tae* prepare you *tae* take me, and I need *tae* move slowly. If you keep touchin' me I won't be able *tae* hold back."

He skimmed a finger down her cheek. "We have all night and the rest of our lives *tae* do a lot of different things. All right?"

She nestled back down into the pillows. Her provocative smile and eyes darkening with such exquisite passion, intensely alluring and inviting, Shawn felt as if her hand was still clasping his hard flesh. His erection pulsed, stretched, begging to shove inside her.

He scooped a condom off the nightstand he'd placed there and already opened so he wouldn't have to stop to do it. With as little movement away from her, Shawn rolled the condom on.

He kissed her smiling rosy lips, when he felt her heated response, he prodded her thighs apart with his knees and put his shaft against her opening.

Lifting his mouth from hers, he said quietly, his voice thick, "I'll go slow, baby, your body will expand *tae* accept me. You have *tae* know that it will hurt, at first, but it will cease. If I hurt you badly, tell me, we'll stop. Okay?"

Her big blues trusting on him, she nodded.

Guiding himself into her, he pushed the blunt head of his shaft through her soft pink opening, *God she is so tight*-soft and smooth and tight, and silky wet.

Propped on his elbow, his arm was long enough he could brush the side of her face with caressing fingers. With the other hand, he cradled each breast molding them ardently in the cup of his fingers. He teased her nipples and kissed her until he felt her legs relax then buckle with the erogenous sensations.

While pushing slowly, he felt her body opening like a satin flower, accepting him. He skimmed his hand down to stroke her clit. Her hips shimmied against his fingers, he felt her humming purr vibrate against his skin.

His body tightened when he felt the resistance of her virginity. Shawn moved his mouth to her neck, sucked hungrily then said quietly near her ear. "This will hurt baby," he warned in a quiet regretful voice. "It can't be helped, but it will ease," and he thrust and broke through her hymen.

Her body stiffened violently, her sex squeezed him so hard he almost came. Her breath was lost, then she gulped a deep pained inhale, he covered her mouth with his to take her scream down his throat.

Shawn could feel her body cringing from him, her hands went against his chest to push him away from her. Leaning his head back, he brushed at the sweat dampening her temples.

In a small tight voice she whimpered, "Shawn, it hurts."

Chapter Twenty-Three

*H*e held still. "I know, honey, I won't move for a minute. Just relax, feel me, feel me inside of you with your hot velvet sheath." He knew she could feel his swollen erection throbbing at her feminine walls.

His mouth surrounded hers, he swept his tongue plundering inside until her lips responded and her tongue joined his in his seductive lure. He felt her easing around him.

Moving slowly, he pushed carefully, when she didn't protest he moved deeper. The deeper he went the more he felt her hips tremulously come up to meet his. Her hands moved from pushing against his chest to wildly clutching his shoulders.

He raised his head to see the passion misting her eyes again and her slight smile up at him.

Almost fully inside her, Shawn's lips ruffled slightly on hers, tugging at her upper then her lower pout with his teeth, teasing with his tongue. Finally, he was completely buried in her warm juicy body.

He propped on his forearms and started unhurriedly pulling carefully almost all the way out then pushing slowly back in.

"Cherriana," he crooned, his accent thick with emotion. "I have been dyin' *tae* be like this with you. I knew you'd feel good, but, *ahhh*," he groaned, plunging less gently in her. "You feel insanely more amazin' than I imagined," his breath slid out in an aching hiss.

"I want this *tae* be good for you, *leamin*." Her hips rhythmically rose to meet his, her slick wetness making the slide easier, he started plunging harder, moving with long, increasingly rapid deeper strokes.

Cheri's neck bent, her head rolled back, her voice exhaled in small sharp puffs, breaking breathy between words she huffed, "This is what I was so afraid of those nights we slept together, uhh-" her skin quivered at his vivid thrust.

His voice strained, his words a husky croak, "I had *tae* hold you, baby, I tried not *tae*, but I needed you safe and warm against me. I fought *tae* resist your exquisite allure, *ahh*, but I couldn't."

Plunging and groaning in short deep growls, he hesitated, "You were afraid I would force you? Cherriana, you know I would never-"

She cradled her hands around his face pulling him down for a searing kiss. "I was afraid you would take me," she sighed, "and I was afraid you wouldn't. I wanted you too, Shawn. You frightened me, and angered me, and yet I still wanted to be with you," she kissed him harder.

Rocking in her again, he parted from her lips and admitted, "I wanted you the second those terrified, gorgeous blue eyes flashed at me. I was a goner, like I was hit by a bolt of lightnin'." He groaned, "You feel so damned good," and he moved faster.

His words in a hush, he said seriously, "I wanted all of you, you know that, right? Almost from the start I wanted you like how we are now in my bed, but I also knew I wanted you in my life, forever."

"Shawn…"

"You okay, baby?" He dipped his head to watch her expression.

Her cheeks were shiny and rosy, her heavy lidded eyes sparkling. She licked her lips, making him lower his head to do that for her. She smiled against his mouth.

"With you inside me, I feel like we're- united, like all one- person, one body-" her breath cut in sharply at his hard thrust, she shivered.

Announcing, "I love you, Cherriana," he thrust harder. "I love you so much, baby, more than life." He could feel her tightening around him, her body quaking. She clutched his shoulders digging her nails into his skin.

Her breaths panted faster, her head lolled back, the blue irises deliriously gleaming.

"Go with it baby," Shawn hissed. His neck strained, he grit his teeth trying to hold back until she was ready.

Her skin vibrated against his hands, her spine arched, her eyes rolled back, she cried out, "Shawn!"

Feeling her shaking and gasping, he dove in faster pushing as deep as he could. When she convulsed against him he let himself go. Her body milked him with spasms.

When she lifted her hips so he could penetrate deeper, a flood of uncontrolled violent thrusts unleashed. He thrust with rapid hard plunges, until waves of primitive agony cascaded down his body.

Split between quenching pain and consuming pleasure, Shawn clutched Cheri shouting out her name as he surged in her again and again until he pounded against the very end of her, then he froze.

His climax shooting through him, his seeds erupted, undulating into the shield, he wished instead they were releasing into his beloved.

Convulsions latched onto his body and shook him straight down to hell and burst back up to heaven. Finally, his wrenching body collapsed on her.

Hearing his own breathing so fast and loud it was deafening, his lungs trying to gulp deep inhalations, his heart beat out of his chest.

Cheri squirmed under him. He shrugged slightly off her to the side, loathing to leave her body. She pushed her flying hair off her face, then reached up with a tender smile to pluck damp spirals of her hair off his sweating face.

"Cherriana," his voice a gushed rasp, his pulse palpitating like a raging gale. He gathered her tightly against his chest, kissed her fiercely then more gently before he dropped back down beside her, panting depleted onto the mattress.

Shawn rolled on his back pulling her to lie on his chest and wrapped his arm around her holding her securely. She brushed her head against his muscled chest, the hair tickling her chin.

"What?" he asked as she giggled, snuggling closer to him.

She smiled. "I can feel your heart racing, Shawn, like mine."

"Are you all right?" he asked with a hint of worry in his voice. Was he too rough, too big for her, too impatient? What if she didn't like it? "I know I hurt you," he shifted slightly so he could look at her face. Her glowing eyes and happy curve of her lips expressed how she felt.

"Yes," she agreed, frowning slightly. "It did hurt. You warned me but it was still a shock. But once the pain ebbed and you," her voice shy, cheeks grew even pinker, "you know, what you did, it was," she sighed heavily, "wonderful. Really incredible, Shawn."

She moved to brace on her elbow, tracing the line around his lips with a fingertip. "When can we do it again?"

His chest jumped with his surprise. "Really?" He stared at her to see if she was serious. She was grinning at him, still tracing his lips.

"Yes. How long do we wait before it's…um, acceptable to do it again?"

Shawn gathered her up in a ball over his body holding her in a cuddled embrace. "There is no acceptable time, silly." He wiggled his brows wolfishly at her, "You're probably pretty sore, but, I'm ready when you are-"

They had three more days together before Shawn had to leave to meet with the authorities. They tried to spend some time with Beau and Daf, they usually ate dinner with them and Shawn managed to take her for a tranquil boat ride.

But, most of the time they spent in their room exploring each other, discovering as many aspects of one another that they could in the short period of time.

They did their study of each other mostly in bed, but there was the secluded cove on the lake, and the porch when the guys weren't there, and a few other places they christened.

Cheri walked with Shawn out to the car. His arm was heavy around her shoulders, she didn't seem to mind, it was the tears in her eyes that tugged at his heart.

He opened the backseat door and tossed his small suitcase in and closed the door, then moved to lean his back against the driver's door. He grasped her hand and pulled her up against him.

"Don't, Cherriana, please." He wiped at her tears with his fingers. "Tis hard enough." He wound his arms around her and tilted her face up for his long lingering kiss.

Leaning back he smiled sadly. "I can taste the salt of your tears, *leamin*, they're killing me."

She slid her hands up around to net his face. "I'm sorry, Shawn, I can't help it. We finally get together and you have to leave." Her beleaguered sigh drew out. "The last few days have been the best days of my life."

Feeling his own eyes welling up, Shawn whispered against her lips, "Mine too." He kissed her and hugged her like he never wanted to let go.

Reluctantly setting her from him, he opened the car door. "I will call you every day, baby. You call me any time you want *tae*, okay?" He touched the tip of her nose.

Sliding in behind the wheel, Shawn rolled down the window and stuck his arm out. "I'll miss you, baby. I'll be back as soon as I can. Promise me you won't leave this house for any reason at all unless Beau or Daf are with you, all right?"

She nodded and set her hands on the edge of the open window. "I'll be here when you get back, Shawn."

The strain of leaving her showing on his face, the lines around his mouth tightened. "C'mere baby, one last kiss."

Cheri leaned in the window and they kissed like it was their last one forever.

He turned on the ignition, she stepped back, and he was gone with a wave.

On the front steps Daf and Beau waited.

When she was ready, she trod up the steps on heavy legs.

Beau tried to grin at her to lift her spirits, but he could see her heart was breaking.

The two men ushered her inside and closed the door to wait until all the business Shawn had to deal with was completed and he could return.

Chapter Twenty-Four

Derrick Masterson stuck his key in the front door, stepped inside the living room like he did every day after work and closed the door behind him.

The sun had set and the house was dark. For no reason he could fathom, the hairs on the back of Masterson's neck rose.

An uneasy feeling gripping his stomach, he set his keys quietly on the table near the door then crept across to an end table next to the couch. Silently, he pulled the drawer open, and stuck his hand inside.

He patted his hand all around inside the drawer, but it was empty. A quailing jitter roiled, tightening his throat. Pulling his hand back out he reached for the lamp and switched it on.

"Looking for this?" A bodiless voice carried across the quiet dark room.

His shoulders raised, Masterson turned around very slowly. He saw a large, muscular man sitting placidly in his chair, a baseball cap pulled down over his brows.

"What the hell?" Masterson stuttered, "Who the...who the hell are you and how did you get in my house?" His shaking gaze dropped down to the man's lap, he was holding a gun. Black gloves covered his hands. "How...why do you have my gun?"

Shawn rose calmly, tucking the gun in the back of his jeans leaving his hands free. He pushed the cap back off his forehead, wavy tufts of black hair slipped out to curl over his brow. "Are you Derrick Masterson? *Professor* Derrick Masterson?"

Masterson's eyes narrowed, his hands jerked with a slight tremble. "Who wants to know?"

Shawn crossed his arms over his chest. Expressionless, his toneless voice even more daunting in the sheer starkness of emotion, he said, "Do you recall a young woman, a beautiful, innocent student by the name of Cherriana Delighya?"

Brows drawn down over dark green eyes, Masterson dragged a hand through his short, freshly trimmed brown hair then stuffed it in a pocket. His mouth tightened into a straight line.

Again not answering the question, the professor snapped rudely, "What's it to you?" He looked to be in his late thirties with basic classical features. A Roman nose, strong jaw. He was wearing a tan pullover sweater over a white shirt with a green tie knotted at his neck and grey slacks.

Braver now that it appeared Shawn had no plans on using his gun on him, he pointed to the door and ordered, "Get the hell out of my house whoever you are and give me back my gun you thief."

Shawn's lips pursed, he stroked his chin perplexed. "I don't get it, *Professor*, you're a good looking, fairly young guy, why would you need *tae* force a woman *tae* be with you? What's that all about?"

Masterson's mouth quirked guiltily. His brows staggered up to his hairline, then like lasers drew back down in anger. He took a few steps backwards towards his door.

"Listen, mister, I don't know who the hell you think you are busting into my house, I'm calling the police." He stuck his hand in his pocket to grab his phone, but froze when Shawn moved several steps towards him.

Shawn bent slightly and picked up something that was leaning against the couch.

Masterson's eyes widened at the baseball bat he held in his hands. Gleaning Shawn's intent, suddenly keenly apprehensive, he sucked in his lips. Keeping his hand in his pocket and his eyes on the bat, his voice shook, "What...what...what do you want?"

A caustic bite darkening Shawn's voice, he said, "I asked you if you know Cherriana. Answer my questions or I will knock your head off your shoulders."

Raising the bat to his shoulder, his ominous glower at odds with the slightly crooked grin, he offered, "Trust me, I am dying *tae* knock your fucking head clean off your *bluidy* shoulders and stomp it 'til tis flat as the bleedin' floor we're standing on."

He took a step closer. "Now, your last chance, do you know Cherriana Delighya?"

Masterson held his palms up. "Okay, okay." He dragged in a deep breath and answered, "Yes, I know Miss Delighya. What in God's name is this about?"

Another step closer, Shawn said coldly, "I am asking the questions. You could get any woman, why, you little prick, are you trying *tae* force her *tae* marry you?"

The professor carefully lowered his hands, shrugged like it was no big deal. "I just wanted her, man. She refused me. I planned on, uh..." he eyed the bat, "to uh, just take her anyway but that would ruin my career if she told." He snorted with a wry grimace. "Plus jail time and registering as a sex offender."

Masterson shrugged again. "I had even thought of disposing of her, uh body, you know, after." His mind picturing Cheri and what he wanted to do to her, he didn't see the murderous glint in Shawn's eyes.

Rubbing the back of his neck, Masterson squeezed it as if reducing the tension suddenly tightening there. "But I feared I wouldn't tire of having her, for quite a long time. I didn't know for how long I would want her," he had the gall to chuckle.

"I found besides wanting that lush little body, I had grown quite fond of her sweet shyness. What an incredible aphrodisiac thinking of her so sweet and untouched on her little knees in front of me, looking up at me with those big blue eyes with my dick in her-"

His face dark, mouth clenched, Shawn advanced raising the bat up and to the side ready to swing it.

Shifting his head from Shawn with a wince, the professor muttered. "Uh," and cleared his throat. "Never uh mind, just a fantasy of mine. Anyway," his face crimped in a scowl. "Then there's the fact that she refused me." He jabbed his thumb at his chest in incredulity. "Me, she rebuffed me! Can you believe that?"

Not waiting for Shawn to reply, he snarled, "I showed that little bitch what it is to refuse me. We could have had a relationship until I tired of her and moved on, but no. She had to spite my ego and say no to sleeping with me. Then I tried to show her my respect by asking her to marry me, and, unbelievably the bitch said no to that too."

He shook his head like he couldn't believe a woman declined to not only not have sex with him, but refused to marry him as well.

Shaking his head, Shawn said, "Gee, I can't fathom why the girl said no." His face already smoldering turned harsher with suppressed anger. "Now, this is the part where you tell me where the evidence is that you have on her."

His dark eyes like faceted onyx, glittered with black bloodlust from beneath the cap. Shawn watched the pique clear the man's face to make room for obstinacy.

Masterson folded his arms across his chest and declared, "I'm done talking with you, whoever the hell you are. I am calling the police." He reached back down and started to pull his phone out of his pocket-

Shawn pulled his cap off and put it back on with the bill facing backwards and raised the bat again.

His brows arching in sarcasm, pulling out his phone, the professor said, "Oh, come on, you don't really expect me to believe you're going to strike me with that thing over a little bitch-"

Wham-

Shawn slammed the bat into Masterson's ribs, the crack echoed in the room.

The professor's eyes bugged like he couldn't believe Shawn hit him. His hands went to his ribs and he crumpled to the floor screaming in agony.

Shawn calmly stood over him holding the bat horizontally in both hands. Impassively watching the man writhing on the floor, clutching his broken ribs. The poor guy struggled to breathe, maybe a lung or two had collapsed.

Shawn was reminded of when Cheri had taken her last breath in the cave. He wiped his forehead with the back of his hand, he had no pity for the creature writhing like a stomped on snake below him.

The actions Masterson had taken against Cheri almost cost her life. Beyond the raping and beatings she would have received in prison, and from Malone and Marx and Zach in the woods, she almost died in a fucking cold dark cave in the forgotten wilderness, tied up and alone.

He brought the bat down bashing it against Masterson's shoulder crushing the bones.

The professor screamed and almost passed out from the pain.

Shawn crouched down beside him looking impassively at the man's tortured face. "The first hit was *tae* get your attention you fuck. The second was for what you put the girl through. The next ones will be for each time I ask you where the evidence is and you don't tell me."

One hand on his ribs, he couldn't move the other one with the broken shoulder, Masterson curled into a fetus and cried, "Please, don't, for God's sake! What do you-" he sobbed in agony turning his face he gasped and sniveled into the rug.

His voice all the more deadly from the quiet of it, Shawn said, "I've been *tae* the prosecutor. He said the evidence they currently have is ambiguous, equivocal. It was enough *tae* arrest her but might not be enough *tae* prosecute her, but that you indicated that you have strong evidence and was about *tae* hand it over when Cherriana was caught and extradited."

He put the bat to Masterson's broken shoulder and prodded it. The man screamed then broke into choking whimpers.

Shawn said calmly, "You tell me where the evidence is, right now, or I start bashing the bones in your fingers crushing each one, then your arms, your legs. You'll be a paraplegic vegetable by the time I'm done with you, so I recommend you start talking, Masterson, now." He badly wanted to beat the man with his bare fists but he didn't want his own DNA all over the place.

"All- all right," Masterson stammered, choking the words out. "It's- in my- my safety deposit box at Rand Imperial Bank," his voice shuddered into the rug as he cried pitifully.

"Give me the key *tae* the box," Shawn demanded. "Where is it?"

Sobbing, on his side, Masterson shook uncontrollably. His spit spluttered on the rug as he spoke, "In- in the drawer, there," he motioned with his head, the desk. "Top right drawer. It's- hey what are you doing?" he cried as Shawn stuck his hand in Masterson's back pocket and pulled out his wallet.

As he took out the professor's ID and tucked it in the pocket of his jeans, Shawn said coolly, "Now, I need the account number and password."

"But- what- what are you going to do with me?" Realizing his perilous position, Masterson's voice rose to a strident squeak.

Standing up, Shawn tossed the wallet on the floor. "Well, that depends. If I get the evidence and clear Cherriana's name, you might get *tae* live. For now," he nodded towards the kitchen, "my friend will be keeping you company while I get the evidence, you know, in case you've lied to me."

Unmitigated hate in his dark eyes, Shawn glared enraged at the man who tried to destroy an innocent, helpless woman just because he lusted after her. He glanced over as Beau came out of the kitchen. Daf stayed at the house to watch over Cheri.

"Hi there," Beau said cheerfully, freckled face grinning, the blue eyes twinkling. "I'm going to be your babysitter." He viciously kicked Masterson in the gut.

"Oh," Beau exclaimed, "sorry about that misstep there, but I like Cheri a lot and it just kills me to have witnessed the hell you caused to happen to her."

He shook his red head sadly. "Boy, I do hope my mate here is quick, I'd hate to have any more accidents while he's gone." Also wearing black leather gloves, he went and retrieved a chair from the kitchen, set it next to Masterson and sat down.

Masterson cried to him, his voice a pleading warble, "I-I need a doctor, man, please, I need a doctor!"

Beau gazed amicably down at him. "Hmmm. Yeah, you probably do." He sat back comfortably in the chair and lazily crossed his legs.

Wrenching sobs hitched out of Masterson. With every sob it hurt his ribs and made him cry all the more.

Shawn crouched down beside the prone man. Pulling off a glove, he said, "After I have the evidence then we will start working on prosecuting you for the man you murdered, and for framing the girl. I'll be seeing you."

He grabbed him by the hair and lifted his head up- then punched him so hard in the face he heard the man's nose crack. He released the unconscious man letting his head drop on the floor, the blood gushed soaking into the rug.

Beau whistled, "Bro, what was that for? I thought you said no DNA?"

Standing up, Shawn shook his head then shrugged. "I just had *tae* feel my fist against his face."

He started for the door, when he reached it he tossed over his shoulder, "I'll be back, you two have fun." With a mirthless grin, he swung out the door.

Chapter Twenty-Five

After collecting the evidence, Shawn dragged the broken professor to the Montrail Police Department.

He'd had conversations with Assistant State Attorney Dick Burke, explaining the false charges against Cheri and the murder Masterson had actually committed to frame her with.

They had scheduled this appointment for Shawn to bring Masterson in to face the music.

Prior to dragging the professor out of his house, Shawn and Beau discussed with him what would happen to him if he brought charges against them for beating and holding him hostage in his home.

Beau explained that Masterson would be in jail awaiting trial for a long damned time, and, Beau advised Masterson how many inmates were there that owed him favors.

Leaving the professor in the officials' good hands where they'd see to his medical care after charging him, Beau drove Shawn to the safe house where they'd left Cheri with Daf.

Beau shot quick glances at his friend as he drove the several hours. "So, what's the plan, Shawn, you guys think through what's next?"

Shawn yawned, scratched his chin, smiled. "Aye. We plan *tae* visit my folks, have my sisters meet Cherriana. We're going *tae* live at my place for now." His grin a lopsided smirk, he said, "I'm going *tae* marry that girl. I'm dying *tae* ask her but I'm afraid, I don't want *tae* rush her and frighten her off."

He chuckled, canting a grin at Beau. "But as soon as my mother latches onto her she'll be planning the wedding anyway. Cherriana wants *tae* go back *tae* school, but I'm hoping maybe she'll do online classes for a while."

"Uh huh, sounds like that's your idea to keep predators like Masterson away from her. You can't protect her from life forever."

Nodding, Shawn admitted, "I know. But just for now, after all she- we- went through, I just want *tae* hold her and keep her safe for a while. This time apart has been killing me. Thank God Daf has been staying with her otherwise I'd never get any sleep worrying." He yawned again.

"Bro," Beau said, "I would be thinking you would be grinning ear-to-ear to be about to see her. You haven't seen her since you left her at the house. But you look..." Beau struggled for the words to describe Shawn's somber expression.

"You look, shut down, closed in, like you're going to work instead of seeing the love of your life after months of screwing with Masterson and the court system. What's that all about?"

Shawn sat with his back against the car seat, his knees bent, legs slightly spread to accommodate their length, his hands clasped in his lap. He stared unblinking out the window.

A slow smile brewed up his face, warming his dark eyes. "Aye, Beau, I am closed in. Tis all I can do *tae* keep in my damned feelings for her. I'm shaking more inside thinking about seeing her than I was with terror chasing that damned grizzly down that day in the woods. I have *tae* shut down or I'll explode knowing I'll be with her…in a few hours…"

Shawn turned to grin wider at his friend. "I can't damned wait, bro, I can't wait." He closed his eyes, suddenly a little anxious wondering if she was as excited to see him as he was to see her.

He squirmed in the seat. After all, they'd been apart for months, maybe her ardor for him had cooled.

"I don't know, though, Beau, if she still wants me. You know that she is so young and we have lived such different lives. Sure, we talk on the phone every day, sometimes several times a day, but tis not the same as holding her luscious little body safe in my arms, my lips on hers. Wake up every morning with her beside me, under me…" his eyes rolled shut.

"Uh, yeah, too much info bro," Beau's grin aimed out the window.

"Yeah, tis just," Shawn stretched his neck working the kinks of stress out. "I've bounced back and forth all this time worried that since we've been apart she might come *tae* her senses and realize we are too different. That I am *tae*-hardened for her, that she really would want a more gentle, ah, non-violent man."

"Apparently you haven't seen the way she looks at you, bro."

"That's just it. We've been apart for months, she's had time *tae* comprehend she is free now *tae* live any life she wants. And, I'm afraid I won't fit into that. She's young, beautiful, smart, brave, she can have any man she wants. Why would she want some hard-bitten guy like me?"

"Shawn, bro-"

Shawn sat up straight and forked his fingers in agitation through his black hair. "*Na*, I'm a fool for thinking there could be anything but friendship between us. If anything she's feeling tis gratefulness for my saving her. That's not the relationship I want. Crap, Beau, just…crap."

His shoulders slumped. "What the hell am I going *tae* do without her? I can't imagine getting up every day and not seeing that gorgeous face, brilliant blue eyes and perfect lips smiling at me."

Shawn sighed and shut down again until he felt the car stop and Beau turn off the engine.

"Bro."

Shawn could hear the smile in Beau's voice. His lids rose wondering what- he sat up straight and reached for the door handle.

Cheri was sitting on the porch steps with Daf. She was waiting for him. As soon as the car stopped she leaped off the steps and started running.

Shawn scrambled out of the door and caught her as she flung herself into his arms.

He dropped his face into her hair, inhaled her scent. "God, baby, I've missed you so damned much." He pushed her hair back to cradle her face, the tears in her eyes made his stomach do a bunch of flip flops.

Her hands wound around his waist. Standing on tiptoes, Cheri whispered, "Me too, Shawn, I've missed you every second of every day." She smiled shyly, her eyes dipped then shone up at him. "That giant bed is so empty without you in it."

He grinned in pure gleeful contentment. Lowering his mouth on hers, Shawn wrapped his arms around his sweetheart holding her as tightly as he could.

Cheri lifted her hands to string around his neck and welcomed him with her lips, her hands, her heart.

Beau sauntered over to join Daf on the step, they fist-bumped.

Flopping down on the step, Beau sprawled beside his friend chuckling, "How long do you think they'll stay glued together like that?"

Daf shrugged. "Dunno, the grill is already hot and waiting. They'll come when they're ready." He clapped Beau on the shoulder, "Come on, let's go eat."

The two men strolled up the steps and into the house leaving the lovers in their adoring embrace.

It was a long time before Shawn finally pulled himself from her soft lips. The sun had almost set. Fireflies blinked like miniature popping flashlights around them in the gentle breeze.

"*Ma nesh leamin*, are you hungry, or should we take my suitcase *tae* our room first?"

The sultry glow in her eyes and flagrant desire curving in her bowed lips left no mistaking what she wanted.

Cheri took his hand, leaned against his strong shoulder. Looking up at his handsome face smiling, she murmured, "Let's get your things into the bedroom, first. We can always eat…later…"

Shawn's grin filled his entire face. Then, he immediately dropped to one knee and quickly fished out the tiny box.

Opening the box, he pulled the diamond ring out and held it up to her.

Cheri's hands covered her mouth, her blue eyes wide over at them blossomed with tears.

Dark eyes filled with tender love, Shawn said, "Baby, Cherriana, love of my life, will you do me the greatest honor and be my wife?"

Her heart pounding, tears slipping down her cheeks, she stared speechless at him.

"Baby," Shawn pried her trembling hand away from covering her mouth and slid the ring on her finger. "Don't keep me in suspension, tell me, my most precious *leamin*, will you marry me?"

Her head nodding vehemently, Cheri sobbed, "Yes! Yes Shawn! Yes!"

He jumped up and lifted her off her feet. Her legs wrapped around his waist as he lowered his head taking her lips in a deep, vibrant, marvelous kiss.

Finally separating their mouths to inhale heavy happy breaths, Shawn smiled at Cheri and rested his forehead on hers.

Gazing into her eyes, he said, "We need *tae* get inside before Daf burns the steaks, and annoying Beau comes out and makes those irritating little kissy noises he makes when we're kissing. I'm afraid we'll have to put off celebrating until after dinner."

"Okay." Cheri grinned at him.

Shawn gave her a quick buss on the lips and said, "The hard part will be figuring out which one *tae* ask *tae* be my best man. They are both like brothers *tae* me."

Smiling shyly, Cheri suggested, "I have no family, perhaps one of them can be my maid of honor? I've come to love them both dearly, like brothers, or best friends I never had."

Shawn threw back his head with a bark of laughter at the picture of either Beau or Daf wearing a pink prom-like dress. "Sweetheart, I think that's a grand idea. They're both going *tae* want *tae* do it. They'll have *tae* draw straws."

He grinned at her, then the grin grew tender and so full of love he looked like he was going to burst and shower love confetti all over their world. "My life, my cup is full, Cherriana. With you and my friends, and my family, I have it all. I am so freaking blessed."

Cheri stroked his face. She said reflectively, "I've always wanted family or friends, even one friend. I've been so alone for so long."

He embraced her tightly, bumped their noses together. "But now you have it all. You have my friends who have become yours, just as my family will also be yours. And, of course," his lips spread showing gleaming white teeth.

Her brows arched as she waited to hear what he was going to say.

He told her, "You have me. And, down the road, our family will grow bigger when we have our own wee ones." Squeezing her, Shawn said, "Our lives, baby, will only grow bigger and better."

Her sigh morphed from sad to joyful. "Yeah," her smile turned glorious. Her hands strung around his neck, Cheri pulled him down for more kisses. "I can't wait."

Carrying her across the grass, Shawn said against her lips, "Let's save dinner for later, I'm hungry *tae* get started on that family now." He hurried with her in his arms up the steps, and into their future.

The End

Dear Reader, thank you for purchasing or receiving a free copy of

Shawn's Prisoner!

I know you could have picked any number of books to read, but you picked this book and for that I am extremely grateful.

I hope you enjoyed this novel, and if you did, **please leave a review where you purchased it**, *and look for other exciting titles in my name!*

About the Author

Louise Furley loves writing romance with a huge helping of suspense. She finds it exciting to study new lands and learn everything she can about the area and the natives that call it home.

Sunny Florida is home where Louise is a graduate of St. Thomas University with a master's degree in Mental Health.

Louise is the author of numerous published novels. When not researching or writing, she is dreaming of unique plots, and discovering fresh ventures she hasn't yet experienced in the world.

Ride along with her as she travels new and thrilling journeys!

www.ingramcontent.com/pod-product-compliance
Lightning Source LLC
Chambersburg PA
CBHW020912200626
46814CB00001BA/302